Philadelphia Fire

John Edgar Wideman's books include *Writing to Save a Life*, *Brothers and Keepers*, *American Histories*, *Fatheralong*, *Hoop Roots* and *Sent for You Yesterday*. He is a MacArthur Fellow and has won the PEN/Faulkner Award twice and has been a finalist for the National Book Critics Circle Award and National Book Award. In 2017, he won the Prix Femina Étranger for *Writing to Save a Life*. He divides his time between New York and France.

ALSO BY JOHN EDGAR WIDEMAN

Fanon: A Novel

Briefs: Stories

God's Gym: Stories

The Island: Martinique

Hoop Roots: Basketball, Race, and Love

Two Cities: A Novel

The Cattle Killing: A Novel

Fatheralong: A Meditation on Fathers and Sons, Race and Society

All Stories Are True

The Stories of John Edgar Wideman

Fever: Stories

Reuben: A Novel

Brothers and Keepers: A Memoir

Sent for You Yesterday: A Novel

Damballah: Stories

Hiding Place: A Novel

The Lynchers: A Novel

Hurry Home: A Novel

A Glance Away: A Novel

Writing to Save a Life: The Louis Till File

American Histories: Stories

Philadelphia Fire

JOHN EDGAR WIDEMAN

CANONGATE

Published in Great Britain in 2018 by Canongate Books Ltd,
14 High Street, Edinburgh EH1 1TE

canongate.co.uk

1

First published in 1990 in the United States by Henry Holt and Company

British Library Cataloguing-in-Publication Data
A catalogue record for this book is available on
request from the British Library

ISBN 978 1 78689 203 4

Typeset in Minion Pro by Palimpsest Book Production Ltd,
Falkirk, Stirlingshire

Printed and bound in Great Britain by Clays Ltd, St Ives plc.

*To Judy—who teaches me more
about love each day*

Let every house be placed, if the Person pleases, in the middle of its platt . . . so there may be ground on each side, for Gardens or Orchards or feilds, that it may be a greene Country Towne, wch will never be burnt, and always be wholsome

INSTRUCTIONS GIVEN BY ME WILLIAM PENN,
PROPRIETOR AND GOVERNOR OF PENNSYLVANIA,
TO MY TRUSTY LOVING FRIENDS . . .
[30TH SEPT. 1681]

PART I

On a day like this the big toe of Zivanias had failed him. Zivanias named for the moonshine his grandfather cooked, best white lightning on the island. Cudjoe had listened to the story of the name many times. Was slightly envious. He would like to be named for something his father or grandfather had done well. A name celebrating a deed. A name to stamp him, guide him. They'd shared a meal once. Zivanias crunching fried fish like Rice Krispies. Laughing at Cudjoe. Pointing to Cudjoe's heap of cast-off crust and bones, his own clean platter. Zivanias had lived up to his name. Deserted a flock of goats, a wife and three sons up in the hills, scavenged work on the waterfront till he talked himself onto one of the launches jitneying tourists around the island. A captain soon. Then captain of captains. Best pilot, lover, drinker, dancer, storyteller of them all. He said so. No one said different. On a day like this when nobody else dared leave port, he drove a boatload of bootleg whiskey to the bottom of the ocean. Never a trace. Not a bottle or bone.

Cudjoe watches the sea cut up, refusing to stay still in its bowl. Sloshing like the overfilled cup of coffee he'd transported this unsteady morning from marble-topped counter to a table outdoors on the cobblestone esplanade. Coffee cooled in a minute by the chill wind buffeting the island. Rushes of wind and light play with rows of houses like they are skirts. Lift the whitewashed walls from their moorings, billow them as strobe bursts of sunshine bounce and shudder, daisy chains of houses whipping and snapping as wind reaches into the folds of narrow streets, twisting tunnels and funnels of stucco walls, a labyrinth of shaky alleyways with no roof but the Day-Glo blue-and-gray crisscrossed Greek sky hanging over like heavy, heavy what hangs over in the game they'd played back home in the streets of West Philly.

Zivanias would hold his boat on course with his foot. Leaning on a rail, prehensile toes snagged in the steering wheel, his goatskin vest unbuttoned to display hairy chest, eyes half shut, humming an island ballad, he was sailor-king of the sea, a photo opportunity his passengers could not resist. Solitary females on holiday from northern peninsulas of ice and snow, secretaries, nurses, schoolteachers, clerks, students, the druggies who'd sold dope and sold themselves to get this far, this last fling at island sun and sea and fun, old Zivanias would hook them on his horny big toe and reel them in. Plying his sea taxi from bare-ass to barer-ass to barest-ass beach, his stations, his ports of call along the coast.

But not today. No putt-putting around the edges of Mykonos, no island hopping. Suicide on a day like this to attempt a crossing to Delos, the island sacred to Apollo where once no one was allowed to die or be born. No sailing today even with both hands on the wheel and all ten toes gripping the briny deck. Chop, chop sea would eat you up. Swallow your little boat. Spew it up far from home. Zivanias should have known better. Maybe he did. Maybe he couldn't resist the power in his name summoning him, Zivanias, Zivanias. Moonshine. Doomshine. Scattered on the water.

Cudjoe winces. A column of feathers and stinging grit rises from the cobblestones and sluices past him. Wind is steady moan and groan, a constant weight in his face, but it also bucks and roils and sucks and swirls madly, sudden stop and start, gust and dust devil and dervishes ripping the world apart. Clouds scoot as if they're being chased. Behind him the café window rattles in its frame. Yesterday at this same dockside table he'd watched the sunset. Baskets of live chickens unloaded. Colors spilled on the sea last evening were chicken broth and chicken blood and the yellow, wrinkled skin of plucked chickens. Leftover feathers geyser, incongruous snowflakes above stacks of empty baskets. The island exiled today. Jailed by its necklace of churning sea. No one could reach Mykonos. No one could leave. Dead sailorman Zivanias out there sea-changed, feeding the fish. Cudjoe's flight home disappearing like the patches of blue sky. Sea pitches and shivers and bellows in its chains. Green and dying. Green and dying. Who wrote that poem. Cudjoe says the words again, green and dying, can't remember the rest, the rest is these words repeating themselves, all the rest contained in them, swollen to bursting, but they won't give up the rest. Somebody keeps switching a light on and off. Gray clouds thicken. White clouds pull apart, bleed into the green sea. A seamless curtain of water and sky draws tighter and tighter. The island is sinking. Sea and wind wash over its shadow, close the wound.

Take that morning or one like it and set it down here in this city of brotherly love, seven thousand miles away, in a crystal ball, so it hums and gyrates under its glass dome. When you turn it upside-down, a thousand weightless flakes of something hover in the magic jar. It plays a tune if you wind it, better watch out, better not cry. Cudjoe cups his hands, fondles the toy, transfixed by the simplicity of illusion, how snow falls and music tinkles again and again if you choose to play a trick on yourself. You could stare forever and the past goes on doing its thing. He dreams his last morning on Mykonos once more. If you shake the ball the flakes shiver over the scene. Tiny white chicken feathers. Nothing outside the sealed ball touches what's inside. Hermetic. Unreachable. Locked in and the key thrown away. Once again he'll meet a dark-haired woman in the café that morning. Wind will calm itself, sky clear. The last plane shuttles him to the mainland. Before that wobbly flight he'll spend part of his last day with her on the beach. There will be a flash of fear when she rises naked from the sea and runs toward him, crowned by a bonnet of black snakes, arms and legs splashing showers of spray, sun spots and sun darts tearing away great chunks of her so he doesn't know what she is. They'll lie together on the sand. She will teach him the Greek for her body parts. Hair is . . . eyes are . . . nose is . . . the Greek words escaping him even as he hears them. But he learns the heat of her shoulders, curve of bone beneath the skin. No language she speaks is his. She doubles his confusion. He forgets how to talk. When she tests him, pointing to his eyes, he traces with a fingertip the pit of bone containing hers. He closes his eyes. He is blind. Words are empty sounds. Saying them does not bring her back. He'd tasted salt when he'd matched his word for lips with hers.

Cudjoe is remembering the toy from his grandmother's cupboard. A winter scene under glass. Lift it by its black plastic base, turn it upside-down, shake it a little, shake it, don't break it, and set the globe down again watch the street fill up with snow the little horse laugh to see such a sight and the dish run away with the the spoon. He wonders what happened to his grandmother's souvenir from Niagara Falls. When did she buy it? Why did he always want to pry it open and find the music and snow wherever they were hiding when the glass ball sat still and silent? He wanted to know but understood how precious the trinket was to his grandmother. She would die if he broke it. She lay in bed, thinner every day the summer after the winter his grandfather died. She was melting away. Turning to water which he mopped from her brow, from her body parts when he lifted the sheets. Could he have saved her if he'd known the Greek for arms and legs? His grandmother's sweaty smell will meet him when he returns to the house on Finance and walks up the front-hall stairs and enters the tiny space where he cared for her that summer she melted in the heat of grief. Her husband of forty years dead, her flesh turning to water. Sweat is what gives you life. He figured that out as life drained from her. Her dry bones never rose from the bed. You could lift her and arrange her in the rocking chair but life was gone. He'd wiped it from her brow, her neck. Dried the shiny rivers in her scalp. Leg is . . . arm is . . . He learned the parts of a woman's body caring for her, the language of sweat and smell they spoke. He had been frightened. He knew everything and nothing. Why was he supposed to look away from her nakedness when his aunts bathed her? He loved her. Shared her secrets. If he sat in the rocker keeping watch while she slept, she would not die.

The crystal ball long gone. He can't recall the first time he missed it. Nothing rests in the empty cup of his hands. Not the illusion of a chilly winter day, not snowfall or a dark-haired woman's face, her skin brown and warm as bread just out the oven. *Ladybug, Ladybug. Fly away home. Your house is on fire. Your children burning.* He is turning pages. Perhaps asleep with a book spread-eagled on his lap, the book he wishes he was writing, the story he crossed an ocean to find. Story of a fire and a lost boy that brought him home.

He had taped what she said. She is Margaret Jones now, Margaret Jones again. Her other names are smoke curling from smashed windowpanes of the house on Osage. A rainbow swirl of head kerchief hides her hair, emphasizes the formal arrangement of eyes, nose, lips embedded in blemishless yellow-brown skin. No frills, no distractions, you see the face for what it is, severe, symmetrical, eyes distant but ready to pounce, flared bulk of nose, lips thick and strong enough to keep the eyes in check.

She thinks she knows people who might know where the lost child could be. And she is as close to the boy as he's come after weeks of questions, hanging around, false leads and no leads, his growing awareness of getting what he deserved as he was frowned at and turned away time after time. The boy who is the only survivor of the holocaust on Osage Avenue, the child who is brother, son, a lost limb haunting him since he read about the fire in a magazine. He must find the child to be whole again. Cudjoe can't account for the force drawing him to the story nor why he indulges a fantasy of identification with the boy who escaped the massacre. He knows he must find him. He knows the ache of absence, the phantom presence of pain that tricks him into reaching down again and again to stroke the emptiness. He's stopped asking why. His identification with the boy persists like a discredited rumor. Like Hitler's escape from the bunker. Like the Second Coming.

What Cudjoe has discovered is that the boy was last seen naked *skin melting, melting, they go do-do-do-do-do-do-do like that, skin melting stop kids coming out stop stop kids coming out skin melting do-do-do-do-do-do like going off—like bullets were going after each other do-do-do-do* fleeing down an alley between burning rows of houses. Only one witness. A sharpshooter on a roof who caught the boy's body in his telescopic sight just long enough to know he'd be doomed if he pulled the trigger, doomed if he didn't. In that terrible light pulsing from the inferno of fire-gutted houses the boy flutters, a dark moth shape for an instant, wheeling, then fixed forever in the cross hairs of the infrared sniperscoped night-visioned weapon trained on the alley. At the same instant an avalanche of bullets hammers what could be other figures, other children back into boiling clouds of smoke and flame. The last sighting reports the boy alone, stumbling, then upright. Then gone again as quickly as he appeared.

Cudjoe hears screaming *stop stop kids coming out kids coming out* as the cop sights down the blazing alley. Who's screaming? Who's adding that detail? Could a cop on a roof two hundred feet away from a ghost hear what's coming from its mouth? Over crackling flames? Over volleys of automatic-weapons fire thudding into the front of the house, over the drum thump of heart, roar of his pulse when something alive dances like a spot of grease on a hot griddle there in the molten path between burning row houses? The SWAT-team rifleman can't hear, barely sees what is quivering in the cross hairs. Is it one of his stinging eyelashes? He squints and the vision disappears. Did he pull the trigger? Only later as he's interrogated and must account for rounds fired and unfired does it become clear to him that what he saw was a naked boy, a forked stick with a dick. No. No, I didn't shoot then. Others shot. Lots of shooting when the suspects tried to break out of the house. But I didn't shoot. Not then. Because what I seen was just a kid, with no clothes on *screaming*. I let him go.

Cudjoe reminds himself he was not there and has no right to add details. No sound effects. Attribute no motives nor lack of motive. He's not the cop, not the boy.

Tape is rewinding on his new machine. The woman with the bright African cloth tied round her head had not liked him. Yet she was willing to talk, to be taped. She'd agreed to meet him again, this time in the park instead of the apartment of the mutual friend who'd introduced them. You know. Clark Park, Forty-third and Baltimore. He'd nodded, smiled, ready after an hour of listening and recording to say something about the park, about himself, but she'd turned away, out of her chair already, already out the door of Rasheed's apartment, though her body lagged behind a little saying good-bye to him, hollering good-bye over her shoulder to Rasheed. She'd watched the tape wind from spool to spool as she'd talked. Rasheed had waited in another room for them to finish. Cudjoe might as well have been in there, too. He spoke only once or twice while she talked. Margaret Jones didn't need him, care for him. She was permitting him to overhear what she told the machine. Polite, accommodating to a degree, she also maintained her distance. Five thousand miles of it, plus or minus an inch. The precise space between Cudjoe's island and West Philly.

Somehow she knew he'd been away, exactly how long, exactly how far, and that distance bothered her, she held it against him, served it back to him in her cool reserve, seemed unable ever to forgive it.

How did she know so much about him, not only her but all her sisters, how, after the briefest of conversations, did they know his history, that he'd married a white woman and fathered half-white kids? How did they know he'd failed his wife and failed those kids, that his betrayal was double, about blackness and about being a man? How could they express so clearly, with nothing more than their eyes, that they knew his secret, that he was someone, a half-black someone, a half man who couldn't be depended upon?

He peels a spotty banana down to the end he holds. Bites off a hunk. Rewraps the fruit in its floppy skin and rests it on a paper towel beside the tape recorder. Spoons a lump of coffee-flavored Dannon yogurt into his mouth. The tastes clash. One too sweet. One too tart. The cloying overripe odor of unzipped banana takes over. In an hour he should be in the park. Will Ms. Jones show up? If he admits to her he doesn't know why he's driven to do whatever it is he's trying to do, would she like him better? Should he tell her his dream of a good life, a happy life on a happy island? Would she believe him? Fine lines everywhere to negotiate. He knows it won't be easy. Does she think he's stealing from the dead? Is he sure he isn't? Tape's ready. He pushes the button.

. . . Because he was so sure of hisself, bossy, you know. The big boss knowing everything and in charge of everything and could preach like an angel, they called him Reverend King behind his back. Had to call him something to get his attention, you know. James didn't sound right. He wasn't a Jimmy or Jim. Mr. Brown wouldn't cut it. Mr. Anything no good. Reverend King slipped out a couple times and then it got to be just King. King a name he answered to. Us new ones in the family had to call him something so we called him King because that's what we heard from the others. Didn't realize it kind of started as a joke. Didn't realize by calling him something we was making him something. He was different. You acted different around him so he'd know you knew he was different. Then we was different.

He taught us about the holy Tree of Life. How we all born part of it. How we all one family. Showed us how the rotten system of this society is about chopping down the Tree. Society hates health. Society don't want strong people. It wants people weak and sick so it can use them up. No room for the Life Tree. Society's about stealing your life juices and making you sick so the Tree dies.

He taught us to love and respect ourselves. Respect Life in ourselves. Life is good, so we're good. He said that every day. We must protect Life and pass it on so the Tree never dies. Society's system killing everything. Babies. Air. Water. Earth. People's bodies and minds. He taught us we are the seeds. We got to carry forward the Life in us. When society dies from the poison in its guts, we'll be there and the Tree will grow bigger and bigger till the whole wide earth a peaceful garden under its branches. He taught us to praise Life and be Life.

We loved him because he was the voice of Life. And our love made him greater than he was. Made him believe he could do anything. All the pains we took. The way we were so careful around him, let him do whatever he wanted, let him order us around like we was slaves. Now when I look back I guess that's what we was. His slaves. And he was king because we was slaves and we made him our master.

He was the dirtiest man I ever seen. Smell him a mile off. First time I really seen him I was on my way home from work and he was just sitting there on the stone wall in front of their house. Wasn't really stone. Cinder blocks to hold in yard dirt. Sucked four or five high and a rusty kind of broken-down pipe fence running across the top of the blocks. Well, that's where he was sitting, dangling his bare legs and bare toes, sprawled back like he ain't got a care in the world. Smelled him long before I seen him. Matter of fact when I stepped down off the bus something nasty in the air. My nose curls and I wonder what stinks, what's dead and where's it hiding, but I don't like the smell so I push it to the back of my mind cause nothing I can do about it. No more than I can stop the stink rolling in when the wind blows cross from Jersey. Got too much else to worry about at 5:30 in the evening. I'm hoping Billy and Karen where they supposed to be. Mrs. Johnson keep them till 5:00, then they supposed to come straight home. Weather turning warm. Stuffy inside the house already so I say OK youall can sit out on the stoop but don't you go a step further till I'm home. Catch you gallivanting over the neighborhood it's inside the house, don't care if it's a oven in there. Billy and Karen mind most the time, good kids, you know what I mean, but all it takes is one time not minding. You know the kinda trouble kids can get into around here. Deep trouble. Bad, bad trouble. One these fools hang around here give them pills. One these jitterbugs put his hands on Karen. I'm worried about that sort of mess and got dinner to fix and beat from work, too beat for any of it. My feet ache and that's strange because I work at a desk and I'm remembering my mama keeping house for white folks. Her feet always killing her and here I am with my little piece of degree, sitting on my behind all day and my feet sore like hers. Maybe what it is is working for them damned peckerwoods any kind of way. Taking their shit. Bitterness got to settle somewhere don't it? Naturally it run down to your feet. Anyway, I'm tired and hassled. Ain't ready for no more nonsense. Can't wait till Billy and Karen fed and quiet for the night, safe for the night, the kitchen clean, my office clothes hung up, me in my robe and slippers. Glass of wine maybe. One my programs on TV. Nothing but my own self to worry about.

When I step off the bus stink hits me square between the eyeballs. No sense wrinkling up my nose. Body got to breathe and thinking about what you breathing just make it worse so I starts towards home which is three and a half blocks from where I get off the Number 62. Almost home when I see a trifling dreadlocked man draped back wriggling his bare toes. Little closer to him and I know what's dead, what's walking the air like it ain't had a bath since Skippy was a pup. Like I can see this oily kind of smoke seeping up between the man's toes. He's smiling behind all that hair, all that beard. Proud of his high self working toejam. I know it ain't just him stinking up the whole neighborhood. It's the house behind him, the tribe of crazy people in it and crazy dogs and loudspeakers and dirty naked kids and the backyard where they dump their business, but sitting the way he is on the cinder blocks, cocked back and pleased with hisself, smiling through that orangutan hair like a jungle all over his face, it's like he's telling anybody care to listen, this funk is mine. I'm the funk king sitting here on my throne and you can run but you can't hide.

See, it's personal then. Me and him. To get home I have to pass by him. His wall, his house, his yard. Either pass by or go way round out my way. Got my route home I've been walking twelve years. Bet you find my footprints in the pavement I been walking home from work that way so long. So I ain't about to change just cause some nasty man sitting there like he's God Almighty. Huh. Uh. This street mine much as it's anybody's. I ain't detouring one inch out my way for nothing that wears britches and breathes. He ain't nothing to me no matter how bad he smell, no matter if he blow up in a puff of black smoke cause he can't stand his own self. Tired as my feet be at the end of the day I ain't subjecting them to one extra step around this nasty man or his nasty house.

So I just trots on by like he ain't there, like ain't none of it there. Wall. Pipe he's got his greasy arms draped over. House behind him and the nuts in it. You know. Wouldn't give him the satisfaction. What I do do is stop breathing. Hold my breath till I'm past him, hold it in so long when I let it out on the next comer, I'm dizzy. But I'm past him and don't give him the satisfaction. Tell the truth, I almost fainted before I made it up on the curb. And wouldn't that have been a sight. Me keeling over in the street. He woulda had him a good laugh at that. Woulda told all them savages live with him. They could all have a good laugh together. The hounds. But what I care? Didn't happen, did it? Strutted right past him like he wasn't there. Didn't even cross to the other side of Osage like I knew he was sitting there betting I would. Hoping I would so he could tell his tribe and they could all grin and hee-haw and put me on their loudspeakers.

No. No. Walked home the way I always walk home. Didn't draw one breath for a whole block. Almost knocked myself out, but be damned if I'd give him the satisfaction.

Doesn't make much sense, does it? Because the day I'm telling you about, the first time I seen him eyeball to eyeball, wasn't much more than a year ago. Three months from that day I was part of his family. One his slaves that quick. Still am in a way. Even though his head's tore off his body and his body burned to ash. See because even though he did it wrong, he was right. What I mean is his ideas were right, the thoughts behind the actions righteous as rain. He be rapping and he'd stop all the sudden, look over to one the sisters been a real strong church woman her whole life and say: Bet your sweet paddy boy Jesus amen that, wouldn't he now? Teasing sort of, but serious too. He be preaching what Jesus preached except it's King saying the words. Bible words only they issuing from King's big lips. And you know he means them and you understand them better cause he says them black, black like him, black like you, so how the sister gon deny King? Tell that white fella Jesus stop pestering you. Tell him go on back to the desert and them caves where he belong.

Got to her Christian mind. Got to my tired feet. Who I been all the days of my life? A poor fool climb on a bus in the morning, climb down at night. What I got to show for it but sore feet, feet bad as my mama's when, God bless her weary soul, we laid her to rest after fifty years cleaning up white folks' mess. My life wasn't much different from my mama's or hers from her mama's on back far as you want to carry it back. Out in the field at dawn, pick cotton the whole damned day, shuffle back to the cabin to eat and sleep so's you ready when the conch horn blows next morning. Sheeet. Things spozed to get better, ain't they? Somewhere down the line, it ought to get better or what's the point scuffling like we do? Don't have to squat in the weeds and wipe my behind with a leaf. Running water inside my house and in the supermarket I can buy thirty kinds of soda pop, twelve different colors of toilet paper. But that ain't what I call progress. Do you? King knew it wasn't. King just told the truth.

My Billy and Karen in school. Getting what they call an education. But what those children learn. Ask them where they come from, they give you the address of a house on Osage Avenue. Ask them what's on their minds, they mumble something they heard on the TV. Ask them what color they are, they don't even know that. Look them in the eye you know what they really thinking. Only thing they ever expect to be is you. Working like you for some white man or black man don't make no difference cause all they pay you is nigger wages, enough to keep you guessing, keep you hungry, keep you scared, keep you coming back. Piece a job so you don't never learn nothing, just keep you busy and too tired to think. But your feet think. They tell you every day God sends, stop this foolishness. Stop wearing me down to the nubs.

Wasn't like King told me something new. Wasn't like I had a lot to learn. Looked round myself plenty times and said, Got to be more to it than this. Got to be. King said out loud what I been knowing all along. Newspapers said King brainwashing and mind control and drugs and kidnapping people turn them to zombies. Bullshit. Because I been standing on the bank for years. Decided one day to cross over and there he was, the King take my hand and say, Welcome, come right in, we been waiting. Held my breath walking past him and wasn't more than a couple months later I'm holding my breath and praying I can get past the stink when he's raising the covers off his mattress and telling me lie down with him. By then stink wasn't really stink no more. Just confusion. A confused idea. An idea from outside the family, outside the teachings causing me to turn my nose up at my own natural self. Felt real ashamed when I realized all of me wasn't inside the family yet. I damned the outside part. Left it standing in the dark and crawled up under the covers with King cause he's right even if he did things wrong sometimes, he's still right cause ain't nothing, nowhere any better.

Cudjoe stops the tape. Was Margaret Jones still in love with her King, in love with the better self she believed she could become? He'd winced when she described King lifting the blanket off his bed. Then Cudjoe had leaned closer, tried to sneak a whiff of her. Scent of the sacred residue. Was a portion of her body unwashed since the holy coupling? She had looked upon the King's face and survived. Cudjoe sees a rat-gnawed, bug-infested mattress spotted with the blood of insects, of humans. Her master's face a mask of masks. No matter how many you peel, another rises, like the skins of water. Loving him is like trying to solve a riddle whose answer is yes and no. No or yes. You will always be right *and* wrong.

Not nice to nose under someone's clothes. Cudjoe knows better. He had cheated, sniffing this witness like some kind of evil bloodhound.

The spools spin:

My lads wouldn't have nothing to do with King. When I moved into his house they ran away. I think Karen might have moved with me but Billy, thank goodness, wouldn't let her. Went to my sister's in Detroit. Then Detroit drove to Philly to rescue me. A real circus. I'm grateful to God nobody was hurt. King said, You nebby, bleached negroes come round here hassling us again I'll bust you up. He was just woofing. But he sounds like he means every word and I'm standing in the doorway behind him amening what he's saying. My own sister and brother-in-law, mind you. Carl worked at Ford. My sister Anita a schoolteacher. Doing real good in Detroit and they drove all the way here to help me but I didn't want no help. Thought all I needed was King. They came out of love but I hated them for mixing in my business. Hated them for taking care of Karen and Billy. See, I believed they were part of the system, part of the lie standing in the way of King's truth. The enemy. The ones trying to kill us. Up there in their dicty Detroit suburb living the so-called *good life*.

Cudjoe fast-forwards her story. Would she tell more about the boy this time? Or would the tape keep saying what it had said last time he listened.

. . . Had the good sense not to sell my house when I moved out. Rented it. Gave the rent money to King. If I'd sold it, would've give all the money to him. Wouldn't have nothing now. No place for Billy and Karen to come back to, if they coming back. Don't want them here yet. City spozed to clean up and rebuild but you see the condition things in. My place still standing. Smoke and water tore it up inside but at least it's still standing. Next block after mine looks like pictures I seen of war. Look like the atom bomb hit. Don't want Karen and Billy have to deal with what the bombs and fire and water did. They see the neighborhood burned down like this, they just might blame me. Because like I said, I was one of them. King's family. Rented my house and moved in with them. Yes. But for the grace of God coulda been me and my kids trapped in the basement, bar-b-qued to ash.

I still can't believe it. Eleven people murdered. Babies, women, didn't make no nevermind to the cops. Eleven human beings dead for what? Tell me for what. Why did they have to kill my brothers and sisters? Burn them up like you burn garbage? What King and them be doing that give anybody the right to kill them? Wasn't any trouble till people started coming at us. Then King start to woofing to keep folks off our case. Just woofing. Just talk. You ask anybody around here, the ones still here or the ones burnt out, if you can find them. Ask them if King or his people ever laid a hand on anybody. You find one soul say he been hurt by one of us he's a lying sack of shit.

King had his ways. We all had our ways. If you didn't like it, you could pass on by. That's all anybody had to do, pass us by. Hold your nose, your breath if you got to, but pass on by and leave us alone, then we leave you alone and everybody happy as they spozed to be.

The boy?

Cudjoe is startled by his voice on the tape, asking the question he's thinking now. Echo of his thought before he speaks it.

The boy?

Little Simmie. Simmie's what we called him. Short for Simba Muntu. Lion man. That's what Clara named him when she joined King's people. Called herself Nkisa. She was like a sister to me. We talked many a night when I first went there to live.

Little Simmie her son. So afterwhile I was kind of his aunt. All of us family, really. Simmie's an orphan now. His mama some of those cinders they scraped out the basement of the house on Osage and stuffed in rubber bags. I was behind the barricade the whole time. Watched it all happening. Almost lost my mind. Just couldn't believe it. I saw it happening and couldn't believe my eyes.

Those dogs carried out my brothers and sisters in bags. And got the nerve to strap those bags on stretchers. Woman next to me screamed and fainted when the cops start parading out with them bags strapped on stretchers. Almost fell out my ownself watching them stack the stretchers in ambulances. Then I got mad. Lights on top the ambulances spinning like they in a hurry. Hurry for what? Those pitiful ashes ain't going nowhere. Nkisa and Rhoberto and Sunshine and Teetsie. They all gone now, so what's the hurry? Why they treating ash like people now? Carrying it on stretchers. Cops wearing gloves and long faces like they respect my brothers and sisters now. Where was respect when they was shooting and burning and flooding water on the house? Why'd they have to kill them two times, three times, four times? Bullets, bombs, water, fire. Shot, blowed up, burnt, drowned. Nothing in those sacks but ash and guilty conscience.

What they carried out was board ash and wall ash and roof ash and hallway-step ash and mattress ash and the ash of blankets and pillows, ashes of the little precious things you sneaked in with you when you went to live with King because he said, Give it up, give up that other life and come unto me naked as the day you were born. He meant it too. Never forget being buck naked and walking down the rows of my brothers and sisters each one touch me on my forehead. Shivering. Goose bumps where I forgot you could get goose bumps. Thinking how big and soft I was in the behind and how my titties must look tired hanging down bare. But happy. Oh so happy. Happy it finally come down to this. Nothing to hide no more. Come unto me and leave the world behind. Like a new-born child.

My brothers and sisters and the babies long gone and wasn't much else in the house to make ash, so it's walls and floors in those bags, the pitiful house itself they carting away in ambulances.

His mother died in the fire.

All dead. All of them dead.

But he escaped.

She pushed him and two the other kids out the basement window. Simmie said he was scared, didn't want to go. Nkisa had to shove him out the window. He said she threw him and then he doesn't remember a thing till he wakes up in the alley behind the house. Must of hit his head on something. He said he was dreaming he was on fire and took off running and now he doesn't know when he woke up or when he was dreaming or if the nightmare's ever gon stop. Poor Simmie an orphan now. Like my Karen and Billy till I got myself thinking straight again. Till I knew I couldn't put nobody, not even King, before my kids. They brought me back to the world. And it's as sorry-assed today as it was when I walked away. Except it's worse now. Look round you at the neighborhood. Where's the houses, the old people on their stoops, the children playing in the street? Nobody cares. The whole city seen the flames, smelled the smoke, counted the body bags. Whole world knows children murdered here. But it's quiet as a grave, ain't it? Not a mumbling word. People gone back to making a living. Making some rich man richer. Losing the only thing they got worth a good goddamn, the children the Lord gives them for free, and they ain't got the good sense to keep.

You've talked to Simmie?

Talked to people talked to him.

Do you know where he is?

I know where to find somebody who might know where he is. Why do you want to know?

I need to hear his story. I'm writing a book.

A book?

About the fire. What caused it. Who was responsible. What it means.

Don't need a book. Anybody wants to know what it means, bring them through here. Tell them these bombed streets used to be full of people's homes. Tell them babies' bones mixed up in this ash they smell.

I want to do something about the silence.

A book, huh. A book people have to buy. You want Simmie's story so you can sell it. You going to pay him if he talks to you?

It's not about money.

Then why you doing it?

The truth is, I'm not really sure.

You mean you'll do your thing and forget Simmie. Write your book and gone. Just like the social workers and those busybodies from the University. They been studying us for years. Reports on top of reports. A whole basement full of files in the building where I work. We're famous.

Why don't you leave poor Simmie alone, mister? He's suffered enough. And still suffering. Nightmares. Wetting the bed. Poor child's trying to learn what it's like to live with people ain't King's people.

Will you help me find him?

I don't think so.

Can we meet again at least? Talk some more?

Saturday maybe. That will give me time to ask around. Not here. In Clark Park. I don't like being in here with that machine sucking up all the air.

I'll meet you anywhere. Anytime. Tape or no tape.

Saturday morning. Clark Park.

What time, Saturday?

Early.

I'll be there.

I bet you will. Tell you a secret, though, my feelings won't be hurt if you ain't.

Clark Park. Forty-third and Osage. Saturday early. I'll be there.

One more thing . . . is that damned machine still running?

Yes . . . no.

Click.

If the city is a man, a giant sprawled for miles on his back, rough contours of his body smothering the rolling landscape, the rivers and woods, hills and valleys, bumps and gullies, crushing with his weight, his shadow, all the life beneath him, a derelict in a terminal stupor, too exhausted, too wasted to move, rotting in the sun, then Cudjoe is deep within the giant's stomach, in a subway-surface car shuddering through stinking loops of gut, tunnels carved out of decaying flesh, a prisoner of rumbling innards that scream when trolleys pass over rails embedded in flesh. Cudjoe remembers a drawing of Gulliver strapped down in Lilliput just so. Ropes staked over his limbs like hundreds of tiny tents, pyramids pinning the giant to the earth. If the city is a man sprawled unconscious drunk in an alley, kids might find him, drench him with lighter fluid and drop a match on his chest. He'd flame up like a heap of all the unhappy monks in Asia. Puff the magic dragon. A little bald man topples over, spins as flames spiral up his saffron robe. In the streets of Hue and Saigon it had happened daily. You watched priests on TV burst into fireballs, roll as they combusted, a shadow flapping inside the flaming pyre. You thought of a bird in there trying to get out. You wondered if the bird was a part of the monk refusing to go along with the program. A protest within the monk's protest. Hey. I don't want nothing to do with this crazy shit. Wings get me out of here. Screeching and writhing as hot gets hotter, a scarecrow in the flame's eye.

Same filthy-windowed PTC trolley car carries you above and below ground, in and out of flesh, like a needle suturing a wound. You hear an echo of wind and sea, smell it. As you ride beneath city streets there are distant explosions, muffled artillery roar and crackle of automatic weapons, sounds of war you don't notice in the daylight world above. Down here no doubt the invisible warfare is real. You are rattling closer to it. It sets the windows of the trolley vibrating. Around the next blind curve the firefight waits to engulf you.

Above the beach at Torremolinos was another city of tunnels

and burrows. Like a termite mound. Once, instead of following the shore path, he'd taken the vertical shortcut from beach to town. Haphazard steps hacked from rock, worn smooth by a million bare feet. You couldn't see very far ahead or behind as you climbed up the cliff. Quickly the tourists baking like logs on the beach disappeared as you picked your way through a warren of dugout houses, the front stoops of some being the stations that formed a pathway from beach back up to hotels, shops and restaurants. Children sat at the mouths of caves and you planted your bare feet over, under and around their bare bodies, afraid of contamination, embarrassed by proximity, trespass. Bony gypsy children. Eyes dark as mirrors draped with black cloth. Eyes that should flash and play, be full of curiosity or mischief, but stare past you, through you. Riding these trains sunken in the earth, the sound of the sea waits in ambush. Near and far. Turn a corner and there sits one of these world hunger poster children silently begging to be something other than an image of disaster. Fingers of rib bone grasp the swollen belly like it's a spoiled toy.

He recalls the sound of waves lapping the pilings, breaking and shimmying slow motion against a golden slice of beach three hundred yards below the outcropping of stone where he had paused. He's naked except for bikini briefs, a gaudy towel slung like a bandolier over his shoulder. He's ashamed of his skin, its sleekness, its color, the push of his balls against the flimsy pouch of black nylon. No pockets to empty, no language to confess his shame. He couldn't make things right for the hollow-eyed, big-bellied children even if he had a thousand pockets and dumped silver from every one and the coins sparked and scintillated like the flat sea when a breath of wind passes over it, sequins, a suit of lights rippling to the horizon. From where he'd stood on the steep cliffside, eyes stinging from shame at having everything and nothing to give, the sea reached him as whisper, the same insinuating murmur that can seep from under his bed at night in this city thousands of miles away, that can squeeze from behind a picture frame on a wall, that hums in this subway tunnel miles beneath the earth.

He'll tell Margaret Jones we're all in this together. That he was lost but now he's found.

I could smell the smoke five thousand miles away. Hear kids screaming. We are all trapped in the terrible jaws of something shaking the life out of us. Is that what he'd tell her? Is that why he's back? *Runagate, runagate, fly away home / Your house's on fire and your children's burning.*

Should he admit to her he'd looked into the eyes of those gypsy children and shrugged, turned his hands inside out? The pale emptiness of his palms flashed like a minstrel's white gloves, a silent-movie charade so he could pick his way in peace past stick legs and stick arms, the long feet that looked outsize because they sprouted first then nothing else grew. Big heads, big feet. Everything in between wasted away, siphoned into the brutal swell of their bellies. Skin the color of his, the color those tourists down on the beach dreamed of turning.

The subway takes you under ground, under the sea. When the train slows down for a station you can see greenish mold, sponge-like algae, yellow and red speckling the dark stones. Sometimes you hear the rush of water behind you flooding the tunnel, chasing your lighted bubble, rushing closer and closer each time the train halts. Damp, slimy walls the evidence of other floods, other cleansings, guts of the giant flushed clear of debris. He groans, troubled in his sleep as his bowels contract and shudder from the sudden passage of icy water.

When Cudjoe's aboveground, heading toward Clark Park, the sidewalk's unsteady under his feet. Should he be swimming or flying or crawling.

He will explain to Margaret Jones that he must always write about many places at once. No choice. The splitting apart is inevitable. First step is always out of time, away from responsibility, toward the word or sound or image that is everywhere at once, that connects and destroys.

Many places at once. Tramping along the sidewalk. In the air. Underground. Astride a spark coughed up by the fire. Waterborne. Climbing stone steps. To reach the woman in the turban, the boy, he must travel through those other places. Always moving. He must, at the risk of turning to stone, look back at his own lost children, their mother standing on a train platform, wreathed in steam, in smoke. An old-fashioned locomotive wheezes and lurches into motion. His wife waves a handkerchief wet with tears. One boy grasps the backs of her legs. The other sucks his thumb with a fold of her skirt that shows off her body's sweet curves. His sons began in that smooth emptiness between her legs. They hide and sniffle, clutch handfuls of her silky clothes. It hurts him to look, hurts him to look away. Antique station he's only seen in movies. A new career for his wife and sons. Wherever they are, he keeps them coming back to star in this scene. Waving. Clinging. But it's the wrong movie. He's not the one leaving. *All aboard, all aboard.* Faces pressed to the cold glass. Caroline had never owned a silk handkerchief, let alone a long silky skirt.

A trolley begins its ascent of Woodland Avenue, the steep

curve along the cemetery where rails are bedded in cobblestones older than anything around them. A fence of black
spears seven feet tall guards the neat, green city of the dead.
When you choose to live in a city, you also are choosing a city
to die in. A huge rat sidles over the cobbles, scoots across steel
tracks, messenger from one domain to the other, the dead and
living consorting in slouched rat belly.

Teresa, the barmaid once upon a time in Torremolinos,
would listen to anything you had to say, as long as you bought
drinks while you said it. Beautiful and untouchable, she liked
to shoot rats at night after work, in the wee hours neither light
nor dark over on the wrong side of town, in garbage dumps,
the pits dug for foundations of luxury hotels, aborted high
rises never rising any higher than stacks of debris rimming
the edges of black holes. She'd hide in the shadows and wait
for them to slink into exposed areas. Furry, moonlit bodies,
sitting up like squirrels, a hunk of something in their forepaws,
gnawing, quivering, profiled just long enough for her to draw
a bead between their beady eyes. She never missed.

She was English. Or had lived in England long enough to
acquire a British accent, a taste for reggae. Teresa never took
Cudjoe seriously. He could amuse her, tease out her smile, but
she never encouraged him to go further. She knew his habits—
endless shots of Felipe II, determined assaults on each new
batch of female tourists—and he knew she shot rats in the old
quarter gypsies had inhabited before they were urban-removed.

He'd daydream of leaving the bar with Teresa, her alabaster
skin luminous in the fading moonlight. They were survivors.
No one else in the streets, the only sound their footfalls over
wooden sidewalks, then padding through dusty alleys as they

entered the ghetto. He'd watch her do her Annie Oakley thing. Her unerring aim. Her face pinched into a mask of concentration as she sights down the barrel. When she tires of killing, when she leans her rifle against a broken wall and huddles in her own skinny, pale arms, he'll create himself out of the shadows, wrap her in his warmth, the heat of his body he's been hoarding while she shot. He loves this moment when she's weak and exhausted, the pallor of her skin, the cold in her bones, the starry distance of all those nights at the bar when he made her smile but could trick nothing more from those sad eyes. Yes. Take her in the stillborn shell of a building that is also the grave of a gypsy hovel, abandoned when the urban gypsies fled to join their brethren in caves above the sea. Make love to her in the ruins that had never been a city, ruins that were once a wish for a city, a mile-high oasis of steel and glass and rich visitors. Surprise her and take her there, loving her to pieces while rats scuttle from the darkness to eat their dead.

Yes. Clark Park. He knew the location of Clark Park. He'd nodded at Margaret Jones. Yes, I know Clark Park. He'd beaten up his body many a day on the basketball court there. Drank wine and smoked reefer with the hoop junkies many a night after playing himself into a stupor. Clear now what he'd been trying to do. Purge himself. Force the aching need for Caroline and his sons out of his body. Running till his body was gone, his mind whipped. Till he forgot his life was coming apart. Keep score of the game, let the rest go. The park a place to come early and stay late, punish the humpty-dumpty pieces of himself till they'd never want to be whole again.

Clark Park where he'd see a face like Teresa's. A woman sat

in the grass, on a slope below the asphalt path circling the park, in a bright patch of early-morning sunshine. She was staring at the hollow's floor, a field tamped hard and brown by countless ball games. This woman who could be Teresa, who would be Teresa until Cudjoe satisfied himself otherwise, rested her chin on her drawn-up knees. No kids playing in the hollow, no dog walkers strolling on the path, just the two of us, Cudjoe had thought as he stopped and ambled down the green slope, lower than she was, so he could check out her face. He'll smile, one early bird greeting another. Pass on if she's a stranger.

Under her skimpy paisley dress, the woman was naked. She hugged her legs to her chest. Goose bumps prickled her bare loins. At the center of her a dark crease, a spray of curly hairs, soft pinch of buttocks. Cudjoe expected her to raise her chin off her knees, snap her legs straight, but she remained motionless, staring at the hollow. It could be Teresa's face perched on the woman's bare knees, a perfect match even though the body bearing it no way Teresa's. But still it could be Teresa's face. Right head, wrong body, like a sphinx. The eyes are dreamy, express a vulnerability Teresa never exposed. Teresa's eyes were mirrors. You saw yourself, your unhappy secrets in them. Nothing in Teresa's gaze suggested you could change her or change yourself. This woman, girl in Clark Park whose face was Teresa's, whose body was compact, generously fleshed where Teresa was lithe and taut, this woman who let him see under her dress, had finally smiled down at him over her knees, a smile saying no more or less than this gift of sun feels good and I'm content to share it.

Then she had leaned backward catching her weight on her

arms, knees steepled, eyes closing as she tilted her forehead into the light filtering through the trees. Cudjoe's throat had tightened; he was afraid to swallow, to move an inch. He stared at the dark hinge between her legs. Though she seemed unconcerned by his presence, she wasn't ignoring him. She was stretching, yawning, welcoming, returning to him after centuries of sleep. She'd chosen her spot and he was part of it, so nothing was foreign, nothing could disturb this moment of communion when what she was was boundless, new, Eve to his Adam, Cudjoe had told himself, half-believing, as he peered into the crack between her legs, the delicate pinks, soft fleece. Born again.

Her green-and-white minidress clearly an afterthought. Didn't matter to her if it was off or on. She rolled slowly onto her side. From where Cudjoe stood the dress disappeared except for a green edging along the top of one bare flank. Neat roundness of her buttocks, graceful drape of thighs glowed in soft morning light. He couldn't see a face now. Teresa disintegrates in the smoky shafts of sunlight painting the bank. Above him the remnant of a statue, a woman perfectly formed from marble.

He'd been stuck. Like a fly in honey. He couldn't look away. Couldn't go on about his business. What was he looking for then, now as he remembers her, remembers her wisp of dress and the sun, his throat dry, loins filling up, growing so heavy he believed he was sinking into the ground, remembering how she was Teresa, then she wasn't, then she was, and the loud clanking of trolleys up Woodland, down Baltimore, cables popping, laughing at himself, believing none of it was real? At some point she'd risen, awkward, stiff from sitting too long.

A flash of red-dimpled white cheek before she smooths down the flowered hem of her dress. How long had he stood there like a dummy, gazing into the empty stripe of sunlight?

On Mykonos scuffing his way through hot sand he'd seen naked bodies every size, shape and color stretched for acres between green sea and rocks spilled at the base of cliffs, bodies so casual, blasé, he ignored them, preferred them at night, clothed, in the restaurants and discos. Funny how quickly he'd gotten used to nakedness. Hair, skin, bones. What was different, what was the same about all the bodies. Blond, dark, lean, stubby, every nation represented, all shapes of male and female displayed in any angle he could imagine. What was he looking for in women's bodies? Surely he'd have tripped over it trudging up and back those golden beaches on Mykonos. But no. The mystery persisted. His woman in the park. A daydream till she brushes bits of straw from the seat of her paisley dress. Runs away.

Rules posted in the park, but the signs, blasted by spray paint, unreadable. No rules, no signs when he'd lived here a decade ago. He'd remembered a green oasis. Forgotten those seasons, months when the park was the color of the neighborhood surrounding it. No color. Grays and browns of dead leaves. July now. Trees should be full, the grass green. He'd been hoping for green. Hoping the park sat green and waiting between Woodland and Baltimore avenues, that it had not been an invention, one more lie he'd told himself about this land to which he was returning.

A statue of Charles Dickens. Only one in the world at last count. Little Nell at his knee stares imploringly up at the great man's distant face. They are separated and locked together by her gaze. Both figures larger than life, greener than the brittle grass. Both blind. In a notebook somewhere Cudjoe had recorded the inscription carved into the pedestal. For his story about people who frequent the park. A black boy who climbs on Dickens's knee and daydreams. A crazy red-haired guy muttering and singing nonsense songs to himself. A blind man who shoots baskets at night. A boy-girl vignette about a baby the girl's carrying, how the couple strolls round and round the path, kids on a carousel, teaching themselves the news of another, unexpected life.

Twenty blocks west the fire had burned. If the wind right, smoke would have drifted here, settled on leaves, grass, bushes. Things that eat leaves and buds must have tasted smoke. Dark clouds drifting this way carried the ashy taste of incinerated children's flesh. Could you still smell it? Was the taste still part of what grew in the park? Would it ever go away?

Cudjoe watches a runty little boy terrorize other children in a play area off to his right. The kid's a devil. He screams and stomps his feet, laying claim to a domain invisible to the other kids till they encroach. Then he goes wild, patrolling his turf ferociously with shoves, screeches, the threat of his tiny fist wagged in somebody's face. He's everywhere at once, defending, shooing, hollering. Tough little bastard, Cudjoe thinks. All the other kids are buffaloed. Till one boy goes after the tyrant with a gun from outer space that squeals like a lost soul. The bully loses it. Screams and trucks away as fast as his stubby legs and miniature Adidas will carry him to a group of women sitting on a wall. Little guy's so shook up, he crashes into the wrong lap, hiding his face till another woman, who must be his mother, snatches him up, fusses at him and plops him down beside her.

The moral, Cudjoe says to himself, is everybody's afraid of something. Or everybody, sooner or later, meets their match. Or any port in a storm. Or if he hadn't been thinking of pussy a few minutes before, he wouldn't have glanced over at the young women perched on the wall around the play area and he'd have missed the whole show. And the moral of that was . . .

Circling the park, he passes benches set in concrete just off the main path. Built to last forever, they weren't going to make it. Somebody had expended enormous energy attacking them. Not casual violence but premeditated murder. You'd need heavy-duty weapons to inflict this damage. Sledgehammers. Crowbars. Why kill these benches whose sole purpose was offering people a place to rest their asses and enjoy the park? Why would anybody need to go declare war on a bench? Whose life was that fucked up? One or two benches survived, hacked, splintered. When would they get theirs? At night or in broad daylight? When all the benches were gone, what part of the park would be wasted next? Cudjoe hears the hobnailed boot tramp of soldier ants, the metallic grinding of their jaws as the column chews its way through a sleeping city.

He checks his watch. No guarantee she'd show up. Why should she trust him? He'd been surprised when she agreed to talk into the tape machine. Surprised when she said she'd meet him in the park. Clark Park between Baltimore and Woodland, around Forty-third. Yes, he knew the place. Yes, he'd be there. Would she?

Three blocks away the basketball court, the hollow. Nothing shaking as far as he can tell. A few people that from this distance, at this hour of the morning are silhouettes, dull shadows until they step beyond the border of trees and then their edges catch fire, bristle in the shimmer of sunshine bathing the far end of the park. One of those figures, wiggling in its nimbus of light, could be hers. Difficult from where he stands to be sure. No chance he'll miss her if she wants him to find her.

He crosses Chester Avenue, takes the lower dip of the path toward the court. Benches here, above the hollow, spray-painted and carved but intact. Cyclone fencing encloses three sides of the basketball court. All those new courts erected in the sixties had four high metal sides. People said they were part of the final solution. Lots more had sprung up in the ghetto since he'd been away. It ain't over yet, Cudjoe reminds himself.

This rusty fence seems higher, the court smaller. He can't remember the asphalt rectangle ever looking as forlorn, abandoned. In the old days when he'd arrive early to shoot around, the court might be deserted, but he'd never felt alone. Only a matter of time before other players would bop in. He wishes he'd brought a ball today so he could pat it, make it boom in the stillness. Glory hanging on every shot. He surveys the backboards, the crooked, netless rims. No clue anybody will play here today, tomorrow, ever. Was the court dead or just sleeping?

Best action migrated all over the city. Years ago Cudjoe knew where they'd be playing any night of the week, they being the bad dudes, the cookers, superstars. If your stuff wasn't ready better not bring it out there. They'd put a hurt on you. Send you home with your feelings hurt. Don't care what college you play for. On the neighborhood courts no coaches, no referees, no scholarships, nothing but you and what you can do and a whole lot of bad brothers who could play some ball. Some Sunday afternoons the action came to Clark. Court up at Sixty-ninth and Haverford packed and people cruise by Clark, get it on here instead of lining up for winners at Sixty-ninth. Knuckleheads tore down one rim at Forty-seventh and Kingsessing, couldn't run full court there, so Clark be it. The Big Time. Joint rocking. They all be out here.

Nothing like it. Cudjoe can't help smiling as he thinks of himself in the thick of the action. Pushing past the point of breaking but you don't break, a sweet second wind gets you over and it's easy then, past breaking or not breaking. Doing your thing and nothing can touch you. Past turning back. You're out there. Doing it. Legs and heart and mind and breath working hard together. You forget everything you know and play. The wall you can't move, that stops you and makes you cry when you beat your head against it, is suddenly full of holes. A velvet-stepped ladder tames the air. You can rise over the wall or glide through it. Do both at once. Unveil moves you didn't know you owned. You don't remember the wall till you're past it, over on the other side and a guy runs up to you and sticks out his palm and you slap skin low, high, higher, and the winos, junkies, bullshitters and signifiers jamming the sidelines holler amen like they just seen Black Jesus.

Cudjoe watches bodies flash past. A sound track explodes with crowd noise. The court's full, then just as abruptly empty again. Seconds pass quietly as the camera pans splitting wooden backboards. Droopy rims. Asphalt cracked with dry riverbeds and tributaries. A view of the empty court shot through interlocking squares of chain-link fencing to suggest how things might look from the steel-meshed window of a prison cell.

Inside looking out or outside looking in. Then the court's full again. Music blasting. Players grunting, panting, squeak of sneakers, cheers from the sidelines, thud of strong bodies every shade of black and brown and ivory colliding, tangling, flying. Cudjoe inserts himself into his film, a solitary figure, narrow shoulders framed by the emptiness of the court that is quiet again. A man caught up in reverie, shuttling at warp speed between times and places, a then and a now. Cudjoe is an actor embarrassed by the cliché shot, a director who can't resist filming it this way. Camera whirs behind his back, inside his skull. Court full, then empty. Sooty clouds, right on time, roll in from the west.

He senses Margaret Jones behind him, moving closer. Coming the long way round, under the canopy of trees, then into a band of light where her body blurs, disintegrates, her steps slower as warmth drops on her shoulders. Her eyes are fixed on his back, sure now it's him. Measuring, assessing the pose he's held too long now, but won't alter because he wants her to find him this way, wants her to shorten the distance between them, do some of the work to bring them together. He hopes she's wondering what he's thinking, that she'll realize she doesn't know everything about him. She reaches the trail worn through the grass alongside the far wing of the three-sided fence. He must not turn around too soon. He'll break the spell, she'll disappear. She's wearing an intricately wrapped turban, a robe with swirls of bold color. A few more paces will free her image from the disciplined strands of wire. He pivots abruptly and finds no one there. His timing's off. He's scared her away. Would she have been there if he'd held out just an instant longer? Too late now, charm's broken. Back across

Chester Avenue a woman sitting apart from the others smokes a cigarette on the stone wall enclosing monkey bars and slides.

Nkisa used to bring Simba here. I brought my kids, Billy and Karen, when they were little ones. Wasn't nothing so great about the park. This dinky playground stuff been here forever and half of it been busted forever but I liked the walk down from Fifty-ninth and liked getting out the house. Somebody different to talk to. Other women stuck at home like me with little babies. So once in a while I'd truck all the way down here to Clark with one in the stroller and one holding my hand.

Ten years or so ago.

About that.

Well, I might have seen you then. I lived on Osage. Spent half my life in the park. Played a lot of ball here.

They still play. Or call themselves playing. More drinking and snorting and smoking reefer than ball playing. A rowdy bunch now.

Used to be good hoop.

I wouldn't know anything about that, but I'd skin Billy or Karen alive if I caught them hanging around here. Pimpmobiles and dopemobiles. Sell you anything you big enough to ask for. And if I know what they're doing, the cops got to know. You think the police do anything about it? Hell no. Not till one these little white chicks slinking around here ODs and turns up dead, then they'll come down on that corner like gangbusters.

So the park's not what it used to be.

What is? Tell me if you know what is.

You might have run into my wife and boys here.

You have children?

Yes. Two boys. Probably about the age of your lads. They live with their mother now.

She stares at him as if none of this is news.

Thanks for meeting me this morning.

We been through all that once, ain't we? Started off with that polite, nicey-nice do. Don't need to go back to that again. I'm here. You're here. Got my reasons. I'm sure you have yours. You might want to take back some of that thank-you when you hear what I have to say. The boy's gone.

Gone? Gone where?

Nobody knows. Just disappeared.

Are you sure?

Sure as I'm sitting here.

Gone.

Like a turkey through the corn. My friends haven't seen him for a week. Finally got him to where he'd play with other kids. Had him a few little buddies come by every day and seemed like he was getting better. Simba even talked some with the kids. Grown-ups thought he'd forgot how. Said they saw him smile for the first time too, when he was around other kids. My friends who were keeping him said they'd let Simba go off and play with his gang because he was improving. Being around other kids doing him a world of good. He learned to ride a bike. Buddies taught him and one day he rode off nobody ain't seen him since.

Have they tried to find him?

What do you think, mister? They was taking care of the child. They nursed him, put up with his craziness. A little wild animal for weeks after the fire. They loved him back from craziness and now they scared to death somebody's done something else to hurt him. Trying every way they know how to find him. But nobody knows nothing. Had a lawyer who lives in the neighborhood check downtown. If the cops know something, they're not talking. Seems like that poor boy rode his bike right off the end of the earth.

Jesus.

That's what I say. This whole ugly business keeps getting worse. People murdered and burnt up is bad enough, but it won't stop there. Can't stop it seems. Worked so hard to make Simba better and now he disappears. Don't make sense. Something going on that's deep-down bad. Something nasty and ugly that's bound to get worse.

Will your friends talk to me?

Best for you to stay away from my friends. I sic you on them they won't be my friends anymore. They're upset. And got a right to be. Ain't hardly a time for strangers to come around asking questions. Too many questions already. People want answers.

If somebody doesn't keep asking questions, how will the boy be found?

Don't you worry about that. Folks don't need any interference right now in what they're trying to do. What I'm saying is leave it be. Butt out. Whatever's going on, people around here can handle it. They got to. No choice. This where they live. We're not looking for help from you or nobody else. Help is what started this mess. Somebody called himself helping is the one lit the fire.

*   *   *

What starts the action, two young bloods shooting around. Gradually six or seven others saunter onto the court. If you're listening for it, drumming of the ball on asphalt carries for blocks. The game's one on one on one. Every man for himself. You keep the pill as long as you can score. Make a shot from the field with somebody guarding you then make three free ones from behind the key then you try and score from the field again, with somebody checking you and so on till you miss. Whoever rebounds the miss is next up. Anybody can guard the one with the ball, but the last one who missed has to check him. Keep track of your own points. Call out your score each time you hit a shot. When you close in on twenty-one the whole mob comes chasing you. No out of bounds, no fouls. Point is you got to get the ball. Show what you can do with it when you got it.

A way of loosening up. A way of seeing who can play. No passing, no teamwork, no slowdown or fast break. Everybody up against it. One on one on one.

Even after enough bodies to run full court, no game starts because older players begin to straggle in. Some sit on the sidelines. One or two join in the one-on-one game, wolfing, joshing, schooling the young guys. Clearly stronger, more experienced, able to dominate and talk trash and have it their way.

A box is set up and begins blasting. Players synchronize their dribbling, head fakes, spins and stutter steps with the tunes. Music's inside the game. If you can't hear it, you can see it. Somebody always getting off, doing his step in the middle of the action. On time. Younger players drift off to a single basket behind the fence where they mess around during the whole court run. People shoot for teams. Everybody takes a turn on the foul line till ten make it or the first two choose squads. Somebody calls winners. Somebody shouts. Got next after you. First out's decided by another shot from the top of the key, make-it-take-it, and the run's on.

That's how it was supposed to start. And it did. They got that part right.

Been awhile, Cudjoe is thinking, and that's why he missed. On line but not enough arch. He'd returned to the park to find a game and now he was trying to guide the ball rather than shoot it. Shooting's all in the mind. You must believe the ball's going in. Confidence and the amen wrist flick of follow-through. You reach for the sky, launch the ball so it rotates off your fingertips and let it drop through the rim. When you hold on too long, when you don't relax and extend your arm and let nature take its course, you shoot short. Because you don't believe. Because you're trying too hard to maintain control, you choke the ball and it comes up short.

First go-round only six made it so a second chance for everybody who blew. This time Cudjoe's too strong. Ball boomerangs off the back of the iron. He sits out the first run. Takes winners with two other guys who missed their free throws.

Game was rag ass. Too much like one on one. A neighborhood run. No surprises. Too much assumed and conceded. A few good players who weren't half as good as they thought they were, sloppily doing more or less what they felt like doing. A few possessed one outstanding skill or talent and slipped it into the game when they could, often when they shouldn't. Defense nonexistent. Everybody going for steals or blocks instead of hanging tight with their man. Chump city. More action cooking around the court than on it. Block long Eldorado drop top docked at the curb. Deals going down. Basketball game like a TV set playing in a crowded room and nobody watching.

Who's next?

There's a spot for you, O.T.

My man wants to run, too.

He's five then. You, your man, that dude over there talking to Peewee, this brother and me.

Solid.

My name's Cudjoe.

This Mike. They call me O.T. What's the score?

Just started, man.

Ain't much out there.

Early. This the first run.

Cudjoe. My oldest brother used to play with a dude name Cudjoe.

What's your brother's name?

Darnell.

Darnell Thompson?

Yeah.

And you're Skeets?

When I was little I was Skeets.

How's Darnell?

He's in the slam, man. Five years now.

Damn.

Dope, man. Into the dope shit, you know.

Darnell?

Yeah. Surprised everybody. My big brother always a together dude. Never in no trouble. He looked out for me. More like a daddy to me, you know. Then dope, man. He just couldn't handle. Stealing and shit.

Damn. I'm sorry. Ran with Darnell many a day. Right here. Darnell could bust the jumper.

He was tough. Used to watch his every move and wanna be like him some day. I remember you now. Cudjoe. Kind of a different name, you know. Remember the name. Now I'm remembering seeing you play with my brother. You had a nice game. You still busting?

Up next with you.

Can you still do it?

I'm in shape. I can run. But it's been awhile since I've played. Not much ball where I was.

Ain't nothing out there on the court. We'll win a few and you be cooking like the old days.

Skeets grown up.

Been a long time since they call me Skeets.

You in school?

Was, man. I'm working now, you know, so I can go back.

Did you play ball?

First semester. Then the books. I fucked up. Lost my free ride. Had to drop out. I'm going back, though. Working now so I can pay my way. Coach say, you know, if I make the team, he'll go to bat for me. See if he can, you know, get me some money.

Good luck with it.

Yeah. I'ma get myself together. Make something of myself, man. It's been nice talking to you.

Sorry about your brother.

That's the way it goes.

Cudjoe watches O.T. move off. Darnell Thompson all over again. Big, black, graceful. Broad shoulders, narrow waist, short, bouncy, almost delicate steps. Darnell's soft, easy manner. Eagerness in his voice as he leans into a conversation. Enjoying what he's saying, what you have to say. Taller by inches than his brother. O.T. had grown a body to fit Darnell's enormous hands. Ten years. Did anything get better instead of worse? Why couldn't he believe Darnell's brother? Why did he hear ice cracking as O.T. spoke of his plans? Why did he see Darnell's rusty hard hand wrapped around his brother's dragging him down?

One guy on their squad a leaper. About Cudjoe's height, six one or six two, only leaner, younger. Not much of a shot, but he'd go after everything that missed. Quick as a frog off his feet, a hustler, battler who loved running the court, banging underneath. Then a short dude, runty and arrogant, who pushed the pill downcourt helter-skelter, advantage or no, constantly jamming himself up. Favored behind-the-back, through-the-legs, over-the-backboard passes. Disappeared when the ball not in his hands. When it was in his hands, he forgot about the other four people playing with him, dribbled himself into trouble so he could dribble out again, feeling taller and slicker each time he escaped a trap he'd created for himself. O.T.'s friend Mike was solid, skilled, understood the game; he was dependable, fun to play with. O.T. a monster, operating a foot or so above everybody else. Took what he wanted. Changed gears when he wanted to. Let the other team stay close enough to believe they had a chance. Then blew them away—steals, slams, blocked shots.

Cudjoe did his bit. Hit a lay-up and a couple jumpers from the wing. Fed the free man. Dealt the ball away from the dribble-happy dude. His legs gave out in game three. Downhill from there. A question of holding his own then, not being a liability, not making dumb mistakes, playing tough D.

No wheels. Knew what I wanted to do but my wheels just wouldn't turn.

His team retired undefeated. Only one serious challenge all evening. A squad had loaded up for them. The best of the rest and Dribble King had decided it was show time, doing his roadrunner act, and they were down three hoops, 6–9, in the twelve-basket game. Finally O.T. glared at Mr. Pat-Pat and brought him back to reality. The little guy sulked but stayed out the way long enough for the others to get it done. Pulling that game out was the best moment. Many high fives and a good, deep-down sense of pushing to the limit and bringing something back. After the winning basket they gathered under the hoop still shuddering from Sky's humongous dunk. Their eyes met, their fists met for a second in the core of a circle, then just as quickly broke apart, each going his own way.

If you keep playing, the failing light is no problem. Your eyes adjust and the streetlamps come on and they help some. People pass by think you're crazy playing basketball in the dark, but if you stay in the game you can see enough. Ball springs at you quicker from the shadows. Pill surprises you and zips by you unless you know it's coming. Part of being in the game is anticipating, knowing who's on the court with you and what they're likely to do. It's darker. Not everything works now that works in daylight. Trick is knowing what does. And staying within that range. You could be blind and play if the game's being played right so you stay out past the point people really seeing. You just know what's supposed to be happening. Dark changes things but you can manage much better than anyone not in the game would believe. Still there comes a point you'll get hurt if you don't give it up. Not the other team you're fighting then, but the dark, and it always wins, you know it's going to win so what you're doing doesn't make sense, it's silly and you persist in the silliness a minute or two, a pass pops you in your chest, a ball rises and comes down in the middle of three players and nobody even close to catching it. You laugh and go with the silliness. Can't see a damn thing anymore. Whether a shot's in or out. Hey, O.T., man. Show some teeth so I can see you, motherfucker. Somebody trudges off the court. Youall can have it. I can't see shit. The rest laugh and give it up, too. You fade to the sidelines. It's been dark a long time at the court's edges. People's faces gloomed in deep shadow. A cigarette glows. Night sure enough now. Cross a line and on the other side it's been dark for days.

Mellow reggae thumps from the open door of a car. A light crowd of hangers-on in groups by the curb, against the chain-link fence, around a bench on the court, huddled at another bench farther away where the hollow drops off from the path. Riffs of reefer, wine, beer. You smell yourself if you've been playing. Cudjoe's in the cluster of men lounging around the bench in the middle of the court's open side. Night dries his skin. He feels darker, the color of a deep, purple bruise. He won't be able to walk tomorrow. Mostly players around the bench, men who've just finished the last game of the evening, each one relaxing in his own funk, cooling out, talking the game, beginning to turn it into stories. Cudjoe knows the action will flash back later, game films on an invisible screen above his bed. All those years of playing and it still happens. While his stiff muscles unknot, too tired to sleep, the game movie will play in his head whether he wants to watch or not.

If he told his story to the other men, if he wasn't a newcomer content to listen to the others, if he wasn't too tired and beat to say his own name three times in a row, his story would be about night dropping on the city, how deep and how quietly it settles over the park. Nothing the same now. Trick about night is it changes things but you can't see exactly how. You know the park is different, you feel it in your bones. Night air cools your skin, contours of the ground rise and fall in unfamiliar rhythms, spaces open which haven't been there before, the hollow loses its bottom, a black lap you'd sink into forever. Night can shrink things. The players beside him are smaller, parts of them lost, stolen by shadow, their voices husky, pitched to the night's quiet, movements slowed as if night's a medium like water and they must conspire with its flow. When night's closing down it shuts things in on themselves and that's why you are on a ship with these other men thousands of miles from everywhere else, floating through darkness, and you can't help sensing the isolation, the smallness because night cuts you off drastically as a knife. But since you can't see clearly, you can't really tell. Night expands some things. Trees explode silently, giant black puffs hovering like clouds against the sky. You know night's different and you guess at why. Can't help guessing, wondering, even though you understand you'll never understand because night is about hiding things. About things changing. And Cudjoe knows it would make a good story. They'd all be in it. Would the players testify, help him tell his story as they cool out after the game?

The other fact about night—it doesn't last. Night's temporary. But you can't really be sure about that, either.

My poor, aching wheels.

I can dig it, bro.

My mind's right there. Tells me just what to do. But my legs ain't with it. In their own world. I send the message and by the time they move, it's too late.

Like the mayor.

That cat missing more than wheels.

You can say that again.

He's not stepping down, is he? You watch. He'll run again. Probably win again if the party's behind him.

Why you think they wouldn't be behind him? All he did was torch a few crazy niggers. That's why he's up in office in the first place. Keep youall ghetto bunnies in line. Sure, he goofed. But things so fucked in this city whoever's in the mayor's chair bound to fuck up. Mayor don't run the city, city runs him. Them slick dudes own the mayor are grinning from ear to ear cause if it had been a white boy dropped the bomb, bloods would have took to the street and the whole city nothing but a cinder now.

Tell the truth.

Leave the mayor alone, youall. Cat's doing his best. Hate to hear people bad-mouthing him. Specially black people. Finally voted in a black man, and now nothing he does good enough for you.

Ain't about black.

Bull-shit. You think they'd let him burn down white people's houses? Sheeit. He be hanging by his balls from some lamppost. Mayor's not in office to whip on white folks. Nigger control. That's what he's about.

New houses they building up on Osage spozed to be pretty nice.

No stoops, man. How you spozed to have a neighborhood with no stoops?

Check it out. What's up there mostly holes in the ground.

Where the people living lost their homes?

Not in City Hall. Not in the mayor's neighborhood.

At least they're living.

Don't care what nobody says. It was murder, man. Murder one and some of those lying suckers ought to pay.

They appointed a commission.

Hey, bro. Commissioners all members of the same club. Thick as thieves. Downtown chumps all eating out the same bowl. They come in where I work. Smiling and grinning and falling over each other to pay when I bring the check. You think they going to hang one their own? Watch. Commission will claim some poor blood lit the match.

Papers been spreading that lie already. Like the brothers poured gasoline on the roof and locked theyselves in the basement and set fire to the house. Who's spozed to believe that shit?

Have they found the little boy?

The one survived?

They say he survived. If he did, hope he's a million miles away from here. They'll fuck with him if they find him.

Blame him.

If he ain't dead already. Papers say eleven dead. Means at least eleven. Lie about the numbers like they lie about everything else. If they admit eleven it means that's how many bodies they caught red-handed with. Don't know how many dead in those ashes in the basement. Papers say a boy escaped. Maybe he did. Maybe he didn't.

Anything left in that bottle, man?

Here, dude. You got the rest.

Cudjoe decides not to ask about the boy again. Cheating in a way when he asked the first time. This mood, this time belongs to nobody. Each man free as long as they relax here letting night close over them. If a city lurks beyond the borders of the park, it's no more real than the ball games they play again as they talk. They are together in this. No agendas, interviews or interviewees. Are the streetlamps dimmer or has the city slipped into a deeper fold of night? Faces around him are masks. Would he recognize any of these guys if he saw them in clothes on the street tomorrow? Music doo-wops in thick pure phrases from the car on Forty-third behind the chain-link fence. Music reigns supreme and there is nothing not listening. Cudjoe holds his breath. Doesn't need breath as a high sweet tenor and voices trilling behind it shine like silver, shine like gold.

Could you bring down a city with trumpets? Could a song lay waste skyscrapers? Scour the hills, cleanse the rivers, wipe the sky? Everything in creation had been listening to the music. Now sirens and jets and horns and trolleys, dogs howling, babies screaming had started up again. Thump of Cudjoe's heart again. That shield of filth the city flings up at the sky in place again. Stars spatter against it like rain on a tin roof trying to get in. Hushed for a moment but now a river of noise again and the tune from a tape deck is a twig drifting along with everything else caught in the current. Waters above and waters below the firmament, and earth a wafer in those wet lips that are light-years thick. He tastes earth as he drains a can of beer. O.T. smoking a cigarette. Darnell sucking on a joint. Or was it the other way round? Too dark to tell. If the lips opened to sing, to kiss, to tell a story. If they opened, and the earth wafer slipped out. Wouldn't there be a long time when nobody'd know what was happening? Centuries out of kilter, askew, but no one understanding the problem. Just this queasiness, this uneasiness. This tilt and slow falling. You are in a city. You look up and can't see the stars and that doesn't bother you as much as it should. You don't know what's wrong but maybe more's wrong than you want to know.

*   *   *

Cudjoe doesn't know why he piled into the car going to Papa Joe's. Why he drank six more drafts with the fellas when the first one cooled him out. Doesn't know why he's decided to walk back to West Philly when his legs already wobbly and stupid. He's at the top of many broad steps, near the entrance of the art museum, whose stones on a good day are golden in the sun. A neat ingot enthroned on a hill. He is sighting down a line of lighted fountains that guide his eye to City Hall. This is how the city was meant to be viewed. Broad avenues bright spokes of a wheel radiating from a glowing center. No buildings higher than Billy Penn's hat atop City Hall. Scale and pattern fixed forever. Clarity, balance, a perfect understanding between the parts. Night air thick and bad but he's standing where he should and the city hums this dream of itself into his ear and he doesn't believe it for an instant but wonders how he managed to stay away so long.

I belong to you, the city says. This is what I was meant to be. You can grasp the pattern. Make sense of me. Connect the dots. I was constructed for you. like a field of stars I need you to bring me to life. My names, my gods poised on the tip of your tongue. All you have to do is speak and you reveal me, complete me.

The city could fool you easy. And he wonders if that's why he is back. To be caught up in the old trick bag again. Love you. Love you not. Who's zooming who? Is someone in charge? From this vantage point in the museum's deep shadow in the greater darkness of night it seems an iron will has imposed itself on the shape of the city. If you could climb high enough, higher than the hill on which the museum perches, would you believe in the magic pinwheel of lights, straight lines, exact proportions, symmetry of spheres within spheres, gears meshing, turning, spinning to the perpetual music of their motion? Cudjoe fine-tunes for a moment the possibility that someone, somehow, had conceived the city that way. A miraculous design. A prodigy that was comprehensible. He can see a hand drawing the city. An architect's tilted drafting board, instruments for measuring, for inscribing right angles, arcs, circles. The city is a faint tracery of blue, barely visible blood lines in a newborn's skull. No one has used the city yet. No one has pushed a button to start the heart pumping.

He can tell thought had gone into the design. And a person must have stood here, on this hill, imagining this perspective.

Dreaming the vast emptiness into the shape of a city. In the beginning it hadn't just happened, pell-mell. People had planned to live and prosper here. Wear the city like robe and crown.

The founders were dead now. Buried in their wigs, waist-coats, swallowtail coats, silk hose clinging to their plump calves. A foolish old man flying a kite in a storm.

Cudjoe decides he will think of himself as a reporter covering a story in a foreign country. Stay on his toes, take nothing for granted. Not the customs nor the language. What he sees is not what the natives see. The movie has been running for years, long before he was born, and will sputter on about its business long after he is dead and gone. At best he can write the story of someone in his shoes passing through.

He is not alone. At this late hour museum busy as an anthill. Steady traffic of cars up and down driveways curving around its flanks. If you swept the night visitors together they'd form a crowd, but the museum's spacious grounds—terraced, grot-toed, thickly planted with trees and shrubs—offer privacy to anyone who wishes it. Most of the young people wish it, play hide-and-seek in couples or small groups. Here comes some fool bounding up the hundred stairs from Logan Circle. Rocky Balboa, arms raised in triumph, claiming the city.

Patrol cars take leisurely passes up and down the circular drive. No one pays attention. The mood is mellow, cops and kids ignoring each other. As long as everybody follows the rules, there wouldn't seem to be any rules. Music and dope in moderation. Little tidbits of sound, of hashish smoke reach Cudjoe. These white kids had been granted a zone. Everybody had zones. Addicts, prostitutes, porn merchants, derelicts. Even people who were black and poor had a zone. Everybody granted the right to lie in the bed they'd made for themselves. As long as they didn't contaminate good citizens who disapproved. As long as the beds available to good citizens who wished to profit or climb in occasionally. As long as everybody knew they had to give up their zone, scurry down off this hill, no questions asked, when the cops blow the whistle.

Maybe this is a detective story, Cudjoe says to himself. Out there the fabled city of hard knocks and exciting possibilities. You could get wasted out there and lots did. His job sleaze control. Bright lights, beautiful people, intrigue, romance. The city couldn't offer those rushes without toilets, sewers, head busters and garbage dumps. Needed folks on the other side of the fast track and needed a tough cookie to keep them scared and keep them where they belong. The fast movers would pay well for that service. Let you sample the goodies once in a while. Just enough to spoil you. Not enough to dull the edge you required to do their spadework, to get down where it was down and dirty.

Limousines out there. And sleek women in dresses slit up to their assholes. Everything bought and sold. You could buy day or buy night. This circus of lights enticing him could be turned off or on at someone's command.

He remembers waterfalls framing the broad museum stairs. At night the pumps rested but during summer days twin stairstepped cascades of water turned the wells at the end of each landing into swimming holes. City kids in their underwear played in the pools. Colonies of little brown monkeys splashing and squealing and sliding down green sheets of water. Beating the heat. Shirts and shorts discarded where they were peeled off sweaty bodies. Shoes were what got to him. Piles of sneakers all colors, shapes, low-rent versions of adult styles, beat to shit the way kids' shoes always are, but these, scattered around on the wet steps, these were worse, gaping holes in the bottoms, shredded uppers, laces missing, shoes taped, patched, lined with cardboard. Cheapest concoctions of glue and foam and canvas that money could buy.

Cudjoe constructs a room to match the shoes, fills it with sleeping bodies, many funky pairs of sneakers set out overnight to dry. Constructs a row house to hold the room, matches it with house after house till there is a street, then a neighborhood matching the sorry-assed shoes he's ready to lace now and thinks of miles of streets he must negotiate to reach the fountain, how pebbles and grains of glass punch through the thin soles, how after a while with his brothers and sisters in tow, it's like walking barefoot on burning coals, you don't stop and wait for a light to change, you charge through intersections, daring cars to hit you. Constructs a city to hold the neighborhood, to match the rags on their feet, broad boulevards to carry traffic to the art museum, monumental buildings to hold treasure. As the boy probes inside his shoe, rubbing lumps, loose fibers, fingering holes that caused yesterday's calluses and blisters, Cudjoe hollers, Stop. Don't stick that rotten thing back on your foot. Hollering as if the boy could hear him, as if the boy could fling down the shoe and everything would be different, as if the shoe isn't already here on the stone steps, the boy's fresh cuts bleeding somewhere in sheets of green water.

Kids played rough and loud in the pools below the fountain. No adults in sight. Kind of place Cudjoe had only seen from a distance when he was growing up. Not nice. Not safe. White bodies rare. Lines were drawn in his family. Poor as his family was, certain distinctions were important, clarified early. He wasn't allowed to play in fountains, in roachy public pools because he wasn't like those children running loose who did. Not a matter of pretending he was a white child, just that he wasn't that kind of black one. Scraped from the streets. Ragmuffin from God-knows-where, infected with God-knows-what, and you'd catch it no doubt about it playing in the water they play in. Nobody's children trekking here for a few hot summer days, then gone, back to wherever they came from, wherever they're going. You stay right here in your own backyard, boy. Be grateful somebody's keeping an eye on you.

The pitiful shoes and how happy the kids seemed. Both those things get to him. He thinks of all those hours on his back steps staring into the alley. Could you lose track of how to be happy. If you learned to wait too early, would the waiting ever end? Didn't take very much to have fun. Splish-splash half naked in the city's water on the steps of this monument. Wasn't that as good as it ever was going to get? What sense did it make to wait? Wait for what? Already time for some of the girls to keep their undershirts on. Breast buds poking through wet cotton pasted to their skin. One year. Two years. How long before the journey here seems silly, not worth the trouble? Tired of being teased, embarrassed by the tricks of a body growing too fast. You bring your little brothers and sisters but hang back because of the bra, hairs under your arms, between your legs. Boys won't leave you alone but some are sweet and you listen and suck on a piece of hard candy and sing to yourself the song you daydream the sweetest one could

sing to you if he cut those other pestering, lame dudes loose,
if you didn't have to keep an eye on all those babies paddling
in the water. Over your shoulder you scope a twin of your old
self, no hips, no titties, wild and stronger than the boys,
hollering because nobody can catch you as you slither and leap
over the falls. Brown and slick as a seal. She's you all over
again. She catches your eye and you're both places at once,
free as a bird, stuck in the honey these boys churn swarming
round you.

Piles of shoes, a mountain of discarded clothes. A shower
bath on the museum steps.

Then smoke rising in the west. The city cringes and holds
its nose and points a finger. Nothing is lost. In the blink of an
eye a new crop playing on the steps, in the fountains flowing
down the hill when summer days turn long and hot again.

He's imagined more than he wanted to. The boy. The girl.
The fire consuming their few belongings. All the evidence up
in smoke. No warehouses of shoes and eyeglasses and clothing
left behind to convict the guilty. The dead were dead. What
they possessed gone with them. On Osage Avenue bulldozers
and cranes comb the ashes, sift, crush, spread them neat as a
carpet over vacant lots. Cudjoe's business concerns survivors.
If any had survived. Simba Muntu lost, found, and lost again.

Some city lights like planets, others like stars. Some burn
steady, others twinkle and bend. Lights pulsate, crackle, hum,
lights blink off and on like insects Cudjoe used to hunt in the
evening, on the bushes in his backyard. He can blot out great
chunks of city by positioning his hand in front of his eyes.
With his hands over his ears he can quiet sirens, the babble
of traffic. Maybe he's missed the city. Or maybe he's home to

remind himself how much he hates the whole stinking mess, the funky air, the slow belly rub of everybody's nerves on everybody's nerves till some poor soul can't take it and lights a match and burns the gig down around his head.

Cudjoe sits on a hard bench. The first shall also be last. The basketball court's empty. During the walk west he was sure he'd never make it back. Then he'd found himself collapsing on this bench. Need a crane to lift him now. He's bolted to the wood slats. His muscles locked in a sitting position and that's how they'll discover him in the morning, frozen solid like one of the Lamed-Vov, the thirty-six Just Men, God's hostages who must thaw a thousand years after they've done their turn of suffering on earth. The court, the whole park empty. No one's passed since he'd sunken into the bench. Crickets and dull roar of the city all he hears behind him. Trolleys farther and farther apart. One must be due soon, clattering up Baltimore or Chester. Traffic diminished to a few madmen racing cars around the dark streets.

At first he believes he's hallucinating, the night chill getting to his brain as well as his muscles. He'd probably nodded off and the voices a dream he can shake off now he's awake. He blinks. Rubs his eyes. The sound, barely louder than the sawing crickets, won't go away. Rising from the hollow, from the bottomless black pit daybreak will change back to the hollow, are sure enough voices, a muted conversation growing more real the more intently he listens. Voices. Voices teasingly close to intelligible. He recognizes speech rhythms, single words, familiar silences between exchanges. Sounds like several different speakers though he can't distinguish what any says. An oddness on top of the oddness of hearing voices in Clark Park in the dead middle of the night, a quality he can't put his finger on as he strains to pick out phrases. Is the language foreign? Are these spirit voices? Little folk who emerge from their hiding places at midnight and rule the park. Is he slipping in and out of a dream? He listens. It's not elves or extraterrestrials. It's kids. He realizes he's been holding his breath and exhales. Kids talking in the hollow in the middle of the night. Up past their bedtime. Like he was up past his. Maybe he should walk over. Hey, youall. It's late. Time to go home. Where are their mothers and fathers? Where are his kids?

Ten minutes. Fifteen. One voice dominates, rapping, scatting till they complete their business. Was it them after a silence of a minute or so, briefly outlined a block and a half away in the snowy glow of a streetlamp? They barely rumpled the curtain of darkness as they emerged from the hollow and scooted through. Cudjoe tracks cones of light under hooded posts for their bobbing silhouettes.

Like calling roll he coaxes his body parts to attention. Necessary to address each by name, remind each of its function and duty. A first step impossible. Then it's accomplished. And the next is worse. He's the rusty tin woodsman clanking after Dorothy. Wasted, but he's not ready to go home to bed yet. He can't read his watch. Just enough illumination from a streetlight to obscure its glow-in-the-dark hands. If he had a ball, he'd drag his sorry ass onto the court and shoot around. Force his joints to loosen up. He'd be OK after a few minutes. Smooth. Perfect rainbow arc as the ball spins off his fingertips. You hear it sing as it leaves your hands. You reach for the sky. Know it's in the hoop when you let it go. A ball pounding the asphalt would be like a drum summoning the kids. They'd share their secrets with him as they played through the night.

If when you die no heaven no place to go where do you go when you die? You be burnt up and the ashes swept away. A broom makes ashes dust and dust flies up in the sky. Where does it go? Ashes make dust and more dust and the sky's too heavy where do you go?

Dust in the sky. All falls down. You snort dust in your nose. Boogers of it in your eyes. You eat dust when you open your mouth. Sky falls on your head and where do you go if there's no place to go? No heaven. No place but this one where you tramp along beside them. They march beside you. In front and behind. Many of them, many, many. Too much dust for the sky to hold. It falls on your head. We hurry along. We lean forward to catch the weight of the sky on our backs. We are strong. We keep it up. One long step then you hippy-dip your shoulder like something in your way you got to lean and dip your shoulder and knock the thing always in your way night and day out your way. Do not open your mouth or eyes or ears. The others carry you along. Dust will drown you. No place to go it fills all your holes and you die inside a body bag sewed tight as a turkey's butt Thanksgiving. You walk your hippy-hop walk on this street and if you opened your eyes you'd see the tracks where the trolleys slide, the wires, the birds. You can see the park without opening your eyes. You wanted to climb the trees. You are too little to reach the first branches so you can't climb up. When you're taller you'll grab the ladder of branches: climb all the way up into the green belly of the tree. Up, up into its insides you could march till green hairs too skinny to hold you. You'd be a squirrel living at the very top. Where it bends and shakes and almost breaks but you hippy-hop, fly like a bird from one place to another. You never fall. You cool at the top. When the sky falls it won't get you. You're too high. High. High. Squirrels with their rat paws scratch from the bottom where the branches start. Little rat paws get them up. Scratching. Hurry up, hurry up across the floor at night. You throw a shoe and they don't come for a while. Then you play dead here they come again scratching. If you could hold on you could shimmy to the first branches, climb to the top. A tree is a dress. You stand under it and look up. Your mama's dress and squirrels play trapeze under there. You dig but your fingers won't stick. The squirrels scratch trolley tracks straight up. The tree is rough. They bite its skin. You touched it, rubbed it. Skin is what covers you and covers your mama. You touch hers. Rub her arm. Warm and smooth. She lets me touch it. Skin over her blood and bones. Tito wears a handkerchief over his mouth. A outlaw. His eyes are big. He's burnt. His skin is tree skin. It's falling. The house is burning. My mama pushes me. Roof falling in. Bombs. Bombs. Do do do do do. She screams, Children coming out. Children coming out. Tito's skin like tree skin. Tito busting open. Everything needs something to hold it in. Hold it together. They hurry me along. They are my skin. I know this street. No need to look. Sparks on the wires. Birds. Dark is skin over us. No one sees us. We must hurry. We must hide. We must stick together. Inside of night skin so we don't die. So our blood runs warm and safe inside because there is no place to go after you die.

*   *   *

They are discussing the price of oil and laughing. Miniature sheikhs, then the players from the court then the kids in the hollow, each one wearing a hooded, milk-white robe that merges obscurely with the darkness. The hollow's steep black sides rise miles above their heads. You can't see the rim. Shrill voices pipe. Laughter, squeaky, giggling, about to pee their pants because they're laughing so hard. Faces under conical hoods are splashed and flecked and sprayed rainbow colors. Mr. Tambo inquires of Mr. Bones: How many cars can you name that start with *P?* Mr. Bones rubs his nappy Yankee Doodle bearded chin, stutters, P P P P Pontiac, Packard, P P P Plymouth, Por Por Porsche. As he speaks the lads scamper up the slopes, triangles of white scattering, an explosion of moths, blinking off and on in the beams of a car's headlights. They're still cracking up. Whatever was funny is funnier now. Cudjoe watches one of the kids—it's Technicolor high noon, a busy intersection downtown, stylish shops and shoppers, expensive cars lining the street—raise the hem of his garment and P P P piss into the gas tank of a Mercedes. The kid winks at him, waves at the mob of scandalized citizens. Want me check the oil too?

And part of that comic strip simply Cudjoe's bladder making its point any way it can. He crawls out of bed. Manages to remain numb all the way to the bathroom, where he plants his feet and goes back to sleep. Takes hours to finish and he doesn't move for days afterward, staring into the bowl, enjoying silence after the noisy rush of his waters. He needs sleep. Much more sleep. His body clock refuses to adjust to this new hemisphere. Perhaps he lost it on the flight over. Dropped thirty thousand feet from the 747, the hands spin, bells chatter, then it raises a salty geyser in the gray ocean. Nodding on his feet, weary as a whipped dog. For better or worse he is up for the day. Barely day. Barely up. Too late to turn back. Rest is what he wants, what he isn't going to get. Why couldn't he sleep more than a few hours a night since he'd been back?

Mind attached to body. And who is in charge? Which is Roy Rogers and which one the Gabby Hayes sidekick? His body begging for rest. His mind jerking it out of bed, forcing it to sleepwalk. Or did a message from the bladder snatch the ghost awake?

Mind and body. Body and mind. Was he actually someplace else, in a dimension where the stink of this stale cabinet didn't exist? Just the idea of it? Was he sealed hermetically within glass walls manipulating a robot arm? When the titanium fingers touched an object, what did he feel? Could body know mind? Or vice versa? He'd always wondered about other animals. What went on in their heads? If you stared into the eyes of a dog long enough, would it speak, mind to mind, bear doggy witness, give up its doggy secrets? Was the animal his mind rode, the animal staring back at him from mirrors, any more likely to speak than a dog?

He pushes open a blistered rectangle of glass above the toilet. His window on the world. Across an alley no sane person would consider entering after dark, a block of apartments extends to the corner, a row of four-story units, each defined by the zigzag iron railing of fire escape. A window in the building twin to his across the narrow alleyway is a cat's eye in the gloom. Even on the brightest days, sunlight doesn't grope into this valley of the shadow. Why was he up before dawn staring into this black pit? Was someone awake over there? A restless, beat-up, insomniac, lost soul, horny motherfucker prowling his apartment, peering through a porthole above his toilet, counting lighted windows?

Didn't you need a million windows opening, framing views of the city every morning in order for a city to come to life? Wasn't a city millions of eyes that are windows opening on scenes invisible till the eyes construct them, till the eyes remember and set out in meticulous detail the city that was there before they closed for sleep? Wasn't the city one vast window covered by a million miniblinds and every morning every blind snaps open, quickly, like you peel a dressing from a wound? The city appears because this vast window is unshuttered a square at a time. Visible because it's remembered. Coming to life in the blink of an eye, the billion blinks of a billion eyes. Wasn't he performing his civic duty, doing his sleepy-eyed bit. What if he said no to the tacky little postcard in his peephole above the toilet? And if he's seeing, doesn't that mean someone in one of those windows across the way must be seeing him, peeping at him between the slats of a blind in one of the dark apartments, a voyeur returning the favor Cudjoe bestows when he spies on his neighbors and makes their lives real? Weren't countless pairs of eyes, eyes like his, needed to create the cityscape? Were they the mind animating the city's body? Or was the city dreaming them, gathering sticks and stones to make its bones.

She's not up yet. His anonymous foxy friend in the second-floor flat catty-corner to his. Thirty yards maybe, separating them. Would she catch one end of a measuring tape if he tossed it across the column of air. If a sturdy bridge connected his window to hers, he wouldn't cross it. She was close enough.

Untouchable, unreachable, and that's what he liked those hours he watched her going about her business. No name. No history. She was the body of woman. No beginning, middle, end to her life. All women. Any woman.

Dark hair, slim, compact, but generously rounded in butt and breast. Like the woman in the park. Like the woman he'd married. Perfectly formed and proportioned the way only small women can be. When his neighbor walked naked through the rooms of her apartment, he could almost hear Caroline's bare feet thumping. Caroline walked too loud for a person her size, thumping, punishing floorboards with each determined stride. He'd tease her. Wall Shaker, Earth Quaker, Heartbreaker, Thunder Maker. What you grinning at, gal? With the heel of his hand thudding on his desk he'd echo her footsteps. Bram. Bram. Here comes Thumper, the lead rabbit. He'd loved the sound. Her bony ankles and child's feet, the exact harmonies of her figure. He'd memorized certain characteristic postures she'd assume, learned how grace and elegance could be endlessly permutated in her simple gestures, walking up stairs, turning the page of a book, standing at a door, curling up on a sofa. The woman in the window could bring Caroline back, the hurt back, so it was necessary she be other women too. All women. She could bless him with glimpses of a woman's privacy. She could draw the shades and treat him as if he didn't exist. Feast and famine. Like those extremes that were the predictable beat of his life with Caroline, extremes substituting for dependable, easy, common ground they'd never been able to establish. What had they desired from each other? Was there so much anger, so much pain because they always came so close to making it, or because five years, two kids, countless defections and reconciliations never drew them one inch nearer?

Cudjoe knows some answers are easy. All the soft shoulders he'd sneaked away to cry on. The lies afterward. He smirks at the clown face in the smidgen of bathroom mirror. His beastly burden. His beast of burden. The woman across the alley's not awake to keep him company. Windows are blind eyes reflecting each other, seeing nothing.

He closes the porthole, shakes and tucks himself away. Too tired to pull off his sweatpants last night. Too exhausted to shower. Nobody sharing his bed so he'd just plopped down, in all his stinking gear, even the damp, binding jock. He'd promised himself one game, two at most. For old times' sake. One game would be more than enough for the first time in months on a court. Just one game. Give me the strength to play one game and I'll be satisfied. Plant my ass on the bench after one. Let me finish one game and I'm history. I promise.

Then you win and slouch to the sideline and this guy on your team, he says, One more, bro. And you say, I'm beat, bro. No way, bro. And he says, C'mon, dude. Run this last one. And you say, Last one. Last one, he says.

Then it always gets to be the morning after. And you have to pay. Why did I do it? Why'd I go too far? Her face is contorted by grief. Things are past explaining. Hurt can't be undone. She's sobbing. Her head ducked into her shoulder; you can't see her face, just the witchy storm of hair. Why doesn't she comb it? Why is she letting herself fall apart? A ball of misery huddled on the couch. A lead rabbit you couldn't lift to save your soul. Dark hair spilling in deep folds. You don't want to see the circles under her eyes. Her flesh slackens when she's unhappy.

When she's hurt by one of your lies she ages years in minutes. Red welts, puffiness. The flesh sags. Heavy blood pulls down the mask of her face. It droops, wrinkles. Sobs rise off her body like bubbles bursting, blood bubbles, blue and bruised.

You hated the power you had to hurt her. Hated her hurt hurting you back.

You're awake now and she's on your mind. And that's the way it's going to be. Back on the edge of his bed he realizes he's stuck with her this morning, wants her this morning and for better or worse she won't let him go. She's sitting on the toilet. Sizzles like bacon frying. He can smell the coffee she's started. He sniffs his fingertips for the buttery scent of her. Rule was no lovemaking until he showered after ball. Infection. Germs. Her vulnerable urinary tract. The woman in the window possessed no insides. No periods. No illnesses, no female disorders. Wouldn't age or die. Home from her job the woman will undress, shower, spend hours in her apartment doing what she did, bare-ass as Eve. *So near and yet so far.* Didn't Little Anthony and the Imperials sing that? Near and far. Far and near. When he sat reading with Caroline in the quiet of an evening, sharing the couch, his back against one threadbare armrest, hers against the other, why did she always close her robe or shut her knees if she noticed his eyes straying from his book, peering between her naked legs?

The weekend they'd driven to the island, her reluctance had been on his mind. *What are you hiding? What don't you want me to see?* Both kids bawling in the backseat. His nerves unhinged two seconds after the drive began. He trots out complaint after complaint as they plot a path through the map he believes he's memorized and she holds on her lap.

Hiding? What in the world are you talking about?

Forget it.

So they argue over choices the map appears to offer. Alternative routes. Distance versus traffic. Red lines or green. Venture unshakable opinions about roads neither's ever seen. Opportunities for sarcasm, disagreement, nastiness are legion. He decides his elder son is responsible for the war in the backseat. He stops the car to threaten him with mayhem, with abandonment on the highway if he doesn't stop teasing his brother. He's surprised how good it feels to lean over the seat and shout at the top of his voice. A grown-up screaming at a child. Does he actually derive pleasure from scaring a four-year-old? The car rolls along. A three-hour drive stretches close to four. Something is drastically wrong. He's been humping way over posted limits. Must be the directions they'd been given. The map. His wife's command at an intersection.

Why does that marker say West 202? Aren't we going east? The ferry's east.

You said east was left. I said turn right but you insisted on turning left. So we're probably headed away from where we want to go.

Away.

You insisted on going left.

I said east. Always south and east. All along I said east. The goddamned map you're holding says east if you don't believe me.

You turned left. You're driving and you turned left. You ignored me. Don't try and blame me now.

You have the map right in front of you. You're supposed to be giving me directions.

I tried. I said east but you turned left and that's west.

Then we've been going the wrong way. Shit. How far back was the fucking junction. You were just going to sit there, weren't you? Till we ran off the end of the known world. You don't give a damn, do you? Just so you wind up being right.

Right was right. I said right ten times. You said east was left so you went left. Right was right.

Right was right. Right was right. Do you think that's cute? It's not. None of this bullshit's funny. All you had to do was read the map and keep the kids quiet.

They are quiet.

Yeah. Because I made a fool of myself.

You insisted on a left turn.

Fuck the turn. Left. Right. What's the fucking difference?

They're quiet because they're listening to you talk the way you're talking to me.

Thank you, Emily Post. Tell me, dear. How come you're better than everybody else? That's your problem. Holier than everybody. Criticize, criticize, but you, you don't make mistakes, do you? Your way's the right way and the only way. Goddammit. I ask you to do a simple thing—my way for a change—and what kind of answer do I get: Let's just sit and read. Let's just relax together. One of the boys might wake up and wander out here.

What are you talking about?

You know, dammit. Don't pretend you don't.

He's remembering the drive but he's not remembering it accurately. The conversation back and forth continues too long without interruptions. He needs to back it up, add a sound track of unearthly squeals, squalls, cries of pain and brays of

triumph from the kiddies in their car seats. Traffic noise. Rattle
of the loose spare tire cover. The thumping of his heart. A
silent scream boiling in his throat. The wall she slapped together
stone by cold stone between them. The arctic wind in her voice.
Ice cracking beneath the hurtling station wagon.

He couldn't wait to escape the car. He'd make her suffer for
this.

Theirs the last car permitted on the ferry. Tension didn't let
up until the final instant when a grizzled, one-armed sailor
waved them aboard. They'd been wedged somewhere in the
late middle of an endless line of vehicles queuing at dockside.
No doubt in Cudjoe's mind the carnival-striped van in front
of them would be the last one allowed on board. Perfect ending
to a perfect day. A battered, hand-painted VW with a menag-
erie of young, seminude passengers. Bodies shuttled in and
out of the van nonstop. He couldn't keep track of how many.
All tanned, long-haired, scruffy. Beads, headbands, cutoffs,
bare tops, bare legs, spacey blue eyes. Probably fucking in the
funky oven of van this very moment. A squirmy mound of
bare asses white as snow, sucking and fucking and blowing
dope and they'd be delivered to the island stoned, happy as
clams, ferried across the neck of water to pitch their tents while
he'd be stranded with wife and kids in this nowhere place, acres
of concrete, Cyclone fencing, warehouses, stuck in some
cruddy, overpriced motel. Whole family crammed in one room.
No hanky-panky. She'd pat his hand when he reached under
the sheet and laid it on her bare thigh, pat it and slide it off.
Whisper in his ear: You know we can't do anything in here.
No privacy. No trespassing on her side of the bed. The room's
stuffy, hot, in spite of an air conditioner louder than all these

vehicles revving up for a charge at the ferry. One car at a time through the needle's eye. The line inches forward in heart-teasing, heart-stopping little snippets. He's ready to ram the van. Torch it and roast every blond, bronzed hippie occupant if he can just move up one notch.

He'd see the crazy van again on the island, parked above a secluded cove when he'd driven with Sam to buy liquor and visit the dump. Both station wagon and VW had crossed on the last boat of the evening. Red, white and blue curtains across the van's back window. A peace symbol covered the whole front door. Sam would notice him looking over the dunes at the van and point beyond it toward the ocean where the land dropped out of sight. They swim without their drawers down there. Then he'd helped Sam unload plastic sacks of garbage. Sam didn't heave far enough and one split, scattering eggshells, coffee grounds, lemon peels, an empty vodka bottle in the clear space at the foot of a mound of garbage bags.

Losing it, me bucko. Old Sam's losing it. A little boy's face, guilty, ashamed.

Metal rims of Sam's glasses erupted. Tongues of light flicked at the sun. This old man still counting, still worried about measuring up. His eyes are invisible behind thick lenses. Moon focals. A basset hound's droopy dewlaps. Why was Sam still so hard on himself? Cudjoe felt sorry for him. Then sorry for himself. Sam was a great man. A successful writer, editor. He'd learned so much from Sam. Learned because he'd been afraid. Why wasn't there a stop between fear and pity? A long easy pause, space where they could both unbend. Throwing a garbage bag fifteen feet. What did it matter? Who was keeping score? Sam's embarrassment unsettled Cudjoe. They were tossing garbage bags onto a heap of other garbage bags. One fell short, bounced off the pile, tumbled, burst, disgorged its contents on the clear space in front of the mound. Had Sam known he was dying? In less than two years paramedics would find him on the parquet floor of his kitchen, unconscious. They'd breathe in his mouth and attempt to beat life back into his chest, but he awakens only long enough to say two words, *Teach me*, in the rear of an ambulance. Rachel had told Cudjoe the story, related to her by one of the paramedics. *Teach me*. Bolting up for a second *Teach me*. Breaking death's bonds. Sitting up startled that he'd escaped so easily, amazed that death's hold was light, light as feathers, as a spider's web, he popped up, stopped only by a strap securing him to the stretcher. Life, what other people had done to him, the final barrier after all. He'd snapped death's bonds. Was on his way up, back, when the leather safety restraint stopped him, whip-lashed his breath away. *Teach me*. Like a sigh. An exhalation. But clear and distinct. I heard him say those words, ma'am. No doubt about it. Just as plain as I'm telling you now. *Teach me* is what he said. Sure of it. Thought you might want to know, ma'am.

Gulls floated over the dump. Gull cries, the lazy circling of gulls. Gulls had followed the ferry across the sound. A second wake in the air. Gray and white like the plowed sea. Gulls hovering in the squat-bottomed boat's slipstream, patiently sailing, scanning the water for bilge. He'd read that sharks trailed the stench of slave ships all the way across the Atlantic, feasting on corpses thrown overboard. Gulls screech and glide above the refuse of the islanders. Cudjoe tried not to breathe as he helped unpack a week's trash from the trunk and backseat of

Sam's blue Dodge Dart. Sun was a bitch. A minute in the open and you were soaked. You could only hold your breath so long, then you had to inhale stink. Just a couple trips each, back and forth. Heave ho. Hurl a plastic sack. The mounds grow tall as a house, a pine tree. Body bags stacked a mile high rotting in the sun. Bad meat. Dead boys coming home from Vietnam were Cudjoe's age, Cudjoe's color, his high-school classmates. You couldn't see color through the thick, green bags. You could smell corpses, but all of them—red white black brown yellow—stink the same. Sam is careless. The bag bursts, vomits up its guts. He apologizes. His eyes accuse Cudjoe of being younger, stronger, of having many more years to live. Cudjoe is guilty. Others crossed an ocean and died for him. Guilty because he didn't fight, didn't die. Cudjoe thinks of Sam as a sad, failing old man. Can't imagine why he was once afraid of him. Why he'd packed his wife and kids in a station wagon and driven two hundred miserable miles, hat in hand, to pass Sam a manuscript. So scared he turned the trip to Sam's island into a nightmare, found ways to positively, personally put a hurt on his sons and the woman he loves.

That first night on the island he couldn't sleep. Wondering if Sam was reading the manuscript. Mad as hell because they'd whipped through two bottles of wine and most of a quart of vodka, only four of them drinking hard, Cassy, Sam's daughter, might have finished a goblet of wine, maybe two, so it's four of them doing the damage, two really, Cudjoe and Sam, unholy together, bringing out the best and worst in each other, doing most of the damage, especially if you added an ice-cold bottle of Mateus they'd guzzled like soda pop on the ride home from the dump. Couldn't sleep because Sam might be somewhere in the house, spectacles perched on the wings of his nose, in slippers and a robe, glass of brandy near at hand, reading the script so long in coming, reading it and liking it or disliking it. The terrible power in his old, spotted hands again. Would he know what the fuck he was reading? Had his bald head lolled back into the notch of the easy chair in his study, is his mouth open calling hogs, his breath turning the room into a distillery? Had Cudjoe's story put him to sleep? Would they talk in the morning? Would there be anything to talk about? Sam wouldn't dare give the script only a cursory, drunken reading. Of course he'd be his meticulous, conscientious self. Another read-through tomorrow. Up at dawn, crisp, sober as morning, as the sea breeze that worried the front porch swing. Its creaking chains are what woke Cudjoe in the first place. Trying to make sense of that rasping, rhythmic tick in his sleep. The loose, thin sleep of far too much drink. Worried awake by a sound he can't place, can't will away. He eased himself out of the tall four-poster bed, careful not to wake Caroline. He was ashamed now of the way he'd acted on the drive down. She'd hit the bed like a rock, her back to him, motionless in an instant, slamming the door on any possibility of nighttime, bedtime reconciliation. He'd boozed himself into feeling better about everything. Flirted with Sam's wife and daughter, and their smiling approval, the teasing back and forth had reaffirmed for him the charm he believed he exercised over womankind. Trying to piece the evening together, the dinner, drinks before, after and during, he realized he'd made absolutely no contact with Caroline. He'd begun having fun so he'd assumed everyone was enjoying themselves. Now as he searched his memory for one sign, one touch or smile or word that said she'd forgiven him, that her mood had changed, that the bitter ride to the island was forgotten, he was forced to admit he not only hadn't seen positive signs, he'd ignored Caroline's presence entirely.

Like a thief then, he tiptoed across the room. Figures out the noise that had been summoning him. Carried his shorts into the tiny guest room down the hall, next to where the boys were asleep. Shut the door quietly behind himself, slipped into his drawers. He shivers. Why didn't he bring a shirt? More like a walk-in closet than a room. Barely large enough to fit a bed. One oval window with a crack in the glass. This room's on the side of the house away from the sea, faces scrubby pinewoods that are part of a forest belt Sam had said bisects the island. Plenty of moonlight. Cudjoe can see clearly down the back lawn to a black wall of trees. This must be a corner room. To his right the main wing of the house looms perpendicular. The entrance, with its columns and wraparound porch, would be on the far side of this wing. Half a house away, the swing with its cargo of ghosts sways, invisible from where Cudjoe stands, its chains creaking monotonously, tirelessly as potbellied buoys rocking and tolling in the harbor.

Other sounds break through the soughing wind, the protest of the swing's rusty chains. A splash, then the sighing drone of water through pipes. Below him in the moonlight a white body hugs itself, twisting slowly, tentatively into spray from an outdoor shower sheltered in this nook of the house. Cassandra must have been swimming in the ocean and now she's warming herself, rinsing salt and sand from her body before she goes to bed. Her long hair shrinks to a cap of seaweed tight on her skull. She peels off a swimsuit and steps deeper into the gushing

water. Her skin's luminous in moonglow. Wet hair glistens
darkly as blood. The water's invisible except for a nimbus of
white froth at the nozzle and needle slants highlighted momentarily. If you couldn't hear the water, if you ignored the chunk
of soap she'd plucked from its hiding place, what you'd see was
a young woman dancing slow motion in a cascade of silvery
moonlight. Her arms carve space from the darkness, her feet
buried in shadow are never still, turning, sliding, little mincing
steps, rising on her tiptoes. Her fingers caress her breasts, rub
the black patch of groin, preparing them, offering them to the
same god at whom she stares, rapt, when she arches her neck,
leans her head back on her shoulders. She welcomes him,
drinks him into every pore of her body, her skin the thousand-
eyed gate of a great city thrown open to receive him.

At any second from the black margin of woods, satyrs will
hobble out to claim her. Sam's lawn is full of naked hippies,
bronze skins flayed so they're white as marble. They're blowing
flutes, passing jugs of wine, wicker baskets of fruit, dancing in
rollicking daisy chains. Everybody in the house snatched from
sleep by the racket, scrambling from their beds to join the
romp.

Cudjoe hears himself trying to explain to his dead friend
why he's spying on his daughter. Bullshit about her being
everywoman and no woman won't go down. She is Cassandra,
Sam's and Rachel's only child, eighteen years old, born on a
day her family once celebrated, then mourned. Sam had
changed her diapers. Rachel sat up with her through nights of
fever. Cassy had been fed, sheltered, cherished. Her loving
parents in spite of themselves had conspired to drive her a
little mad. Cassy's behavior often erratic, but just as often

charmingly, excruciatingly perfect. She was becoming who she must be by whatever devious paths her imagination could invent, circumventing one Cassy, their Cassy, to be another. Hence solitary midnight swims in the ocean. Long walks alone in cities at night. Dropping out of high school. A shower while normal people are trying to sleep. Cudjoe knows the history of her troubles. The rescue missions, and kiss-and-make-ups. Rachel's and Sam's constant fear she'd go too far and they'd lose her altogether. He understands he's wrong to be stealing from her. Violating her privacy. Poaching the bloom of her young woman's body while she's offering it to the spirits of night. He shouldn't be at this window staring down at her, a hard-on extending his shorts in spite of the slew of classical allusions he rehearses to himself. Unable to be still, staying and leaving, as she plays in water warm as a bed.

No excuses. Sam's no saint. He should understand. No harm intended. How many young editorial assistants had he banged over the years? No harm. Sam, Apollonian light of reason and intellect, knew what happened on full-moon nights when horny maidens cruised down from the hills. So look, Sam. I'm sorry. She's your daughter and I have no right, but . . . He starts some lame apology, not because he intends to cease what he's doing but because Sam is dead, and the dead have power. Sam may be hovering, waiting to avenge this violation of his daughter. The dead on their powdery thrones, looking down, weary, disappointed. He must answer to Sam because Sam's his twin, his cut buddy and drinking pardner, voice of his conscience, stage manager of his art, Sam in the wings silently paring his fingernails. Didn't Sam teach him how to be capable of anything? Technique, technique, my bucko, is truth.

Cassy was special. Sam loved her to distraction. Cassy was another chance. Sam could lavish on her what he'd never been able to grant to Rachel. A great passion replayed, only this time he wouldn't fuck over his woman. No lies. No cheating. A better Sam, reborn penitent, wiser for having sinned grievously. Capable of unconditional love. He's screaming at Cudjoe. Leave her alone. Leave her alone. She's my last goddamned chance.

Cudjoe watches entranced. Cassandra will be dead in nine months, a fiery crash in Mexico. The van she's riding in with her lover careens off a cliff, burns beside the ocean. He's spying on her because there's not much time, never enough time. He must learn her secrets, save her. Sam should understand. He'd be here at the window sucking up his daughter's beauty, every ounce from every angle, a sad feast always because never enough, she'll be gone tomorrow, he'll follow her a year later. So Cudjoe tells himself! Drink her in. Make love to her any way you know that won't hurt her or rob her precious time. If Sam had known how little time they could look forward to, together, alive, wouldn't Sam have been there, beside him, greedily taking it all in? His heart in his throat like Cudjoe's. His old pecker nudging his shorts like Cudjoe's.

No. Not that way. Cudjoe's getting confused, his stories mixed up. The striped van spins through the air, preternaturally slow, bands of color distinct as they turn, you can read the peace sign on the door, then it's gone, then the lumpish shape rotates again and you read again, Peace. Spinning through thin, hot air so slowly you can focus beyond the van, note the scenery, rugged jut of golden mountains shaded with midnight blue. Sharp peaks with crystal blue of sky as backdrop. You marvel. Range succeeds range, a breathtaking panorama spread across the horizon. Lower, there are buttes, desert plateaus, painted in delicate pastels, a patchwork of pinks, turquoises, rose, magenta, aquamarine. The colors inside a vagina. You're able to observe this while the van falls toward the dark maw of sea. No sound. No hint of horrendous impact, buckling metal, pulverized glass, the crackle of a gasoline-fueled inferno incinerating the vehicle when it lands, rendering it into a blackened skeleton on a rocky ledge thirty yards from the foaming surf. The story is Cassy first, then Sam. The story is, Cudjoe knew nothing of their imminent deaths that night in the little room in Sam's house when he'd watched Cassy showering. The story is, Cassy's with her lover in a van Cudjoe cannot picture because he's never heard it described. Never had the heart to ask for one more detail than he'd been given by her dumbstruck parents. This out-of-sync van that plummets forever against a tourist-bureau poster of mountainous Mexican scenery would be full of hippies, boiling, squealing like gulls.

Cassy naked in the moonlight on his first trip to the island. She's gone second time around. He's remembering correctly now because on his second visit, alone, two summers later, he'd imagined telling Sam about that night, what he'd seen. A crazy urge to confess, share his vision, as if the story might have pleased Sam, as if it would be a consolation to hear first-hand Cudjoe's witness to the sexual power of his daughter, how perfectly she'd grown into a woman's flesh, how she'd treated it, enjoyed the fullness thereof, dancing, gilded. A foolish idea. Sam was dead the second time Cudjoe visited the island. And if alive old Sam would have been outraged.

Probably try to kick Cudjoe's ass. Old liver-spotted fists flailing. Battering Cudjoe's hard brown skin. Wings of an angry butterfly till Cudjoe seizes the bony wrists, pins them under one of his hands and talks Sam down from his anger, soothes him like he would a child, patting the bald crown of his head. No harm, old buddy. No harm done. No evil intent. You would have done just what I did if you were there. If you'd found yourself in my shoes. My bare feet, really. Because up on your second floor where you'd stashed us, I tiptoed naked away from my wife and bed. Sleepwalking sort of, and the rest just happened. Believe me. You couldn't have turned away either. You'd have watched and been better for it. That dream of Cassy filed away with the rest. That much more of her inside you, to console you. Haunting you, killing you, sustaining you, for the little time you had left.

Did it for you, my friend. Cudjoe's lying again. He had returned to bed, masturbated, careful not to wake Caroline, his back inches from hers, miles from her in a place with different weather, his face turned up to drink warm rain.

> *Out of a misty dream*
> *Our path emerges for a while, then closes*
> *Within a dream.*

Pretty soppy stuff but Cudjoe had recited it and wept on the anniversary of Sam's death, that cloudy day Rachel had cast Sam's ashes into the wind. Sam retained a soft spot for Ernest Dowson and Lionel Johnson, those melancholy English decadents, their tears-in-a-teapot version of the blues. Sam the tough new critical priest of the text speaking for itself knew everything about the lives of the late Victorian Romantics and found them *simpatico* he said, *boon coons* later when he'd grown comfortable with that phrase he'd pinched from Cudjoe's writing. A gray mottled sky, heavy as iron. Rolling hills, profiles thinly one dimensional, dominoes stretched one behind the other till the last one collapses, melding into the bluish haze of distance. *They are not long.* The survivors drifted away after the ceremony. No one spoke. After Rachel had sprinkled his ashes where Sam had instructed and the sprightly wind, gray as the sky, had lifted them and threshed them, a final separation bit from bit, speaking into that silence would have been like farting in public. The mourners moved off to be alone, to be with one or two others. Cudjoe had observed in their strained, somber faces the panicked helplessness of a person stuck in a crowd needing to pee with no bathroom in sight.

Rachel took him by the hand, led him to the barn. Jesus Christ. They're all gone now. The whole family. Cassy. Sam. Rachel. The whole family. Wiped out. Invisible. As if they never existed. He hasn't thought of any of them for years. He wasn't really thinking of them now. He's dealing with the presence of Caroline this morning. Remembering how he lost her. Remembering a trip to Sam's island when they were together, when their lives had begun to unravel. Cudjoe is exploring the connection. Missing his wife and now he finds himself missing the others. Sam and Rachel and Cassy. *Our path emerging for a while.* Crying for them. Spying on them. Waiting for the lights of the city to come on.

Rachel led him by the hand up to a ladder at one end of the barn. She mounted first. Tail of her pleated skirt bobs as she climbs. Rachel's short legged. She's wearing no stockings.

Sturdy calf muscles jump like animals foraging under her skin. A spidery delta of blue veins on the back of one thigh. He looks away as he climbs after her. She wants to show him a picture she's painted of the island. A surprise intended for Sam, her way of saying thank you for the gift of island he'd presented to her. After thirty years of homes and separations, this house on the island their last stand. Sam sold or mortgaged everything then borrowed more to build a place where they could retire. Though he'd dropped his memoirs, a play, books he'd taken on as editor emeritus, Sam had exhausted himself completing the house project. My grand obsession. Sam's Folly, he called it. And after Cassy was killed, it seemed he had nothing left. Pharaoh content to be buried in the monument he'd constructed because that's what he'd settled into doing, dying by inches. He mopes around all day in his robe and slippers. Won't dress. Barely eats no matter what I cook for him. It's driving me crazy. I lost Cassy and now I'm losing him. Rachel fought back, patient, giving as she'd been all through the marriage, and as Sam gradually returned to her, she'd started painting again. She was hoping to finish her portrait of the island and surprise him with it on the anniversary of their new beginning.

Cudjoe has no trouble recalling the barn's smell in his funky bathroom this morning. An astringent, ammoniac odor of urine dominates here. A lake of aging piss percolating somewhere under the apartment house, seeping up through the toilet neck. Sam and Rachel's barn also a cave of smells. Piss, shit, sweat. Cows and horses long gone but the scent of them was rubbed into the barn wood, their dung stamped into the earthen floor, air weighted with their steamy breath. Sounds of animals rustling in their stalls, chewing cud, pawing the ground had left their echo in the air, turned it brown and warm. The barn was an animal, old, lopsided, walleyed. It swallowed them both as Cudjoe followed Rachel up the ladder to the loft. A bereaved animal, its innards the color Rachel must have been inside as she let Sam go one last time. Ashes. Ashes in the wind.

Swaybacked floorboards buckle under Cudjoe's steps. If Caroline thumped across the loft, she'd punch right through. He didn't have that to worry about. No more. Not here. Not anywhere. Between Cudjoe's visits to the island she'd left him. The book that was to be dedicated to her, his payback for what it cost them both, had been, like Rachel's painting, orphaned. Time was and time wasn't. Cudjoe a big boy now, but still a city boy, with a city boy's fears. The gloomy interior of the barn, its smells, ghostly animals ruminating, bumping around below the loft bothered him. Large, moist-breathed beasts had inhabited this space. Their blood was on his hands, in his belly. Their presence like a hood settling over him. He could feel the texture of their rough hides. He was wearing them. He was inside the steady churning of their guts. He tasted liver, heart, lungs, the sour, salty mash they'd brew into piss.

Between trips to the island Caroline had said she'd had it. Called his bluff. Cashed in her chips. His sons were growing up like exotic plants on a faraway island he'd never visited. He knew them not at all. They spoke another language. They had another father, a man who was finding it easy or difficult to live with their mother, a man who felt better or worse than Cudjoe between her legs.

He'd removed himself absolutely from their lives. All or nothing is how he explained it to himself, to her. Left it on her to explain to the kids. A bastard. He proved himself a cold fish of a bastard. She said she'd known it all along. She said she'd never understand why she tried to hold on. When she knew all along the kind of cold bastard he was. It proved you got what you deserved, she said. Got what you asked for. She knew she was asking for trouble, wanting him. She hated him for the lies, the betrayals. He'd disgraced them both. That's what he couldn't face. The mirror in her eyes. The hurt. The truth. Run. Run. Never look back. A cry from the deepest recess of him, the part nurtured in forest gloom when he dangled from a tree by a three-toed claw. An adrenaline rush as the command formed in his gut. Run. From the nighthawk, the bear, the slithering lizard, the coiled snake. Run. Run. Run.

Not that he ever really escaped. Rachel leaves him and strides to the opposite end of the loft. Tugging on a length of hairy rope depending from the rafters she opens a sliding window set in the steeply pitched upper story of the bam. Light floods the platform. Easels, canvases in various stages of finish, mounted, propped, lying flat, sucked, suddenly pop into view. Cudjoe expected to see Caroline revealed, eyeing him disapprovingly from a corner where the rapid thump thump of her steps had stranded her. No. Nothing. She was ancient history, like the lives of the animals who'd inhabited this bam. Cow dooky, horse dooky, a woman's footsteps exploding old wood, light blazing through slits in the boards, the mewling, murmuring ocean of brown bodies he'd drown in if this rickety floor collapsed. A woman's bare flank flashing through the saffron square of a window, the creaking arrangement, groaning like a swing in its chains, sea in its bowl, of pulley, tackle and rope draws open the loft window, horse dooky, cow dooky, smell of moon trapped in her blood once a month.

Finished now, I think. I need to show someone. You're the first.

Smoky light shivers in the rectangular opening. They used to pitch hay through there to store for winter. Standing on top of a wagon on top of a hay pile you could reach the opening without breaking your back. Heave ho. Light splashes into the loft like a giant pitchforkful of hay.

Do you think Sam would have liked it?

I'm sure he would.

Do you really think so?

The island's in your painting. I can see it. Sam would see more. Much more. Of course he'd love it. It's beautiful.

Thank you. It was important to finish it. Even after. The island started me painting again. Living again.

It's wonderful.

I'm so sorry about you and Caroline. You'll try again, won't you? Such lovely boys.

He could almost reach up and touch the rafters. Shadows up there not so deep now. Not so forbidding. Another world. Cobwebs, dust, filaments strung by spiders. Crawling things, gnawing things up there where the sloping sides of the bam roof joined in a point. The narrow end of a funnel. Tiny creatures in the shadows that are complement and terror of giant beasts below.

Yes. He'd thought that. Not in those exact words. Perhaps it's better to say he felt it. Order. Chaos. Felt himself suddenly exposed by light smoldering in the hay door. A superfluous creature. Not heavy like a cow, no wings or skittering banks of needle legs so he can scurry light and fast. In between. Alone beside another like him, but both alone, marked by aloneness as other creatures are known by their flavor, their bite. She grieved for her lost ones. He grieved for his. Grief was mooing, hooves shuffling aimlessly in a stew of dung, dried grass and pee. No room in the stall for another creature and therefore, no need, no point yearning for one. Grief was being confounded by darting, whirring licks from things that have no bodies, airy impossible things even when you catch one and squash it under your thumb. He's feeling miserable and exposed because he's neither of earth nor of air. He's smoke nodding at this canvas she's tried to fashion into earth, light, wind, water.

I'll come see you again. (He won't.)

Let's keep in touch. (They are already out of touch.)

Your painting is beautiful. (So it is and it changes nothing. He'll hear of the cancer and be afraid to call. He'll forget then be reminded when he hears the cancer has removed her. To the other side. From one place to the other. Out of the goddamned middle.)

She's up and busy. Flitting from room to room, naked as the day she was born. He listens across thirty yards for the thud of heels registering like drumbeats upon whatever it is that covers the floor of her apartment.

He surprises himself and turns away after a thick, choked-up minute. She is who she is and he is who he is. He crossed oceans to find a boy named Lion. He'd like to think finding him is his fate. He slides back the shower curtain. Daffodils, daisies, grimy yellows and greens. If not fate, then duty. A job. Finding him. He examines scratches on the back of his hand, checks for a bump on his sore shin where a knee had slammed him. He'll survive to play another day. His stomach is hard but bulges if he doesn't stand up straight, pull his shoulders back. Body pride. The little volleyball on his tummy will deflate if he plays regularly. A better Cudjoe inside this whipped flesh. Lean, fierce, a fighter, someone who could help the lost boy.

With the pointed end of one of the metal loops that hold the shower curtain on the rod, and squeeze open like safety pins, he pokes holes in the plastic. He's tired of a sopping floor every time he showers. Daffodils, daisies, yellows, greens. He threads curtain through three loops and refastens them. Three new holes, three new connections hike the curtain so it barely hangs past the tub's lip. Plastic's stiff with age. Scratches Cudjoe's skin as he brushes it aside, steps into the tub.

Trick is to finish washing before hot water runs out, or if the hot water's flowing free and strong, to finish before bilgy scum crawls past his ankles. Water pressure problems. Drainage trouble. You get fucked coming and going when you share ancient, inefficient plumbing with four floors of tenants. Cudjoe imagines showering in the condo he imagines Timbo owns. Timbo had class, if class means expensive tastes, the cunning and luck to satisfy them, Timbo surely one class dude. Cultural attaché to the mayor. Did the mayor know how to spell *attaché*? Was the accent over the final *e* acute or grave? When did Timbo learn to spell it, when had any of them learned the foreign words and foreign ways, how to pronounce, to spell, to feign an easy familiarity with places where such words were spoken? Mayor a country boy, he'd been told. Mississippi mud.

Timbo too, born on a farm a long ways inland from the New Orleans he liked to claim when questions about a birthplace were really questions about family, about pedigree and pretensions to civilization. Who the fuck are you? And who's your mama? Your daddy? Timbo had a rap for that species of question just as he possessed answers, slick and convincing, to questions most folks meeting him didn't know they intended to ask, till Timbo drills them with the answers.

Would Tims be different now? How would he have changed? Spray on Cudjoe's back boiled an instant then cooled lower than body temp. He cringed and scooted away from the scalding he was about to receive, skidding, regaining his balance just in time for a rush of chill needles on his backside. Too early in the morning for hot water to be gone. Sky not cracked yet. Still a solid sheet of slate. Who else in his building is up and about showering at dawn? Pipes must be busted again. Somebody's ceiling leaking, plaster bulging, dropping in wet lumps on somebody's kitchen table. He hoped the landlord would at least warn his tenants before he torched this block of decaying flats. Upkeep rising past what rents produce, what else is a good businessman spozed to do, either stuff in more families, a physical impossibility in this case, or burn down the building and collect fire insurance. Water sputters, teasingly hot then cold then a little of each. Cudjoe wipes away the last gobs of soap from his body with a washcloth, steering clear of the spray, cursing it and the landlord's mammy.

Timbo, you son of a bitch. I bet you're soaking your black ass in a Jacuzzi. Sauna and steam bath and geishas massaging your rusty legs every morning before the limo fetches you. A shower in your office. So you can go home to your old lady smelling sweet after a hard day humping your secretary on that buttery Corinthian leather couch beside your desk.

G'wan, man. This is serious bizness. Your man Timbo gots righteous responsibilities. Spons-bilities. Yeah. You like that. G'wan smile, nigger. You know you just as crazy as me. And just as sponsible.

Cudjoe had arrived late. Timbo later. The restaurant Timbo's choice. His treat. On the mayor, you unnerstand. After all, my friend, you are a writer, ain't you? Distinguished Negro Intellectual. Sure. Shit yeah. We gots a budget for that. Ain't that many of youall. We can afford it.

Cudjoe had showered, then flopped across the bed for a few minutes to catch his breath, soothe his pounding head, sneak up on the long morning. Body hung over from hoop, beer, trudging cross half the city, no sleep. Weary to his bones. But his mind wouldn't stay still. Caroline. Sam. Rachel. Cassy. Shit. He had closed his eyes, exhausted. The nap lasted three hours. Sleep at last. Sleep at last. He bolts up. Checks his watch. Time, but none to spare. He figured Timbo for at least a half hour late. Turned out to be more like forty-five minutes so Cudjoe has time to check out the joint. No way he's going to pay this tab. Three flunkies already had performed little flunky services just getting him inside the door good. Price of the ticket would include all that. Waiters, cocktail waitress, busboy, dessert tray still to come. A steep ticket. Don't let Timbo jive his way out of paying.

My man. Cudjoe, my man. How long's it been, brother? How long? Too long. Don't shake my hand, nigger. Come round here and hug me. Men's is lowed to hug and squeeze each other these days. Mmmmm. Yessir. Huggin's hip as Perrier and white wine. Gimme some skin now. Cudjoe, you scarce mothafucker.

You're looking good, Timbo.

Was you expecting otherwise, bro?

Timbo, elegant, skinny, strikes a pose, lead tenor of the Dells *Why do you have to go*, arms to the sides, away from his body, palms faced outward to the audience, shoulder cocked, front knee slightly bent, a curtsy almost, but too much held back, too much power in reserve, he's offering an emblem of himself held just so, sleek lines of his outfit displayed to advantage, a gray, double-breasted, laser-striped suit you don't buy off a rack, tailored so it appears comfortable as a T-shirt, the bad motherfucker he could be reined in, stylized, anticipated and satirized by this little halfway playful bow. He's really not giving a damn thing away, but yeah, he knows the game, he can do them little dances, them soft-shoe forms exchanged before you get down to business, so you can get down to business.

I appreciate you meeting me on short notice, man.

Anything for a brother. We go back, way back, don't we, brother man? Damn. To those thrilling days of yesteryear and shit.

Lemme say this up-front before we even sit down. I understand your official position. What you say to me doesn't go any further than me without your permission.

Whoa. You ain't the *National Enquirer* is you? Sit down, man. Here we are together after all these years. I know who you are. And you know Timbo. I'ma get to the fire, man. Know that's what you want to rap about and we'll get to it by and by. But relax, bro. Tell me bout you. Is the novel finished? Heard about you breaking up with your old lady. But that was long ago, wasn't it? If she swung wit you, she musta been fine. Always cruised with a fox on your arm. You're the baddest. Bet you still are, you devil. Needs to catch up with you, bro. Ain't too many niggers like us left in the world.

Not changed. Not one bit.

Mr. Maurice. Like you to meet my main man here. Mr. Maurice owns this joint. We, the mayor, myself and our very special guests, dine here regularly. Mr. Maurice knows how to set a table. Anything you fancy. Anythang. Mr. Maurice can see to it.

Pleased to meet you, sir.

Cudjoe. Just call me Cudjoe.

My man's a democrat, Maurice. One the people. Not like some these uppity niggers come in here.

Mr. Cudjoe. Welcome to my humble establishment.

Pumps hand. Avoids eyes. He's busy panning the huge room, missing nothing. Lots of Liberace hair, shining, every strand in place.

Humble, my ass. Pulls in a fortune daily. Each and every day. More on weekends. This dago like rust. He don't never sleep. If he ain't racking it in, he's counting it, investing it. Ain't that right, Mr. Maurice. But the man's good. Serves nothing but the best to the best. Day in, day out.

You're too kind, Mr. Timbo, too kind.

Cudjoe doesn't know what to make of the exchange. Who's zooming who. A new language. New license. Niggers and dagos. Cityspeak. No secrets, no history, what you see is what you say. Things have changed since he's been away. Never used to be more than a few black faces in a five-star restaurant like this. Now every third chair occupied by a brother or sister dressed back. Make their white companions look like poor relatives from the country. Clearly the place to be at lunchtime. Even the help swaggers. In his K mart blazer and chinos Cudjoe is one of the country cousins. Timbo at home in these waters as a shark. Things change. Not Timbo though, not blessed Timbo.

Two Absoluts on the rocks. Doubles, babe. You still drink vodka, don't you, home?

Cudjoe orders crab cocktail. Timbo a sampler of pâtés. Gets better from there. Timbo urging him try this, try that. C'mon have some this good life. Election's coming. Goodies might all be gone tomorrow. Get it while it's hot.

The old days. Sure I remember them. And some of them were good. None of us had a dime but we was living good, better than we knew at the time. Academic welfare. Way I look at it now they was testing us. Put a handful of niggers in this test tube and shook it up and watched it bubble. Was we gon blow up or blow up the school or die or was some weird green shit gon start to foaming in the tube? Or maybe the whole idea was to see if we'd come out white. Nobody really knew the answers so they decided to experiment. We were guinea pigs. How many of us in our class at the University? No more than nine, ten total. Set us down in the middle of a place Negroes never been before, wasn't ever spozed to be. Then shook up the tube.

Trouble was they couldn't keep things straight. What was experiment and what was real life. And if they couldn't keep it straight, how the fuck was we spozed to? I'd think I was walking down the street with this cute little white coed, thinking we're minding our business, strolling to the cafeteria for a cup of coffee, and *blam*. Run right dead into the glass wall. Wait a minute, boy. This pussy you trying to scheme up on is real. It ain't part of the goddamned experiment. You still in the tube, nigger, and don't you forget it. Oh yeah. Those was good old days. Sometimes. But the bad days tore up a whole lot of sisters and brothers. Beaucoup casualties. Bump into some of them downtown every day. Walking round like ghosts of they own goddamned selves.

So what's different now? Maybe nothing, Cudjoe. I wonder why we ever believed it was spozed to get better. Who fed us that lie? Why'd we swallow it? What's different? Something ought to be, shouldn't it? Well, to begin with, take the two of us, here, today. We survived. We're eating higher off the hog. That ain't all bad, is it? Food tastes pretty good, don't it? I ain't real sure after that. This city gon be Camelot, right? Our black Camelot. We're in the driver's seat, watch us go, world. Ain't a black city cause whites still outnumber us, and ain't a dead city cause still plenty money here, so wasn't like some these other burgs where they stick in a black mayor cause nobody else want the job. Different situation here. Possibilities here. This an old city with old money. Seemed like we might have half a chance to do our thing here, do it our way. Show everybody. A showcase city. Everybody grinning, shaking hands, making money. But shit, man. I been on the inside two years and you know what I think? I think they experimenting again.

*   *   *

All this area in through here. Remember what it looked like?

Timbo drives like he dresses. The black sedan with the mayor's seal on the door graces the streets, the route it follows synchronized to Timbo's voice-over as they zip along, changing lanes, pace, direction, pausing, whipping through superfluous terrain as if the cityscape had been tailored to accommodate this quick sketch Timbo is drawing.

This used to be stone slum. Raggedy row houses and vacant lots. Stone ghetto, baby. Now every square foot is solid gold. City underwrote the project. Bought up those tobacco-road shacks for next to nothing. Leased the land to private developers and they put up dorms, apartments, town houses, condos. Hard to believe it's the same place, ain't it? I mean if you was a roach and been away on vacation and come back to the old hood, you'd say, Shit. This ain't home. Where my brother roach and cousin rat? Some body done messed up my good thing.

See, down here, paralleling the railroad tracks we're laying a new street. Direct access off and on the expressway. All this mess around in here, warehouses, garages, shanties, all these eyesores got to go. When redevelopment's finished, a nice, uncluttered view of the art museum. That's the idea. Open up the view. With universities just a hop skip down the way what we're trying to create here is our little version of Athens, you dig? Museum's the Acropolis up on the hill. Cross by way of bridges and tunnels to the brainpower and computer power of the universities. Modern urban living in the midst of certified culture. College boys and girls running around on the set looking good and smart and prosperous like ain't nothing wrong with the world. It's gonna work, too. You wouldn't believe the price of real estate. People standing in line to buy. Fortunes being made, brother. And this time round there's some black fingers in the till. Not too black, you dig, don't want to smudge the cookie jar. Gon be some big-time bucks generated by this action.

The folks used to live here. Yeah. Well, you know the answer before you asked that one. S.O.S. Same ole shit. Some went north. A lot got pushed west. Landlords getting fat off that end too. Shortage of housing so they cramming three, four families in one-family houses. Hell. If I owned a house in West Philly I'd rent it and move down here. A damned good investment. Figure it out. Borrow the down payment. Three families each paying to rent your old crib so you can meet your condo note and your loan note. Maybe have change. Nobody would have to burn old Timbo out. I'da been right here, man. In my shiny new pad. Right here where it's happening.

It ain't all a bed of roses, though. Parts of the city, like this, man, are cooking. A new day. The right ingredients in place. Big money making bigger money. They love the mayor here. Black and white. Call him Sambo behind his back but they be grinning in his face. On the other hand, let's just say he ain't universally loved. We still got sections of this great metropolis where nobody don't love nobody. Too ugly. Too mean. No time for love. Niggers scuffling and scheming twenty-four hours a day to survive. That shit ain't changed. In fact since dope been king it's worse. Much worse. Some of us, a few really, are doing better, moving up. A handful doing damned well. But them that ain't got and never had, they worse off than ever. S.O.S., man. Rich richer and poor poorer. Some these pitiful bloods off the map, bro. And they know it. And they ain't too pleased about it. That's the rub cause you know who they blame. Bloods voted for the mayor and he won but they ain't won shit. Same ole. So the natives is restless. Mayor's trying to keep a lid on but, tell the truth, it's driving the cat crazy. Doing everything he can to make the city a better place to live and you can see progress, real progress. Area like this University City wasn't nothing but a gleam in a planner's eye a few years ago. Look at it now. Look at what it's gonna be. Can't argue with progress. At the same time over in the north and in the west where people from here forced to move, what's growing is garbage dumps.

Like in the Third World, man. I was down in Rio for Carnival, dig? Having me a natural ball. This dude down there, does business with the city, he invited me out to his villa. Stone fairy-tale palace out in the boonies. Swimming pools. Stables. A disco. More servants than I got cousins. On the way the limousine had to pass through this slum. Miles of it. Talk bout tent city. These folks lucky if they got a rag to pull over they heads. Most of them just plain-ass living on the ground. The ground, man. Stinks like bad meat. Don't matter all the car windows closed. Stink sneaks in. You feel dirty, like stink's painting you a nasty color. Acres and acres of it, man. A garbage dump. A people dump.

I'm thinking to myself, this is poor. Back in the good ole U.S. of A., we ain't got real poor people. This is poor. Living in boxes and holes. Hard ground and evil sky. When the sun's hot you bake. If it rains, you rained on. People jammed up so tight they shitting and pissing on top one another. Kids playing in open sewers. Couldn't believe it, man, and I seen some bad shit in my day.

I say to myself, Never. Couldn't never get this bad back home in the land of opportunity and the bitch wit the torch. Not so sure now. Already people in this city live off garbage. And I'm not talking about just bums. I'm talking about families, about gangs of kids roving the streets, sleeping outdoors. And plenty people sleeping indoors in rattraps bad as the streets. Everyday people sinking deeper in the hole. Losing people every day. Enough of them go down the tube they gon start climbing back out. Walk up each other's backs and climb out the hole. What we gon say then? What's the mayor gon do when the city starts to cracking and pieces break off the edges and disappear. It's thin ice, man. Damn thin ice and we all dancing on it. We all gon fall through if the shit starts to go.

So what's the mayor intend to do?

Do? What a mayor always does. Grin and lie and shake hands and cut ribbons on new shopping centers. What else he spozed to do? This mess been here long before he was elected and he'll be dead and in his grave before it changes. If it ever changes. You and me. We happened to come along at a time when it seemed things might change. We thought we was big and bad enough to make the world different. That's our problem, believing things spozed to change for the better. Mayor's not like that. He's older, wiser. Not dewy-eyed like we was, but not bent down like our daddies, neither. He's in between. Korea's his war. A police action. He's realistic about power and politics and deals and compromise and doing his jig inside the system. He ain't about change. He's about hanging on long enough so some who ain't never tasted pie can have a bite before the whole shebang turns rotten. A simple, devious, practical man. A nice guy. Hey. He's my boss. Love the nigger. Treats me better than any white boy would.

If the city's coming apart at the seams, nobody's going to be eating cake very long.

Right. But that ain't the mayor's fault. No more than it's my fault or yours, Mr. Cudjoe. Where you been hiding all this time? Could have used a few more good shoulders at the wheel. You copped the education and ran, man. Maybe you know something none the rest of us bureaucrats know. Maybe you holding some answers. The mayor will listen. Maybe you should have stayed home. You could have told the mayor what to do with the King and his bunch of loonies.

Why did anyone have to do anything with them?

They were embarrassing, man. Embarrassing. Trying to turn back the clock. Didn't want no kind of city, no kind of government. Wanted to live like people live in the woods. Now how's that sound? A Garden of Eden up in West Philly. Mayor breaking his butt to haul the city into the twenty-first century and them fools on Osage want their block to the jungle. How the mayor spozed to stand up and talk to white folks when he can't control his own people? The press ate it up. Nonsense in the papers every day. King's people demanding this and demanding that. Letting their kids run around naked, sassing the police and getting their heads busted, cussing out the neighborhood on loudspeakers, dumping shit in their back-yard, demanding the release of their so-called brothers and sisters from the slam. Sooner or later those nuts had to go. Mayor got tired of them mocking everything he was promising. Talk about a thorn in his side. King and them were a natural thorn halfway up his behind. A whole brier patch growing up in the mayor's chest. Sooner or later, one way or another, them and their dreadlocks had to go.

The fire.
The fire.

*   *   *

Timbo cuts the engine. They've parked at the edge of new construction. Beyond a barrier of striped sawhorses dead-ending the street, oatmeal-colored guts of the city have been exposed. Huge chunks of asphalt are stacked, waiting to be hauled away. Heavy equipment. Humming generators. Rows of man-high cement cylinders, coiled snakes of plastic tubing. Cudjoe thinks of veins, arteries, nerves, organs, high-tech replacements for old, worn-out parts. To the east, windows of tall buildings are bronzed by late-afternoon sun. The skyline hovers pale, indistinct through heat haze. Early summer but already heat has begun to reshape the city. By August the city would be a sure-enough patient laid out on a table. Hot sand scalds his bare feet. He steps from shadow to shadow when he can find one, following a path that twists forever up the side of the cliff dividing town from beach. Dark caves. Rotten teeth. Skinny kids stare through him as he passes, a faraway look dulls their eyes. He's a fly on the other side of the glass.

Timbo. Why did we believe we could turn this country around?

Cause we wanted more than we had and that seemed the way.

I'm writing about the fire.

Oh yeah.

About the fire, but about us too. About believing we could take over. Build a better world.

We did take over, didn't we? I mean, shit. We had the whole world in our hands and we blew it. Dropped it like a hot potato. Whew. I don't want it you can have it. Tossed it back to Daddy and exited for goddamn parts unknown. Kathmandu. Wyoming. You know what I mean.

We had them on their knees, man. Begging and pulling out their hair. Tried everything to put us down but we were strong. We were righteous. Couldn't nothing stop us. But our own damn selves. They let us strut around like we owned the Johnson. We was superbad. On the tube. In the movies. They just let us *be* for a while. Let us boogie around till we got bored with our ownselves and wasn't nothing to do but creep in the back door and tiptoe up the stairs into our old rooms and give up the keys. Please let us back in the house. Youall grown-ups go on and take care the grown-up business. We just want to play and have a good time. They said OK. You can come back. And here's some shit to play with. Here's a war in Asia. You can take your music and dope and go fight it. Take the niggers with you. And here's some more dope for when you get back. You can fuck each other's brains out. Fuck till your crotches rot. That's what you wanted, wasn't it? A party. Share a little of the goodies with the niggers. Keep them out our hair. We got business to tend to. Grown-up business of running the world.

They snatched back the car keys, the house keys. We got slogans and T-shirts and funny haircuts. And AIDS. Make love not war. Grateful Dead. Woodstock. Black Power. Sheeit.

Cudjoe is tired. He's been sitting too long in the restaurant, the car. His muscles are stiff. Timbo rapping nonstop about something else now: South Africa, the PLO. Vietnam War, civil rights, marches and protests, he'd dealt with that time of their lives in five minutes. How could Cudjoe have thought it would fill novels?

Cudjoe closes his eyes, listens to Timbo the way he listens to music. Timbo's voice could bring back the feeling of those years they were in school together. A particular succession of notes created a tune. Certain notes started it, you recognized them but the music immediately carried you someplace else, behind the notes, between them. The meaning of the notes was where they took you and how it felt to be there, behind them, feeling again what you felt another time when you heard the notes played. A fast, jumpy tune makes you sad. A slow song thumps you between the shoulder blades and you remember the wings folded back there and they open and fly you away.

Greed's got the deepest pocket, cause see Greed scheming full-time to keep that pocket full. When you want something you go to Greed's pocket. It stinks, it's pukey down in there. Dead babies and disease and children starving with flies and maggots in the pus draining out their sores and assholes. You know Greed got to dig down deep in the shit to give you what you asking for, but you need it and where else you gon get it? Yes. I'll take it. Thank you kindly.

You hate to watch Old Greed stirring around down in his ugly pocket and you damned sure avoid looking at his fingers when he draws out the little piece of change you're begging for. You know good and well the nasty place it's coming from but you ain't hardly refusing what he holds out, blood, vomit, shit, piss, pus and all.

Answer's always yes. Yes, I'll take the money. Don't care how much blood's on it Don't care if it's my blood. Yours. I wasn't the one responsible. I'd prefer clean money but till clean drops down from heaven this will do. Yes. I'll take it. Somebody will take it. Mize well be me. Money's money. None of it's clean.

See, to me, man, that's the bottom line. No matter how you cut it, human nature gets down to a simple fact. You want yours and I want mine, don't matter whose blood on the money, yes, we'll take it. World operates the way it does because that's the bottom line. Survival's the bottom line. Looking out for number one.

How you gon convince somebody democracy's good or socialism or communism or King and his nouveau Rousseau or whatever the fuckism, how you gon preach the morality of one system over another system when all anybody concerned about is the goodies the system delivers to their door? Everybody wants a piece of the rock. What's it matter whose bones broken hacking the rock out the earth, who's dying pushing the rock up the hill, who's ground up underneath it?

Timbo off mankind now, ranking on particular friends and acquaintances. Whatever happened to thus and so? Whichamacallit? What's his name? You know who I mean. The guy. The chick. C'mon. You know who I'm talking about. What's the cat's name? A shooting gallery of faces as Timbo ticks off their signs: bad breath, big tits, the stuttering, dickhead mother-fucker. Mr. Prim and Proper, Miss Fine Ass, Woody Woodpecker square-headed no dancing turkey. The Crab Lady. The Dog Man. Finger-painted in the air, pantomimed, noises in his throat, a giggle, finger pops, silences, bat of his eyelashes, face after face flickers across the screen of Timbo's rap. Cudjoe thinks up a god so prodigal it can't help creating everything it thinks. Runaway creation, people spilling from its orifices as it laughs and farts and slaps its thigh and marvels at the perversity, the fecundity of its mind, the permutations and combinations it can spin off the basic human clay. One leg, three legs, no legs at all. Legs where arms should be. A phantom leg after the real one blown off by a land mine. Legs tangled, twisted, one shorter than the other, legs like flippers, perfect deadly legs, legs undersized and elephantized, suppurating and skin flaking away, black ones on red people, green ones on white, and as fast as the god dreams them, here they come pouring from a cornucopia, flooding the earth, a rickety, crooked, misshapen pair, a joke, a whim, the only set of legs some sorrowful motherfucker will own all the days of his life.

You remember people, Timbo. I have places, almost like stage sets, in my mind. I've been trying to find them since I've been back but they're gone. Buildings, streets, trees. Stores I used to shop, bars where we partied. The Carousel. I can picture it perfectly. But there's no Carousel anymore.

Been gone for days, bro. Guess you have been away for a while. Lemme see. It was the Carousel when we were in school, then the Sunset Grill, then the Hi Hat Lounge, then it didn't have a name. Just a trifling little corner joint. Back part where we boogied torn down. By then most the shit around it torn down, too. They were building those high-rise dorms across on Chestnut and everything north was being urban-removed. Driving down to City Hall and I pass this busted sign, two or three tubes of neon kinda sputtering, red, bright red cause it was a crisp, winter night and nothing else around in there so these squiggle-squaggles of red caught my attention spelling out a message looked like Arabic or Chinese characters, didn't make any sense, then I noticed where I was, between Fortieth and Thirty-ninth on Market so I thought to myself, Yeah. That must have been the Carousel—whatever name it went by then—still holding out on that lonely-ass corner. Thought of you, old buddy, and the rest of the crew used to always be hanging out in there. The good ole days. That sign with the blood barely squeaking through its veins was sure enough pitiful and I was long gone on my way downtown but I could picture the joint jumping again. Ray Charles on the Box. What D'ye Say. Folks wall to wall Saturday night and I just got paid. Hey. Timbo rolling along in his big car courtesy of the City, pocketful of money, the mayor's boy, the city cocking up her big legs for him. Timbo on top the world, but man, I can tell you, and you'll understand. I'd have given it all up in a minute for them old days. Timbo missing the Carousel. Timbo shedding a big, sloppy tear for them golden olden days and all us fools carousing at the Carousel.

Let's go cop us a taste, brother Cudjoe. I want to hear about your life.

*

I lived on an island. Learned another language. Almost like a new life. Born again before born again was big business. When Caroline and I split up, she took the kids and moved in with her parents. She eventually married again, lives in Haiti. After we broke up, nothing made sense to me. I knew I'd fucked up.

Felt dirty, contaminated. And contagious. Yeah. I didn't want to have anything to do with other people. Afraid I'd give them what I had. Or that they'd know on sight how sick I was and shun me. That was an even greater fear. Being found out. Being punished. The man who'd been encouraging me to write died. But not before saying, No, not yet, twice to the book I was struggling with. Nothing here for me so I crossed the ocean. Bummed around a year. South of France, Spain, North Africa. Then I found my island. Mykonos. Wound up staying away ten years.

Ten years. That's a lot of years.

One-two-three-four-five-six-seven-eight-nine-ten. Ten dead Indians. Count em.

What'd you do?

The island was beautiful. I stayed because it was beautiful and I wasn't required to do a goddamn thing. Cool out. Day after day of nothing and nobody gave a fuck. I became an institution. Only splib in the permanent colony of foreigners. Worked at a bar. You could find me there regular as rain. Black face behind the bar at Spiros. A fixture. Part of the island. Like naked beaches and caves and cliffs. Everybody loved me. Then forgot me. Invisible man. Bartending my day job, and sometimes at night I wrote.

Living the life of the expatriate, huh. Beachcomber and pussy-hound and artiste. Sounds good to me, homeboy.

I was lonely lots of the time, Timbo. But shit, I was lonely living with a wife and two kids in a goddamn matchbox apartment you can't turn around in. Missed music and playing ball and the funny stuff you Negroes over here got into, sitting in, occupying buildings, Mau-Mauing the Man. Missed it and missed my family. For a while didn't care if I lived or died. Played it day by day. Minute at a time. I'd read about what was happening over here. Seemed like the whole world was going to explode. Then nothing happened. Don't know today if that made me feel better or worse but I survived. Mad plenty of days. Mad weeks at a stretch. Did lots of drinking and hiding and running. Wrote a lot of bullshit poems and unfinished essays. Letters to Caroline and the boys I never sent. A boring life really. Like a spectator from a distance watching my country kill itself. Watching and waiting for my old life to disappear. And take me with it. Some things never change, I guess.

Hey. Some things do. Ten years is ten years. We grown-ups, good buddy. Middle-age motherfuckers. Wish I'd stole me five or ten years to do nothing.

Never finished the novel about us.

Too bad.

But I can tell you something about it. You were one of the stars.

Would have been some book, then.

Maybe what I'm writing about the fire will make up for the other one. You're in it, too.

Oh yeah. You ain't intending to get me fired, are you? Or strung up?

I need help. The boy who survived is the key. I have to find him.

Write your sixties novel. Make old Timbo a literary hero. Let me play the part in the movies. Forget the fire. Play with fire you know what happens. You'll get burnt like the rest of us. Tell the story about trying to change the world. Fire ain't going nowhere. Be right here when you get back from Hollywood.

Kids Krusade. Kaliban's Kiddie Korps. Cudjoe saw the graffiti everywhere. Triple K's. MPT. Double K's. *Money Power Things.* Anywhere and everywhere. Man-high letters. The words spelled entire. Where did all the spray paint come from? Who was splashing every wall in Philadelphia with these messages? Like a new season. Instead of last-ditch autumn brightness or summer green or gray-white winter this was a season of garish primary colors dashed and slooshed and spilled over the city, rainbow signs signifying things were changing, a new day on its way, breaking out, taking over, a rash of MPTs and K's transforming the city like the stigmata of a galloping disease.

And like a natural season, these messages blasting from every surface struck him as inevitable, not new, just not remembered, the way a blinding snowstorm and freezing temperature are unreal when you're sweating through a T-shirt on a muggy August day. Heat rises up at you from the asphalt and you can't believe the hawk ruled here, just yesterday, his chilled wings flapping through these canyons, his icy talons lifting your shivering ass clean off the ground as you scurry cross Market, humping for the steaming subway entrance. The spray-painted messages defaced or decorated the city, depending on your point of view. Vandalism or tribal art or handwriting on the wall. Whatever the signs meant, they were a transforming presence. For a while, as long as they reigned in plain view, it was their season, and their season was different.

War paint, Cudjoe thought. Gearing up for battle. Kids

priming the city with a war face. MPT. KK. A ritual mask summoning power; a dream, a revelation as the features of the city change before our eyes. Does anyone besides him recognize what's happening? Did it happen too quickly? Nobody paying attention to walls, billboards, sidewalks, fences and then one morning, boom, the signs had appeared. Second nature instantly. Blending into the cityscape nobody ever sees. Kids Krusade. Money Power Things. Kaliban's Kiddie Korps. Unnoticed. Like dead trees, dead rivers, poisonous air, dying blocks of stone.

He knew. He saw. He was afraid.

In the restaurant he had asked Timbo if Timbo knew what to make of the signs. Of course Timbo had an answer.

Kids today are a bitch. Worst problem used to be gang warring. Maiming and killing each other like flies cause they didn't have nothing better to do. Now they kill anybody. Anything. Cold-blooded little devils. You wouldn't believe juvenile court. Not no lightweight run away from home and stealing candy bars and cars shit. Huh uh. Dope dealing and contract killing and robbing and beating people in the neighborhood for drug money and full-scale turf wars with weapons like in Nam. Gangsters, man. Ice water in their veins. And ain't this high yet, ain't twelve years old yet.

I'll send you copies of some stuff the undercover dudes from the Civil Disobedience Unit been collecting. Check it out. You won't believe it. Kids is crazy these days. And cold. Mean and cold. Smart too. Capable of any damned thing. We looking at a cockeyed kiddie insurrection brewing.

They want to take over, man. Little runty-assed no-hair-on-their-dicks neophytes want to run the city. Yeah. Money Power Things. MPT. What you see on the signs is saying they want their share. Claim the only difference between them and grown-ups is grown-ups hold the money, power and things. Funny, ain't it? Same shit we wanted back in the sixties. Only these kids bolder than us. They don't want to be something else. They don't want to be white or shareholders or grown-up. They want it all, everything adults have, the MPT. Then they'll run the world their way. Run it better than we do. So they say. And I halfway believe they could. Know what I mean, Cudjoe? Be hard to fuck up worse than we're fucking up. You know what I mean. They got a point there.

Bottom line is this, though. Get this. When the kids in control of MPT, they gon ship old motherfuckers like you and me away. Old Islands, bro. Ship us off to these elephant grave-yards where we spozed to die. See, getting old is getting greedy and useless. So everybody over twenty-one got to hat up. Live in adult concentration camps is what it comes down to. It's written down in their pamphlets and posters. We'll be sent off to work and grow old and die. Shut away so we don't crowd their space. Everything for the young. Shit end of the stick for the old. It's fair, they say, because everybody's young once. And nobody has to grow old if they don't want to. Hint. Hint. You dig? They say it's just birth control in reverse. Fairer, they say. Cause at least the olds have their chance to be young.

One more piece of this madness we've learned about. Fixers. Fixers are these goddamned cute-little-kid-next-door death squads. Free of charge they'll take out troublesome adults. You know, abusers, pimps, dealers, derelicts, unreasonable teachers and parents. Fix up problems for other kiddies. Half-pint assas-sins. Fixers. And these juvenile delinquents think they're going to change the world.

Who writes the pamphlets?

Pamphlets, leaflets, posters. Some are like comic books. Pictures tell the story for kids who can't read. Recruiting brochures are what they are. That and inflammatory propaganda. Spreading the word. You know. A battle for the hearts and minds of kids. Of course that rapping music's in it. And the stuff on the walls part of it too. A big part. Putting out the message every way they can.

But *who's* the they? Kids doing it all?

There's one long pamphlet. Can't see a kid writing it. It's a manifesto, carefully thought out, cleverly worded, organized. Wish I had somebody in my office who could turn out copy like that. Possibly an older kid could have written it. But it's not kid style. Reads like the prose we used to hammer out in those all-night emergency meetings. Our demands, our grievances, all the bullshit we wasn't gon accept from the Man no more. What I believe is someone's using the kids.

Outside agitators?

What you grinning at? I know what you're thinking but sometimes it's true. Outsiders come in, stir up trouble. A fact. Don't care how dry the straw is and how high it's heaped in the bam, you still need a match.

To light the fire.

Light the fire.

Timbo. Has anyone downtown heard anything about the boy who was saved?

We always talking about the fire, ain't we? No matter what I think we talking about, it comes down to the fire. Well, the answer's no. When you read what I send you, though, you're going to get a shock. The fire's in it. In a list of atrocities that prove adults don't give a fuck about kids. The lousy school system, abortion, lack of legal rights, child abuse, kiddie porn, kids' bodies used to sell shit on TV, kids on death row, high infant mortality. In that list as one of the latest signs. Cause the fire burned up mostly kids. And also because a kid managed to survive. Survived bullets and flames and flood and bombs. Superkid, dig. City used everything in its arsenal but the little mothafucker got away. Simba, right? He's a symbol of kid power. He's a hero, magic, they say. Went through hell to show the others they can do it. Do anything.

Olds are Vampires. They suck youngs' blood.

Schools teach you the 3 Ds. Kids are Dirty, Dumb, Dependent. Schools treat you like beasts who must be tamed. The truth is we are perfect. Our bodies are perfect and clean. Our thoughts make perfect sense. We have a perfect right to Money, Power, and Things.

Being born is good. Growing old is bad.

Play not work.
This truth can set you free.

I don't know, man. Don't know how seriously to take any of this. But something's out there. And it ain't pretty. You ready for a long walk off a short pier, Cudjoe? You ready to be fixed? You ready to slave in a salt mine on an Old Island so some little jitterbug can party?

Cudjoe remembers Timbo's answer. He remembers a waiter

clearing the table. Mr. Maurice cruising by one last time to stroke and be stroked. Recalls thoughts that rose in him. All this ceremony, this help, squads of saucers, plates, glasses, cups and silverware, the dirty pots and pans back in the kitchen that had cooked what they'd eaten. How many hands, how much time and trouble required to fill the stomachs of two black men who probably weren't that hungry in the first place? A wave of shame and humiliation. Where are his children? Caroline? What would any of the people living and dead whose opinions he values think of this lunchtime debacle? What could he say to a starving person about this meal, this restaurant, this possibility of excess made real by the city? Why did he sit still for it? Accumulating. Bloating. Smiling and chattering while piles of bones, hunks of fat, discarded gristle and cores, skins and decorative greens and sculpted peels, corks, cans, bottles, grease, soiled linen, soggy napkins, crumbs on the floor, shells, what was unconsumed and unconsumable, waste and rot and persiflage heaped up, the garbage outweighing him, taller than he was, usurping his place. Eaten by refuse faster than he can cram it down his throat. He'd lunched with his old pal Timbo and whatever it was destroying the city gorged itself upon them and shit them out even as ice cubes dinged in crystal goblets and silver coffee spoons chimed against the edges of bone-china cups. Not so much a thought as a sensation. The experience of being swallowed. Used and abused. Slipping and sliding down into a stinking, slithy darkness. Lost, lost and almost enjoying the ride, the plunge, but sickened too, helpless and pitiful and exhausted. Finally expelled.

What would he say to Simba if he ever found him?

* * *

Timbo. I had a dream.

You too?

Gimme a break. Listen a minute before you laugh.

What's your dream, brother?

I wake up in a park. Right down the street from the fire. Clark Park at Forty-third and Osage. Or dream I wake up. Then I hear a bunch of kids singing. The words are unintelligible. Another language. But the singing gets to me anyway, right away. I can feel what they're singing about. Doesn't matter that I can't understand a word. It's a freedom song. A fighting song. Righteous as those movement anthems. Ain't gon let nothing turn me round, turn me round. Remember? Remember the tears coming to your eyes. Remember how full and scared and strong the singing made us feel? That's what I awakened to. Those feelings. That music. Only different. Another language. Another country. And kids doing the singing, kids I couldn't see because it's pitch-black middle of the night and there's a hollow in the park and that's where the singing seems to be coming from. I stand up. Start to walk toward where I hear the sound. Then I'm lost. Dream time turns me all around because suddenly it's daylight. Or it's been day all along and I've just been walking around with my eyes closed. A grimy, grainy Philadelphia gray morning. Only stark silent. No city babble. Quiet as a grave. I'm still walking toward the hollow and when I pass the basketball court I fall down flat on the ground. I go down fast and heavy and wonder why it doesn't hurt because I fall fast and hard like being chopped off at the knees. Like suddenly my limbs below the knees are gone and I crumple. Then I'm scared. I scream. But it ain't myself I'm screaming at. Dream time, you know. Because I'm chopped on the ground, rolling around with half my legs gone but I'm also a witness, upright, floating, somehow staring down at the basketball court, screaming because a boy is lynched from the rim. A kid hanging there with his neck broken and drawers droopy and caked with shit and piss. It's me and every black boy I've ever seen running up and down playing ball and I'm screaming for help and frozen in my tracks and can't believe it, can't believe he's dangling there and the dumb thing I'm also thinking in this dream or whatever it is, is if they'd just waited a little longer his legs would have grown, his feet would have reached the ground and he'd be OK.

That's all?

I don't know. I don't know how long I'm there. I don't know how I remember it is just a nightmare and cut him down. There's a memory of his weight in my arms. Catching him when the others sawed through the rope. I seem to be relieved. Grateful almost to realize he's just a child. That his body is small and I can bear the weight of it as I back down the ladder.

The ladder?

A basket's ten feet high. We needed ladders.

Then there's more to the dream. You're talking miniseries, man. Child murders. Ladders. Cops. KKK.

I'm not sure if there's more. Certain things had to have happened for any of it to make sense. What I'm left with, what I'm certain of is not very much at all. But indelible. Real. The singing. The broken neck and slumped body. The weight.

Simba? The lost boy?

It could be.

Who killed him?

It was a dream.

Well make up something, then. Wake up and make up. You got my attention. Don't leave me hanging.

Damn you, Timbo.

I ain't trying to be funny. But it ain't fair to start telling me a story then just stop in the middle.

The dream stops there. Everything surrounding it's gone. I want to know the rest, too. Thought telling you might help. But it doesn't. I feel myself beginning to invent. Filling in the blanks but the blanks are real. Part of the dream.

Dream?

Yeah.

Shit, man.

PART II

PART II

On May 13, 1985, in West Philadelphia, after bullets, water cannon and high explosives had failed to dislodge the occupants of 6221 Osage Avenue, a bomb was dropped from a state police helicopter and exploded atop the besieged row house. In the ensuing fire fifty-three houses were destroyed, 262 people left homeless. The occupants of the row house on Osage were said to be members of an organization called MOVE. Eleven of them, six adults and five children, were killed in the assault that commenced when they refused to obey a police order to leave their home. A grand jury subsequently determined that no criminal charges should be brought against the public officials who planned and perpetrated the assault.

Pretend for a moment that none of this happened. Pretend that it never happened before nor will again. Pretend we can imagine events into existence or out of existence. Pretend we have the power to live our lives as we choose. Imagine our fictions imagining us.

In 1850 John Fanning Watson wrote in the Annals of Philadelphia: Many can still remember when the slaves were allowed the last days of the fairs for their jubilees, which they employed (light-hearted wretch) in dancing the whole afternoon in the present Washington Square, then a general burying ground—the blacks joyful above, while the sleeping dead reposed below.

The phone rings. You pick it up and listen. You hope somebody will say a name you recognize. His. Hers. Yours. You've been caught unawares by the ring. You were absent and the ring brought you back. To where? To whom?

Hello.

It is my son and he speaks softly from far away. I can barely hear him. His voice is changing. He's at that age. Adding muscle and thickness. He is probably larger than I am now. The thought of him growing I put out of my mind quickly. Because I am here. Where I am. Growth means time passing, time apart from him I can't do anything about. He is my lost son on the phone and I must answer before I don't have the power to say a single word.

I say, Hey. How are you?

And that's that. We go on with our conversation for a decent interval, until the guard cuts us off or long enough so the little serious joke about not letting Ma Bell get rich off us is appropriate closure. We also don't go on. Can't move past the initial formulas of greeting.

How are you?

OK.

I've learned the hard way that I've always known next to nothing about him. Except I do know the danger of the place where he's incarcerated, the depth of the trouble he's in, the innocence and terror and guilt he must cope with day after day and little on the horizon but more of same.

I don't know what words mean when he says them. I don't know if he knows what they mean or knows why he says them. So we can't move beyond the ritual of greeting. To ask how he is opens a door into the chaos or our lives. Perhaps he's unable to tell me how he is. Perhaps I wouldn't understand how to take what he'd say, even if he tried to tell me. Words between us have become useless. Decorative. They can't furnish the empty rooms of our conversation. But the phone rings and he's two thousand miles away so all we have to work with are words. I can't hug him. Smile at him. See how big he's growing. The growth that's cruel irony, a blind, relentless message inscribed in his genes, shoving him into the body of a man whether he stands on the sunlit deck of an ocean liner or is curled in the dark comer of a cell.

We cannot talk, yet we are momentarily connected. Wouldn't the time we're allotted be better spent singing, crying, screaming through this instrument? I can hear his hand gripping. I can feel the power. Then he relaxes, his fingertips brushing and stroking the phone absentmindedly, adrift in some inner space where he retreats while I recite ball scores and game highlights, repeat what he's heard many times before. Small talk. My paltry news. The family's weather. Does any of it get his attention? He hears me. Responds on cue. I can't tell what engages him. When he's just being polite. Sometimes when I ask too much, he'll cut in and end the call. He'll say, I better go now. They're telling me my time's up.

Nothing is more painful than the phone ringing and finding him there at the other end of the line, except finding him not there, the sound of the phone call ending, the click, the silence rushing to fill the void words couldn't.

A Monday night in bed. Push-button scanning of all available channels, flipping, clicking, twenty-nine cable options and none satisfactory so you choose them all and choose none, cut and paste images, you are the director, driver, pilot, boss hoss, captain, the switch is in your hand. Or rather you grip the remote-control gadget with a desperate love-hate possessiveness that melds it to your palm. Your toy. Your game. Part of the fun of the game is the woman beside me who claims she doesn't enjoy clicking around the channels, who's screaming even as she silently indulges my flashes forward and flashes backward and fast shuffles and digital displays popping and muting, exploring every function the gun in my hand allows. She screams without uttering a sound: Don't touch that dial. And in a way I don't. We're in bed. The Sony's ten feet away. I can round first base and scoot into second and slide through a cloud of dust into third without getting my uniform dirty. A city burns on the screen. Any large city. Anywhere in America. CNN. Cable News Network. Row houses in flames. Rooflines silhouetted against a dark sky. Something's burning. We watch. Wonder whose turn it is now. Whole city blocks engulfed. It must be happening in another country. A war. A bombing raid. We're watching a Third World shantytown where there's no water, no machines to extinguish a fire. Flames, true to metaphor, do leap and lick. The sky retreats, jerks away like a hand from a hot stove. We are curious. We are impatient for the voice-over to tell us what to think. Where? When? Why? What? We'd be on the edge of our seats if we were on seats and not lounging in our waterbed in Laramie at 9:05 P.M. with nothing better to do than play this spin-the-bottle sweepstakes of the dial. But here it was, a jackpot consuming all our attention. Philadelphia.

Philadelphia.

West Philly. Osage Avenue.

Shit. We used to live in West Philly. On Osage Avenue. Osage can you see by the night's early firelight. Our old row house somewhere in there, down in the darkness of the silhouette's belly. Long camera shots preferred, sustained. Aerial views, probably from a copter. Perhaps the blaze is too hot to approach any other way.

Details are skimpy. Or we've missed them this time round. They'll return because news is cycled and recycled endlessly on this network. What we don't know always carries the potential to harm us, and we know just enough to believe that, so we stay tuned for further developments. Now we bring you a word from our sponsor. But such courteous, ponderous, time-consuming transitions are a thing of the past. Cut. Cut to whatever, wherever with electronic speed. Warp drive. Chiquita and her banana shoved in your face faster than you can rub the smoke from your eyes. What'd he say? The announcer. Sixty-second and Osage? Powelton Village? That's not Powelton. Too far west for Powelton, isn't it? But the conversation has switched to a woman pulling the oars of a rowing machine. Where's she going? What's she wearing? A miracle fabric or did somebody paint the bitch, brush a shiny second skin over her big boobs and tight butt mashed down into a funny valentine on the bicycle seat of the rowing machine? Do you receive one like her with each purchase? There's the price, sixty twice, then the number you must call to order right away.

Somebody's talking who doesn't know Philly.

Pneumatic woman's gone faster than I could punch her away with my magic twanger. A set of bamboo pots and pans, watertight, indestructible and a wok thrown in free if you call now. Which is May 13, 1985, the day after Mother's Day. I remember that. Remember it as well as I recall the lump of remote-control device in my sweaty palm.

We're both riveted. The channel riveted. We are all set in stone. Judy stops telling me, Don't touch that dial. She's having it her way this once without a fuss or fight. We both wonder what the fuck's going on. Why is Philadelphia burning? How do I know what she's thinking? Why do I assume I do? Her left breast, the one closest to me, or closer, since it's one of a pair, slouches brown nubbed and complacent, doing its own thing. If I touched it or bit it, would I learn what it was thinking? Sexy. I think it's sexy now, paying no attention to itself. Leaving me to make something of it. Whatever. Wherever. Many colors. Many ages coded in this plump breast that is part of this woman, part of this scene which includes the image of a city where we once lived, burning, somewhere, for some reason. Burning in other bedrooms. In other cities. International coverage. I heard later from a friend who said he saw it same moment, same day in Japan. Instantaneous satellite spy-in-the-sky transmission everywhere. So much happening at once. Impossible to keep up. Even if you spin the dial till the colors run together and the tigers melt chasing each other's tails. But Sambo's always caught in the middle of the ring. Puzzled. Appalled by the unforeseen consequences of his good intentions.

In the stillness of our bedroom her breast registers as deep silence. She sighs, extension of the breast, the breast under which she hides in a cage of ribs her heart. One of my ribs, so they say. Never thought to ask which one. To claim it. Many colors. Years coded. Flashing across the screen of this dark room. Forward and backward. On my desk a snapshot of her at fourteen, sweater girl. Pointy, warrior bra that pulls her tits high on her chest. Saluting what? Patient for decades, waiting to relax into this natural, perfect, nubby pout. Flesh after all. Sighs when unbound. Rib bones delicate as rib bones when I trace them with my fingertip and she is fragile as the straw where you might stash eggs for safekeeping and why not think of her chest as a nest, her breasts pouched there for whatever subtle reasons. She is a tree full of nests. Nests of spun light. Nimbus. Swirls of light in branches if you are melancholy and can't sleep and walk Philly streets at night, look up and you'll see what I mean, you'll see wreaths of light, halos in bare branches above the streetlamps. Painterly swirls symmetrically gathering light, spinning it, casting it. Her dark hair used to be long enough to cover her breasts. Now it only reaches the first swell where the flesh softens and understands exactly what it's supposed to do next. Furrows below her shoulders, bones joined at her throat. I pull her silver-threaded hair forward so it drapes the first soft swelling. I run my finger up and down, up and down, curling the ends, learning the texture of fleece, the insistence of flesh beginning to pile up and form a breast. She was younger once and so was I and our whole history's contained in glances. In leftovers and new puzzling mounds and creases that we can't work into other stories. Once upon a time. This time, this age when we huddle under the covers and imitate ourselves as children playing in other rooms, other cities. All over again. Safe the way our children once were safe. Leftovers and remnants and day-old goods tasting stolen and better than ever some nights. Other nights the edginess, the anger, the sense of loss, the fear, so I flip-flop, ply the channels like a ghost, waiting for something to watch.

That's how I learned about the Philadelphia fire.

Giacometti: The more I looked at the model, the more the screen between his reality and mine grew thicker. One starts by seeing the person who poses, but little by little all the possible sculptures of him intervene. The more a real vision of him disappears, the stranger his head becomes. One is no longer sure of his appearance, or of his size, or of anything at all. There were too many sculptures between my model and me. And when there were no more sculptures, there was such a complete stranger that I no longer knew whom I saw or what I was looking at.

Say the word *father*. Now say *son*. Now think of the space between *father* and *son,* as they are words, as they are indications of time and the possibility of salvation, redemption, continuity. Think of these two words in natural order and sequence. One comes before the other, always, forever. And yet both must start somewhere, in order to begin one must break in, say one or the other, *father* or *son*, to begin. The mystery of their connection is that either word will do. I am the son of my father. I am father of my son. Son's father. Father's son. An interchangeability that is also dependence: the loss of one is loss of both. I breathe into the space separating me from my son. I hope the silence will be filled for him as it is filled for me by hearing the nothing there is to say at this moment.

I hope saying nothing is enough to grip the silence, twist it to our need. Which is holding on, not letting go. My breath in him. This temporary contact fallen into silence, into listening for the other's silence. Not because it is enough but because it's all we have.

Gospel at Colonus: Thanks, Frank, for the tickets. The show was great. I'm haunted by the scene in which the old king, blind and weary, led by his daughters who've become his eyes, finally reaches the walls of a city that will grant him sanctuary. He's amazed and grateful to discover dust that will accept his dust without complaint, without conditions, without demanding long speeches from him concerning the wretchedness of his history, the horrors that turned his eyes to stone. The lifting of his burden—incest, murder, exile—is palpable in the music. Oedipus floats, almost kicks up his ancient swollen heels.

After the performance, at a dinner for cast and guests I told one of the singers seated at my table that Oedipus receiving sanctuary was what moved me most about the play. I told him I'd stopped expecting anyone to find sanctuary on this earth, but the song he'd helped sing caused me to believe, for a moment anyway, sanctuary might be possible in spite of whatever evil and calamity a man brought down on himself.

The singer said, God's grace is a gift you can't earn, but you can't throw it away either.

He pushed back from the table, rubbing his heavy hands on a blazing white linen cloth. He was fat and the work of eating caused him to sweat profusely. *Sanctuary.* He beams. Yes, he understands. He sang the song, didn't he, onstage with the others, gospel chorus and close-harmony quartets and rocking brass combo and African drums and didn't they make a mighty noise. Sanctuary. No indeed. The world is not a stroll on a sunny day. Huh uh. No, sirree. You need grace to be saved. That's why they call it Amazing. Grace, that is. Cause it's like God's voice in your heart saying he knows you're tired, and knows you couldn't bear your cross like you wanted to but he understands and says well done. You see, my friend, I've been singing the good news thirty-five years, hard times and harder all over this world and let me tell you, based on what I've seen, the spirit can reach down and touch you, don't matter how low you go. Without the spirit you got nothing. But with it, my, my. Ain't no telling what you can do.

It is a cause for wonder, isn't it? That old blind king dragging around a tail of sorrows long enough to wrap three or four times around the earth. Then, on the very doorstep of his tomb, one quarter inch from extinction, there's time for forgiveness, peace and understanding, time for the cities of his grief to be dismantled brick by brick, time for green grass to start pushing up through the broken stones.

Anyway, we enjoyed the show immensely. Don't know yet when our ongoing troubles will force us west again but when they do, and if we survive them, hope to be in touch.

This thing of darkness / I acknowledge mine.

—THE TEMPEST

As he drove he considered all the moments of his life that had brought him to this particular moment on a winding, divided street in the year 1987, Amherst, Massachusetts, on his way to do whatever it was he'd set out to do. Thinking such thoughts, as if such thinking really was thought, was ridiculous. Even worse it dizzied him. The steering wheel feels arbitrary in his gloved fists. Black leather gloves. Black leather wheel. Arbitrary black skin inside black gloves. A tug right and the car would crumple against a concrete embankment. If he dropped his hands into his lap and let nature take its course, the course would be a parabola with no relation to the curve of the road, a tighter swerve accelerating as he floors the gas pedal, rear tires following front tires for a while, then impatient, climbing their backs. No urge to change the course of his history, however, was part of this moment. Rather, he sat in the driver's padded lumbar-supporting seat in awe. Astounded by the concatenation of accidents, of minute turnings, of one thing after another after another that had brought him to this moment. Choice, will, intent. How could he ever have imagined what the outcome would be that day, any day in his distant, distant past when he decided yes, I'll take another deep breath and after that another one because one day I wish to be negotiating a curve on a cold bright winter afternoon on Larkspur Drive in Amherst, Massachusetts, a middle-aged, middlingly successful writer, teacher, father, husband and all the rest, which for a moment is a marvel, just because it's what it is after all and could have been almost anything else.

For a split second he actually sees the moments of his life. Like a flock of sheep milling beside the road, they are gathered together and he can see them, the collectivity of them that suggests how many, how countless they are. Visible as an idea is visible. Visible as sheep in a dream. The stalled, restless mass

of them unresolvable into individuals, just a woolly blur in the
corner of his eye. He knows they are there. Not there. He thinks
their presence. Does not need to look away from what he's
doing because he's seen enough to know they're there. And he
can proceed. Can hold the idea of them in his mind for as
long as he wishes while he's doing something else. My life was
all those times. Every single little twitch. Every nerve end firing.
Every scream. Every turning away. He luxuriates in the abun-
dance. Could weep at the notion that somehow all of it
happened, happened once to him, was him and would never
happen again, never had before. Oh. He was precious. Oh.
How did the shit get piled so high? And here he was responsible for it. Knowing no other god. No good reason not to rip
the wheel off the steering post. Except he's not strong enough
for that. The moments put together did not equal that power
in his hands. Black hands. Black gloves. He follows the curving
road to the T junction, stops, looks both ways and takes the
left fork. Another choice. Another piece of himself he'll quickly
forget until one day, at another intersection he'll fall prey to
whatever it is making him giddy, nearly sick at the stomach
today. He'll be remembering. It will all come back. None of it.

*   *   *

Tempestas also means time. When the play opens, ship sinking,
society dissolving. Thunder and lightning. Judgment Day the
opposite of sanctuary. Gonzalo says of the boatswain: man
fated to hang cannot drown. In Michael's book about Jamaica
I learn Rastafarians privilege the same belief in a proverb, in
almost exactly the same words.

But it was so hard to write. I'd get an idea of how to describe the moment I was wounded and the period right afterward when my illness began. At last I'd turned up a good idea. So I began to hunt for words to describe it and finally I thought up two. But by the time I got to the third word, I was stuck. I'd rack my brain trying to remember. Hold on, I'd think. I've got it. But before I could manage to write it down, it was gone, along with the other two words I'd had such a hard time remembering. I'd try to dig up another idea and find suitable words for it, and I'd write these down on various scraps of paper before including them in my writing. I'd try to clamp the words to the idea as much as I could. But what a torture it was. I'd always forget what I wanted to write, what I had just been thinking of the moment before. Minutes would pass and I wouldn't be able to remember how far I'd gotten.

So, before I could go on and write my story, I had to jot down various words for the names of objects, things, phenomena, ideas. I'd write these down whenever they came to me. Then I'd take the words, sentences, and ideas I'd collected in this way and begin to write my story in a notebook, regrouping the words and sentences, comparing them with others I'd seen in books. Finally I managed to write a sentence expressing an idea I had for this story of my illness.

—L. ZASETSKY RECORDED BY A. R. LURIA
IN *THE MAN WITH A SHATTERED WORLD*

*   *   *

Arrived Maine Friday. Yesterday and today at old station on dock. Page proofs of *Reuben* to finish. Awake early. Try the old routines. An orderly beginning—succession of tasks, motions, priorities. Gradually give a shape to the morning, a shape to self simultaneously. Stretching exercises while coffee brews. Quiet gathering of things laid out the night before, quiet so I do not wake Judy. All thought, effort directed toward the possibility of sitting in my chair on the boat dock. One step at a time—a discipline, but also letting it happen—rediscovering the routine's logic, appropriateness, rather than simply repeating by rote something that's worked before—a question must be answered—is it possible this morning to begin again, to find within myself what it takes to meet and be met by whatever will be out there when I have the mug of coffee in my hand, the papers and pens spread on the arm of the chair, my eyes opening to the lake's stillness and quiet.

Jackie Robinson broke into the major leagues on April 15, 1947, at Ebbets Field. I read in *Sports Illustrated* that his first time at bat he faced the pitcher Johnny Sain and hit a grounder to third. When Robinson's team, the Brooklyn Dodgers, made their first road trip with him on the roster, they were turned away from a hotel in Philadelphia because Robinson, number 42, was black. Was that the beginning of the fire? I was about six years old then. Two or three years later my family would move from Homewood, a community predominantly black, to Shadyside, a white community with a few streets where Blacks clustered. The move was considered progress. Summer nights on our black end of Copeland Street in Pittsburgh,

Pennsylvania, meant scratchy, booming and fading broadcasts of Dodger games from Mr. Conolly's radio set on the sill of his always open third-floor window. My father rooted for the Yankees and nearly always had the last the word in October, shouting up at Mr. Conolly, wagging his finger, Uh huh, uh huh, I told you so, old man. Those bums will never win.

*   *   *

Our love must survive through the ancient flames. / We must congregate here around the sitting mat, / To narrate endlessly the stories of distant worlds. / It is enough to do so, / To give our tale the grandeur of an ancient heritage / And then to clap our hands for those who are younger . . .

—MAZISI KUNENE, *ANCIENT BONDS*

Every day you get more of what you're going to get and less of it . . . aging and its discontents, or the uneasiness of aging as the span of life increases and the time for it recedes.

—HERBERT BLAU, *MEMORY AND DESIRE*

I must not look on reality as being like myself.

—PAUL ÉLUARD

At all times and in all fields the explanation by fire is a rich explanation.

—GASTON BACHELARD, *THE PSYCHOANALYSIS OF FIRE*

The name *Wagudu* signified "infinitely deep" and it was in fact such a city, complex and profound in its variety and wonders. Whatever men sought after, they went to Wagudu to find.

—HAROLD COURLANDER, *THE*
HEART OF THE NGONI

Ramona Johnson Africa gave policemen a letter addressed to Mayor Goode, Saturday, May 11, 1985: The raid will not be swift and it will not be clean. It's gone to be a mess. If Move go down, not only will everybody in this block go down, the knee joints of America will break and the body of America soon fall. We going to burn them with smoke, gas, fire, bullets . . . We will burn this house down and burn you up with us.

How does it feel to be inhabited by more than one self? Clearer and clearer, in my son's case, that he is more and less than one. Perhaps his worst times are those when he's aware, in whatever horrifying form that awareness takes, that he must live many lives at once, yet have no life except the chaos produced by divided, warring selves. The utter frustration, loneliness and fear accompanying such an awareness are incomprehensible. If there ever is an I, a me beyond the separate roles he must play, its burden would be to register the damage, the confusion wrought by his condition. To take stock, to make sense, to attempt to control or to write a narrative of self—how hopeless any of these tasks must seem when the *self* attempting this harrowing business is no more reliable than a shadow, a chimera coming and going with a will or will-lessness of its own, perverse, delusive as the other shadow selves that vie for ascendancy. Is he doomed to fail? Doomed to come apart no matter how hard he struggles at constructing an identity, an ego, a life, an intimacy with who and what he is? Is madness the inevitable result? A part of himself, a *self* exploding with pent-up rage, another part numb and bewildered, approaching catatonia as it beholds its predicament. Helpless, appalled, avoiding any motion, any act that might aid and abet the furies. Waiting. Playing mindless, repetitive games, locked in but also grateful for the cage of inactivity, the stasis that for a while can pass for peace, control, coherence. Sanctuary. A blessed oblivion consciously sought, an oasis between wrenching, explosive takeovers. He must learn in periods of calm to repeat a story endlessly to himself: there is a good boy, someone who loves and is loved, who can fend off the devils, who can survive in spite of shifting, unstable combinations of good and evil, being and nothingness. Can this story he must never stop singing become a substitute for an integrated sense of self, of oneness, the personality he can never achieve? The son's father. Father's son.

*   *   *

He is sad almost all the time and wonders if it shows in his face. In the course of a day his face is required to take on many different expressions, but no matter what emotion his features mime, the sadness is there, somewhere, because he feels it, burning like a rash, always. In front of a mirror, he bisects his face on the vertical axis with a towel and studies first one, then the other naked half. He believes he'll discover that half his face is frozen by sorrow. That it is raw and sore from the other half pulling it, worrying it to accommodate the mirrors in other people's eyes. Half his face obliged to go on about the business of living, half as if asleep, dreaming over and over again the nightmare of his son's pain.

Just yesterday I returned the call of an old friend, a colleague at the University in Philadelphia when I'd taught there fifteen years before. He's retired from teaching but still active. He'd seen the review I'd written of a book about the fire in Philadelphia. Hadn't been in touch for years so decided he'd call. Just to say hello, touch base. By coincidence he was leading a study group and the object of their inquiry and research was the fire on Osage Avenue. October at a memorial service for victims of the fire, if we both live that long, might be a time we can get together. Yes, he'd stayed on, hung on. After his wife died, he'd sold the big house in Germantown and moved to an apartment in City Center. Plenty of room. I was welcome to stay with him, he said. The University had treated him poorly. His department was deemed superfluous to what the University conceived as its central mission. The School of Social Work was traditionally a hands-on operation, pragmatic, problem oriented, a direct link to city agencies and institutions. A training program and lab with emphasis on practical outcomes, it produced graduates equipped intellectually, technically and emotionally to deal with the everyday runaway chaos of an ailing urban landscape. A commission whose announced goals were academic but whose actual agendas were political and economic declared that the University's responsibility was international, not local, theory a higher priority than practice, research and publication worthier measures of success than ministering to the immediate needs of the dispossessed urban proletariat surrounding the island of University. It was generally understood that the committee's charge was to lay to rest once and for all, for anyone still confused in the late seventies, certain misconceptions about a university's role that had arisen in the sixties.

My friend had served as an example of how far the University was willing to go to prove its point. No other professor in the handful of black faculty members was so deeply rooted in the tradition of service to the community or had labored so long and effectively in a position where scholarship was secondary to professional know-how, experience, courage and skill. You must be anticipating where all this is going. Yes. He was not rehired. What had been for decades a unique and seemingly permanent part of the University was dismantled. Not cost-effective. Not representative of the academic standards maintained in other schools and departments. Some dissenting hue and cry. Letters to the school paper, the provost and president. A little picketing. A strike threatened by black grad students. An attempt to hook up the large number of black workers on campus—cooks, janitors, garbagemen, buildings and grounds—with the scarce black students, administrators and faculty. But these minor storms blew over and the blithe, gray weather of the University prevailed. In a year or so very few people seemed to miss what was lost. Fewer remembered denials of tenure, the wholesale sacking of what had constituted the largest enclave of black professionals on campus.

The whole ugly episode returned in the first sentence my friend spoke. Of course a university has the privilege of undergoing periodic identity crises, and yes, financial retrenchment was necessary when it became clear that the wartime boom of the sixties couldn't last forever, that the University could not attempt to be all things to all people, that its survival as a viable institution demanded clarification of purpose, that it should concentrate on doing well what it had traditionally done best. But should all the above mean simply serving the powerful, legitimizing an elite? Fiscal responsibility became a battle cry, the license to cut back, turn back, cut down. The forces at work in the University mirrored those in the larger society. And the University acted as icily, pragmatically as the federal government. Hunker down. Clarify priorities. Whose University is it, after all? Whom is it meant to serve? Which constituencies laying claims on its resources were qualified petitioners? Who could the University afford to ignore?

In my friend's voice I was hearing the history of an intricate hurt. Objective decisions, policy formulations from hard-working, well-intentioned committees studying and fact finding, a democratic, collegial process, and responsible management by the upper administration, all those neat, clean means that can be trotted out to accomplish the most vicious ends. I heard that hollow, righteous clamor, the weight of arbitrary power rationalizing itself, justifying itself by turning this man away. Of course I also heard echoing in his voice the corrosive emptiness of a house he'd shared twenty years with a woman, the house whose rooms he still haunted even though he'd sold it and driven past it only once in the two years since his wife's death. No one gets by without loss. I heard that too.

The reality, inevitability of personal grief. And racial insult's double-whammy, that's always collective *and* personal. The School of Social Work had to go. Nothing personal about the committee's finding. Incidentally, in the working out of the committee's timetables, conclusions, proposals, directives, certain individuals, most of them black, would suffer, but the harm was not intended personally or racially; the whole busi-ness of shoring up the University, the country, was about ensuring the best deal for everyone, in the long run. Clearly the ax had to fall. Better that it fall systematically, according to a master plan designed to maximize profit derivable from losses. My friend could think of himself as one who'd drawn an unlucky ticket in this lottery. Something's got to go. Too bad it's you and yours. The news wasn't really news, was it? Last hired, first fired. Hadn't he heard words to that effect before? Another reason not to take it personally. Right.

What I heard over the phone was a man who'd speak up and continue to speak up. I heard no sobs, no curses, no grunts or exclamations, no special pleading, no arguing with the inev-itable, no sign of incredulous recognition and bewilderment and throwing up his hands or bowing his gray nappy head, I heard no evil wind howling, as he hums a blues in a segregated army barracks in Texas, no baby Michael singing *Got to be there*, no holler when at last, at last, Kareem whips the Celtics with a championship-winning sky-hook and Magic high-fives the moon, no drawing back his hand when colleagues who couldn't look him in the eye offered their parting shake, no cringing, no outraged condemnation, no sullen teeth-gritting, jaw-grinding silence, no benediction, no sad farewell as he stood on the bank, and she sailed on, sailed on, no chorus answering a sister's perfect laddered solo, I heard none of that, all of it, in the silent interstices binding his words as he spoke to me over the phone.

Some of us ain't gon let it die. You'll hear more and more. We are not going to let it die, John.

What about the official silence?

Man. Don't worry about those folks downtown. You won't ever hear anything from them. Still hiding. Still got their behinds in the air and their heads in the sand. But plenty people out here determined to let City Hall know what they think.

Sounds like I would enjoy your seminar.

Oh, we'll still be carrying on when you come in October. It's been really something so far. People are just beginning to come forward. Lots of facts and material available now that the commission didn't have during their hearings. Don't know how the commission would have handled what we're finding out. Far worse than I first thought it was. A nasty business all round.

You're doing fine then.

I'm here. You know I'm here.

Good to hear from you.

October then, OK?

God bless.

Peace.

Will I ever try to write my son's story? Not dealing with it may be causing the forgetfulness I'm experiencing. Not as bad as pitiful Zasetsky but I do feel my narrative faculty weakening.

A continuous, underlying distraction so that if I look away from what I'm doing, I lose my place. What I'm doing or saying or intending engages me only on a superficial level. I commit only minimal attention, barely enough to get me through the drill I'm required to perform.

Getting by, getting through. But I'm afraid I'm losing even that capacity. Synapses not synapsing, wires crossed or uncrossed, some chemical sentry asleep or hyperactive, arthritis of the mental circuits, whatever. My fate rearing its ugly head. 1 keep recalling how Jonathan Swift paused and stared at a gigantic tree whose upper branches had been blasted by lightning. He said to his companions, I'll go like that one. At the top first.

For every foul-up I catch, every distraction I circumnavigate and get myself back on course, for each success, there are failures, chances lost, plans unraveling. Doubt and insecurity are themselves distracting, reinforce the state of mind that causes them. Second guessing, duplicating and rechecking, treading water, going nowhere fast and also excruciatingly slowly.

> *Made such a sinner of his memory*
> *To credit his own lie.*

                                    —THE TEMPEST

The unmitigated cruelty of the legal system. My son rots in a cell. Courts neither shitting nor getting off the pot. None will act, render a decision yea or nay on our appeal to remove my son's case from adult to juvenile court. So he sits in limbo. Solitary confinement month after month while the appeals court, then the state supreme court sit on the case. Frustration began with the hearing in juvenile court. A judge ignored a day and a half of expert medical testimony, chose the narrowest possible definition of mental illness, and declared my son not committable to a mental institution, and thus not eligible for treatment. Therefore, stuck him in a cell to await trial in adult court. That was a year and a half ago. Hardened criminals crumble after a few weeks in solitary. My son gradually deteriorates. How could he not? He can't treat himself, no outside help is provided. Because of his age, he's in a phase of maximum jeopardy. According to the experts, adolescence is the time when childhood personality disorders almost certainly coalesce into incurable adult schizophrenia. Even with the best sustained professional help, prospects for recovery are slim. He sits day after day alone in a cell because he's a juvenile in an adult jail and the system has no other facility for him. Even if some official recognized the torture, the damage the state is inflicting on my son, that official, if he or she tried to help, would discover what we have discovered: no humane alternatives exist. The state chooses to believe my son's illness is not real and thus accepts no responsibility for treatment.

If my son were wounded or diseased, chances are he'd be treated. The inhumanity of allowing sores to fester, infection to rage, that species of cruelty is universally condemned. Mental illness is just as real, cruel and destructive to mind and body as a gunshot wound. Only a colossal failure of will and imagination allows us to pretend otherwise.

Why is my son left alone to suffer and try to make sense of his imprisonment, the chaos of his personality, his terror and guilt? That's the portion he awakens to each morning and goes to sleep with each night. Is it any wonder he's giving up, turning out the light in his cell, attempting to blot out the world by sinking into a profound stupor? That's the instinctual behavior of a wounded animal. To crawl into its den and curl up and die. Why would we allow anyone, adult or child, to suffer untended, alone, an agony enacted not deep in the forest but in a so-called civilized city, in a building with a number, on a street with a name, in a cell with a tiny window we pay people to watch?

*   *   *

Aside from worrying about his own children, Cudjoe wonders what happened to the kids he taught. Fact is they're grown and have kids. Cudjoe's confused. The kids he's looking at, searching for his students' faces, are the children of the kids he taught. He's a generation behind, lost in time. Standing still while the world passes him by. His kids have disappeared into a hole in the mountainside. Cleaning somebody's house. Washing dishes. Janitors. Cooks. Prisoners. Sanitation workers. Housekeepers. Doing all that invisible shit. Down the tubes, babe. Under the sidewalk we're standing on. This a new crop. Long live the kids. Come up like grass. And get trampled on. And new grass next spring. Youall some prolific people, man. Youall just keeps coming. Teeming loins. Yes indeedy. If babies was gold, youall'd be the King Midasses of the New World.

Today is my grandmother's birthday, my father-in-law's birthday, the birthday of the daughter of my wife's best friend in this town. Tomorrow is Martin Luther King's birthday. My sister's a grandmother again. My niece's baby is not two months old yet. When the baby Cheryl sat on my grandmother's lap they spanned five generations. No one took a picture but next time someone must. Miracles like that don't happen every day. It's a duty to preserve them. The best way to do it would be all five representatives. My grandmother, mother, sister, niece, and grandniece, if that's what the little one is to me—gathered together, perhaps Grandma sitting with the baby in her arms and the others framing them, leaning over the back of the rocker to keep the focus tight so the faces won't be too small. I would love to own a copy of that picture. I would explain to anyone willing to listen, the names, the unusual circumstance, what such a rare, lucky conjunction says about time and blood and family. Into my rap I'd slip a reference to a picture I actually possess. It's no slouch. Even though one less generation is represented. My first son, myself, my father, his father, the male string stretched taut as a bow ready to be fired. I feel a peculiar kind of dizziness when I contemplate the meaning of these pictures, the real one, the imagined are equals when I consider them this way. Dizzy from the intersection, the connection. My grandmother is ninety-three today and if by chance the baby whose face she looks down into lives for the same number of years, what is caught in the picture is two centuries, two lifetimes, which could encompass a skein of time close to the age of this country. Two faces connected here, at this nexus, by a camera, in my mother's house, noticing each other and their two pairs of eyes could be a bridge between an old man rocking my infant grandmother on his lap and another man taking the arm of a frail, tottering, ancient woman to guide her up a step or through a doorway, one man from the nineteenth century, the other from the twenty-first, touching here, linked here, not by a thought or a number but an actual bridge of flesh and blood joining them here and now. The thought could take your breath away. All those years. What transpires in them. My grandmother a witness, living through every event occurring in the twentieth century, the horrors, the slow blooming and death of so many of us as our family slowly climbed the hundred steps. How many has she seen stumble and fall? And the new life she cradles in her arms could endure just as long as hers, longer even, or be gone tomorrow. A life can be a great soaring arch with the shadows and sorrow of a century huddled under its span or shorter than the tick of a clock. There aren't words for what I think as I watch the oldest and youngest females in our family size up each other. Where they're going, where they've been is part of what they're learning, exchanging. Their conversation excludes me. As it must. As it should. A door opens and a wind sweeps over them, sealing the moment, a silence and crystalline murmur too fast, too ancient to register anywhere but in the two pairs of eyes meeting. Neither will forget the moment. The baggage carried forward, the trip still to make. Words fail me because there are no words for what's happening. I am a witness. All I know is that everything I could say about what I'm seeing is easy, obvious and, therefore, doesn't count for much except to locate me, outside, record my perplexity.

My wife said her mother told her it doesn't matter how old you are when your last parent dies. What you feel, however old, is orphaned. You are an orphan in the world. But what is the word for a parent who's lost a child? I have no word, no place to begin. Nothing to start you thinking, no word like my wife's mother's word to tell you how I feel.

If you've lost a child it's like undoing that picture of four generations, or the one yet to be taken of five. Having it but then watching it burn, or be erased, or unwinding, or waking up one morning to the news it was all a mistake. Never happened. Forget it. A child lost cancels the natural order, the circle is broken. The photos of generations set my head spinning because in the face of time they are a record of its incomprehensibility but also its finitude, its peculiar, visceral, sensuous availability. We all swim in the same sea of time. That could be true, couldn't it? We can hold in our hands proof of the endless ebb, flow and possibility. We can remember that what brought us here takes us back and brings us again. We can believe for an instant in this ocular proof, the photo we possess. The mystery overwhelming us also allows us to step back and take a sounding. We aren't able to touch the same place once again but what's there has been there a long time and so we've been there too, and so will again. The photo, though mysterious, offers proof and promise. The lost child, the parent who grieves for the lost child owns an emptiness as tangible as a photo. You carry it around. It's there to show anyone you choose to show it to. You can relate the names, the unusual circumstances, the failure of blood and family and time to persevere. This emptiness, this not having is so palpable you can pass it around a room. A ghost photo going from hand to hand as you spy on each face in turn. You hate pulling it from your wallet but sometimes you can't help yourself. Imposing on people, embarrassing them as you say over and over again the only thing you can say. You say nothing. Because the emptiness has no name, no place. A negative marvel, a phantom pain incomprehensible, inexplicable while the orphaned photo makes its circuit, and you stand tongue-tied, wondering why you exposed it again. Think of a leg that's been amputated. Then think of the emptiness where it once was. The pain resides in that space. I feel it, point to it. But of course the leg is invisible. It's not a leg. Anyone with a leg knows that. I know the pain is not in my leg because my leg is gone. No word for the space where the absence of a leg is real, the pain is real. No word for the confusion. My life forming around an absence we've been in the habit of calling one thing, but now it's another without a name, but I must speak to it, of it, exist with the pain of its presence and absence speaking to me a hundred times a day, every day.

Who am I? One of you. With you in the ashes of this city we share. Or if you're not in this city, another one like it. If not now, soon. Soon enough to make it worthwhile for you to imagine this one, where I am. Sometimes I've thought of myself, of you, of ourselves, as walled cities, each of us a fortress, a citadel, pinpoints of something that is the inverse of light, all of us in our profusion spread like a map of stars, each of us fixed in our place on a canvas immense beyond knowing, except that we know the immensity must be there to frame our loneliness, to separate us as far as we are separate each from each in the darkness.

(Enter Caliban, heavy, heavy dreadlocks resembling chains drag nearly to the floor. A cloak of natty wool. His natural cape, suggesting, repudiating Prospero's dashing midnight-blue silk one with all its devices, astrological symbols, alchemists' calligraphy, Stars, Stripes, sickle moon, comet and tail, etc. Caliban is naked under his dreads, but they cover him without hiding him, his proper, modest fur. His speech queerly accented, traces of the Bronx, Merry Ole England, rural Georgia, Jamaican calypso, West Coast krio, etc.): Wait. Wait please, breddars, before you put your hands together, man. Tis I and I mek for one last word so. This the church. This the steeple. Open sez me. Out come all de peoples. See. Like roach, man. When you light oven in morning. So, breddars, please. No clap now. Sit seats one moment more.

Think of this play this man done. Him broken my island all to pieces. White folk weeping and wailing cause all lost. Ship lost. Fader lost. Storm taken ebryting away. Walls dem all fall down fall. Son on him knee cry for Fader. Dig wet sand for trace of him fader eye. Noting. Wind howl. Thunder and lightning ring deep down in ear chamber. So moist down in dere, so long, so loud, so gone.

Do you listen? Do you hear down dere weeping and wailing? All fall down on golden sand of this island mine.

Or was mine. Once pon time. As that fancy one dere does testify. Mine by way Queen Sycorax my mother. Him say all dat and say my mother am witch. Why him play dozens now? Say island belong to him now. Say my mother dead in nother country. Why he swoop down like great god from the sky, try make everybody feel high? Take ebryting. Den ebryting give back. Go off teach at University. Write book. Host talk show. Jah self don't know what next dis dicty gentleman do.

Ebryting restore but what him first stole. Island mine from my poor mother. Island stole from me.

Noting make self. I be her son and son of some fader. Don't

try guess who. Don't say in de play. I no know, no want to know. Just want island back. Queen Mama back. No time be playing dozens now.

> *Heigh ho and fi fun*
> *Nasty blood of Englishmun*
> *Plow in ditch*
> *Catch him itch*
> *Fee fi foe fun*
> *Bloody end of Englishmun*

We all somebody's chillren. We all Eden born. Eden bound. All claim same two fader, mother. Who am so dirty take what him don't belong? Steal from breddar. Steal from son. Break bond. Break word.

What I say here is dis, Rasta. Make some things better you must make all better. Don't be steal me again. Dis island mine. Been mine always. This mother-humping play can't end no oder way.

The saddest thing about this story is that Caliban must always love his island and Prospero must always come and steal it. Nature. Each one stuck with his nature. So it ends and never ends.

Why this Cudjoe, then? This airy other floating into the shape of my story. Why am I him when I tell certain parts? Why am I hiding from myself? Is he mirror or black hole?

I cannot recall a name. The failure is frightening. Forgetting this name is like forgetting my own. I search through an alphabet of women's names: *A* for Angie . . . *J* for Judy, Jill, etc. I feel myself registering cold, lukewarm, ice as names appear on the screen. *F* is Felicia, Feride, Fran. A scoreboard. Lovers' names pop up at each outpost of alphabet. Can't write this morning on the dock, can't do anything else but wonder what the fuck her name is. I sort through images, listen to conversations. Snap my fingers in exasperation as her nickname dissolves on the tip of my tongue.

She is a friend's daughter. Her siblings' names flash on and on. Tease me because they are so obvious, unforgettable, except when I can't remember them either. If I could only stop thinking, I might think of her name.

R again. *R* teased me first time around. I pull back the *R* curtain. Reba, Rachel, Rene.

Why am I playing this game? I could walk up to the house and ask Judy the name of our friend's daughter. Because yes, last night in Rick's Café we were talking about the awful world adults have made for kids—the desperate measures kids have adopted to cope—in that conversation the name had popped up, maybe I'd said it myself—her name spoken as recently as last night—her complaints remembered—how her friends see themselves as flower children, listen to sixties music, recycle sixties saints, clothes and slang but they're not hippies, she said, they're punk with soft uniforms, selfish, narcissistic, each concerned only about himself or herself and lonely, lonely, always in packs, parading malls, streets, school halls, lonely, lonely. I hear the conversation but sit befuddled, getting crazy because I see her face but can't recall her name. Pull out the drawer of another letter—*K*—it's empty. I'm too embarrassed to ask for help. When I see her next should I admit, I've been thinking of you lately but you had no name?

Searching for clues I resurrect another scene. Remember myself here. In this very chair on the dock. Two years ago. Her family is visiting. Her father and mother, my wife, myself, all on the dock. She's swimming. She parts the water. (I look at it now. The space unoccupied, undisturbed, unparted.) She parts the water slim and white as a candle. A little girl. Shy. Yet her body knows for sure it's on its way to being a young woman and she's ready and anxious to share that knowledge. Still a little girl's body so she can swim without a top in her underwear while the adults sit like blind judges on the dock. Skinny-dip when her mother throws her a bar of soap and yells, Clean up. As she pulls off her underpants she turns her back to us, natural modesty—also coquettish—reminding us of what's coming—the thrill, danger, complication and possibility of a woman's body soon—even though she's safe now, just a skinny breastless unfleeced kid, flashing in the water as she bounces and surface-dives, cavorting, flirting, telling us to look, look, look what I can do, naked and past blushing, apologizing. She cracks the surface and smiles, enjoying what she is, enjoying being watched, secure, teetering on an edge.

In shallow water she flips backward, does a handstand with her head submerged, her spraddled legs kicking in the air, her sex displayed seamed and taut as a fist. A child on her way to being a woman. What she soon will be clairvoyant in her body's promise. I hear her mother yell, Come in now, Becky. The nickname. So easy. The name I couldn't squeeze out, no matter how hard I tried.

Was I compromised by the sexuality of that moment. Seeing Becky as female / woman though she was just a child. One I am bound to protect as a daughter. Is that what was at stake in my forgetting? Must I first own up to a moment of confusion, ambiguity, not just about Rebecca, but her sisters, my daughter, their friends, that flood of young womanly flesh ebbing and flowing around me as I grow older? Am I still trying to find the proper place to file my reactions? Is there still a live wire? A name won't come because it carries baggage that's compromising. A little shame. A sense of cheating. Of being more and less to her than I wish to admit to myself. Did I have to ask the right questions in order to free the name? Free myself. *Open, Sesame*, the magic formula must be relexified precisely. Memory speaking only if addressed in a language it understands. Smell of madeleines. Bite of apple.

Dear Mr. Wideman. On the Move!

I am writing to you because I read an article in a magazine and it featured a story or a piece on you.

In this article the writer gave a brief history of your work and named some of the books you have written including your best-known memoir: *Brothers and Keepers.*

I understand from the article that you are currently at work on a book of short stories and a novel about a group based on Move and this is where my concern comes in; *not* because it is a novel based around my Family only. But because there have been *many* distortions said about the Move org. that was and still are being printed about us that need to be cleared up. I say this to say, I wish that you would get in touch with some of my Family members here in Phila. and I'm sure you will be *well informed* and given some clear information as to what we are about and some profound wisdom from the teaching of *John Africa,* our founder and source of energy, strength. *John Africa* is very much alive. *Long live John Africa!*—There are plenty events, confrontations that we have had with the city of Phila. for the last fifteen years and they need to be told by us. (At least we could enlighten you as to the *truth* about Move as opposed to the perpetual lies and distortions by the mass media and this government and its deceptive mind-molding agencies of treacherously laced propaganda!)

I am presently in jail in upstate Pennsylvania along with ten of my brothers and sisters who was framed for the killing of a Phila. cop in August of 1978. We are serving 30–100-yr. sentences. Enclosed will be a letter that was written recently by the Move org. that will be attached to a zeroxed copy of *City Paper* with a article on *the Move indictments* e.g. Wilson Goode and his blatant murderers of my family on May 13th '85.

I hope this letter reaches you.

Here it was then. The thing he would do with them, the thing. The play. Prove. Ten- and eleven-year-old black kids. Shakespeare.

He would cast about. Cast himself a caste. A cast in his net. Catch of the day. Fresh. Castanet.

He sees them in their seats. Counts. Semicircle on chewed little short-legged chairs gathered round him. Eye of the round.

Their teacher. He reads whose speech? Teaches whose voice? Let it be Prospero. The father in his moony sunglasses. The good tyrant, protector of his island children. The one willing to lose everything to prove a point. In control to the last. Then he gives away the store. Maybe. His daughter gallops off into the sunset. Brave new world. Goody-bye. Goody-bye. The women sing for her. And moan. Spread a meal for her on a patch of earth they've swept till it shines. She'll come and get it when they're gone. When she's ready. If they've fixed it correctly. And, brother, you know they've done it up right. You can tell by the angle of their lean backs as they leave the clearing and are silhouetted an instant in moonlight when they reach the verge of the forest. For a moment they are a city. Frozen skyline that breaks into the narrow-hipped switching of a pack of hunting dogs, every body part they own quivering with the excitement of the chase as they two-step into the woods. Good, broad-beamed sisters who move when they're happy like teenage girls, the tired old flesh then surely nothing but disguise, something they can leave behind like dishes of food on the bare disk of ground to summon a spirit. Buildings. Wolves. Lost in enveloping darkness once beyond the shaft of moonlight that shows off branches like lace, like intricate highways of bone, like an X ray of some dead god's brain.

He'll read Prospero to his ducklings and they'll cue up behind him, all in a cute line, a dragon's tail, kite tail, string of letters on a page. A word for what they must do, *Imprint*. It means they choose one to follow and mirror its behavior. They learn that way what it is to be duck or goose or whatever. Imitation. Sneaking through the looking glass so you are on both sides at once. Looking in and looking out and it seems you know perfectly well how you should act, who you are, what you should say, until you catch the worm of doubt in the other's glance and then you are the other, or not the other, or both or neither and it doesn't really matter does it, who's zooming who, who you imprinted or the shadow imprinting you, who or whom, the bird in the water or bird skimming just above the reflected reversed image of its flight on the still lake. It's all a game. Imprinting never more than skin deep. You walk on water. Learn to shed a whole skin daily. Gimme some, and you smack back, Ahmad's brown, cockeyed, half-pint grin teasing out yours. If you're lucky you grow new skins faster than you wear out the old ones. Luck of the draw. Baby goose waddling behind a water buffalo. Trying to keep up. Snorting and tossing imaginary horns on a huge wedge of head that grows beneath its shoulders.

Luck of the draw. His charges fidget in their seats. Waiting for him to speak. To perform. Will he be the one? The role model as they say these days. Orphans. Dead at an early age. No ducks or geese or sheep in their neighborhoods to follow. To be like. His tabula rasas. If that's the plural. What fucking kind of role model him? An English teacher who don't even know how to form Latin plurals. Little learning. But he possesses the advantage of color. They can't help noticing that, can they? His net. His emperor's clothes. He'll be their drum major and nobody's perfect anyway. Nobody scores 100 on the test except the guy who made it. Made it. Made it. And nobody can be like him. Only him. Like him. Because he made it. Test scores prove the point. Only so much room at the top. What good would a test be that doesn't prove what anybody with good sense knows already to be true. A bell curve. Rings true. For whom? Is it tolling? Bell. Period ends.

He'll do. Do he. He can hear their flat, webbed baby feet paddling behind him. Perfect V's of their wakes gouged into the water's thin skin. That heals instantly. Heedless. Headless. He leads them along the rocky shore, astride the still water. They are on it and in it. Perfect doubles of themselves. I love you he quacks back over his plumy shoulder. They have long curly lashes like Daisy, Donald's love. They sleep behind those butterfly lashes. And dream. Eyes full of dust in the morning. Clotted by sleep. Curtained. Some eyes crust over because they are diseased. A word he can't recall. Eye rot is what? Gum rot is gingivitis. He remembers lurid illustrations on a dentist-office chart. He'd better get started while these kids still own some moving parts. Before their vital parts silently rust away. Mad people cogwheel their limbs like Frankenstein's monster, fluid motion broken into lurching tics. While he's watching and waiting his kids rot away in their seats. Gingybread girls and boys. Little motors idling. Waiting for a prince to come. Or princess. Someone to teach them to be other than what they are. Lost behind snotty, dingy curtains.

Ah hem. Ahhh. Hem. Amen, this morning, children. Say amen.

Amen, Mr. Cudjoe.

Amen, boys and girls. Today's lesson is this immortal play about colonialism, imperialism, recidivism, the royal fucking over of weak by strong, colored by white, many by few, or, if you will, the birth of the nation's blues seen through the fish-eye lens of a fee fi foe englishmon. A mister Conrad. Earl the Pearl Shakespeare, you see. The play's all about Eve and Adam and this paradizzical Gillespie Calypso Island where the fruit grows next to the trees but you're not supposed to touch, see. Point

is, long before Fanon or Garvey or Marley or any of that, before
the spring storm in Memphis that ate the foliage and opened
a line of sight from the window of a motel up on a hill down
to the balcony of the divine Lorraine, long before a bullet
booked down that long lonesome highway and ended the life
of a man who'd just enjoyed a plate of fried fish (the dish still
sits in the room and the dish was what broke my heart,
summoned him back from wherever he was, to stand full of
life and smile and not know it was his last supper, ummmm,
this fish is good, man. Some good fish. Here, have some, brother
Malcolm, brother Chaney, brother Goodman, and here, Addie
Mae, honey, you cute little angel you, taste a piece and take
some for your lovely sister too, you surely look beautiful today,
my children. Help yourself, Medgar. Go on, man. It's good
fish.), long before various events, each of which is a story in
and of itself worth learning, studying, black brown red yellow
female histories like special platters you can choose off a menu,
long before a Third World when there was only One and it
was cakewalking, expanding by leaps and bounds, big fish
swallowing little fishes and little ducklings, in Bermuda, near
the fabulous, infamous, mystical Triangle, your Godfather
Caliban was hatched. And it was a playwright, a Kilroy Willy
who tabulated the plot. Who saw the whole long-suffering
thing in embryo, rotten in the egg, inscribed like talking book
on the tabula-rasa walls of the future. Sentient. Prescient. Yes,
Willy was now. Peeped the hole card. Scoped the whole ugly
mess about to happen at that day and time which brings us to
here, to today. To this very moment in our contemporary
world. To the inadequacy of your background, your culture.
Its inability, like the inability of a dead sea, to cast up on the

beach appropriate role models, creatures whose lives you might imitate.

So let's pretend.

You Ahmad, scratching your ear. I think you'd make a good . . .

He casts about in his mind for good matches. Dry ones. Symmetry, synchronicity. Matches. To light his one little candle. Start his fiery storm of protest. In this void. This dry wilderness of the United Emirates of North America.

The lingo is English landwich. Quack of the baddest, biggest Quacker. King's English. Pure as his tribe. We've heard it before, leaking from a circle of covered wagons, a laager squatting on the veld, a slave fort impacted on the edge of a continent, its shadow athwart the deep blue sea, a suburban subdivision covenanted to a lighter shade of pale. You've also heard it on TV, if nowhere else, boys and girls, the slang of getting and spending. Howdy Doody. Buffalo Bob. Claribel. Walter Klondike. Mister Rogers. Mr. Jellybeans and Mr. Green Jeans. Cork-faced minstrels use it. Black mammies and midgets and clowns. Your own hip babble comes back at you like a yo-yo or boomerang in their smiles, on their tongues. But this Shakespeare not what you'd call everyday paddy-boy speech. Not your common garden-variety blank prose. It's a verse of another color clime and time, the days of old when sailors were bold and beknighted for such exploits as scalping aborigines or laying a cloak over a puddle so my lady's dainty toes saved from the miring clay. This was back when everybody lived on islands and English sounded like the geechie talk you hear today round Charlestown or in Frenchtown, places nice to visit, but like the streets where you live, not exactly desirable full-time residences, not quite up to snuff. But the lingo, mi buckos, my sweet oreos, the talk they talked, Queen's English to be more exact, was down, especially in the pen of this one, the master blaster, bad swan from Avon, number-one voice and people's choice, scratcher and mixer and sweet jam fixer, ripsnorter and exhorter, cool as a refrigerator prestidigitator, have no fear, Mr. Auctioneer is here super pitchman mean as a bitch man, pull my goat and milk my goat ding-dong pussy-in-the-well wheeler-dealer and faith healer, record changer dog-in-a-manger platter-pushing poppa of the rewrite right-eous doo-wopping, skin-popping, hip-hopping got all the ladies' drawers dropping camel-hair benny ain't giving away any but got it all wrapped up tight, tighter than a whore's pussy on Christmas cause she ain't giving away nothing to nobody not today nor yesterday, not to her mama nor yours nor the seven dwarfs nor Bambi nor you my tragic lil indins all in a row, in a line, circled like covered wagons on the Laramie Plains while hostiles swirl around you, howling at the moon, faster and faster, tigers churning you to cocoa butter my lost Sambo children.

But be that as it may. I'm here this morning to tell another story. Listen up. May sound strange at first but it's hip. Got its own hippy-hop cadence and blue notes, same blue been used since the middle ages to designate a state of mind (thank you, Al Murray) among white people when they don't feel quite white. Right. But a blue closer to you. A shade you can turn more naturally than red. So don't be embarrassed. It's your history too in the word. A bit out of sorts, out of breath from running day and night. Blue. As in melancholia. As in blue spirits or the black dog when things ain't the way they spozed to be or how they used to be. See. Now we getting down to origins. Think on Adam and Eve (whose color are they) squatted in the ferns, missing the good ole days, how things used to be, and they ain't been in the garden five minutes, ain't never been nowhere else in time or space and here they sit commiserating about what's been lost, how things used to be, before the fall, and they still unfallen, naked of memory and means to picture past or future. And these pure children, your original mom and pop, got a nostalgia jones plaguing them. Yearning for dusty disks, golden oldies they ain't never heard before, which ain't even been cut yet, ain't no Motown, Vee Jay, no Atlantic, no Apollo but here they sit inventing stuff to be miserable about when there wasn't nothing but just the two of them, looking into each other's moony eyes, all their equipment checked out and A-OK and primed and that's what they seen but didn't know what to do with it so they started crying. And been blue since.

Well, with this kind of history, black white red and blue, you can imagine the devilish fun Mr. Willy had putting words in people's mouths.

He started from scratch. But said it was the itch come first. And folks still trying to figure that one out. So he's off and running. Seventy-five thousand years on Broadway. Great Emancipator, motongator with his bag full of bones and stones and feathers and ugly pills and hallucinogens right on down to our present-day most advanced uses of hoodoo, voodoo, couches and the entire cornucopia of modern dramacology. He did it all with one stroke of the pen. Set this nigger free. Your number-one great great great greater than god grandfather Caliban.

And thereby hangs a tale. Willy said that, too. And one of my jobs as model and teacher is to unteach you, help you separate the good from the bad from the ugly. Specifically, in this case, to remove de tail. Derail de tale. Disembarrass, disabuse, disburden—demonstrate conclusively that Mr. Caliban's behind is clean and unencumbered, good as anybody else's. That the tail was a tale. Nothing more or less than an ill-intentioned big fat lie. And that when all is said and done, sound and fury separated with Euclidean niceness, with Derridian diddley-bop from the mess that signifies nothing, what you discover is the one with the tail was old mean landlord Mr. prosperous Prospero who wielded without thought of God or man the merry ole cat-o'-ninetails unmercifully whupping on your behind and still would be performing his convincing imitation of Simon Legree, of the beast this very moment, in this very classroom, cutting up, cutting down, laying on the stripes, if it weren't for me, girls and boys. Your big boppa, name droppa, cool poppa, daddio of the radio.

Say Amen.

Amen.

Say Free at last.

Free at last.

But don't go yet. Don't clap your hands. Stay awhile and help me mount this authentically revised version of Willy's con. We been in the storm too long, chillun. We gon crank up the volume, crank up the volume, to a mighty tempest and blow the blues away.

And blow (I got to whisper now so lean them nappy heads, that sooty breath, those crusty eyes, lean it closer so I can whisper into the conch shell limbo swirling down down your

earry canals, into the untouched back channels of your brains).
And blow away whole regiments of any honky mothafuckers
gits in our way.

*   *   *

This is the central event. I assure you. I repeat. Whatever my
assurance is worth. Being the fabulator. This is the central
event, this production of *The Tempest* staged by Cudjoe in the
late late 1960s, outdoors, in a park in West Philly. Though it
comes here, wandering like a Flying Dutchman in and out of
the narrative, many places at once, *The Tempest* sits dead center,
the storm in the eye of the storm, figure within a figure, play
within play, it is the bounty and hub of all else written about
the fire, though it comes here, where it is, nearer the end than
the beginning. Think of a gift to the community where he's
been teaching four years. These black children going nowhere
are tapped early and instead of oozing off the comers of the
map—oil spill, sludge, dregs, tar babies—the geyser of their
talent and potential explodes here in the park, an ebony tower
taller than Billy Penn's hat spouting to the stars. Their achieve-
ment cannot be ignored. Suddenly, as they stand above the
footlights, drawn to stage edge by our applause, our hooting
told-you-so and knew-it-all-the-time pride and reflected glory,
as they stand in cruel daylight because after all there is no
electricity in the park, we did it alfresco, on a platform of
sawhorses crossed by planks anchored by railroad ties and a
turret braced by diagonals so from the back the skeleton of
the tower resembles a gallows, as they stand triumphant and
revealed for what they really are, our kids discard flimsy bits

of homemade costumes, fling masks, superfluous ornaments into the threshing crowd, our children's, your children's, my life, your lives are vindicated. The play was the thing. To catch a conscience. To prick pride and dignity and say, Hey, we're alive over here. That was Shakespeare youall just saw performed. And we did it. Blank verse and fustian, shawns and bombards, the King's English. Tripping lightly off their tongues. So look upon these heros. Don't ever forget them. They wave madly. Want your approval. About to implode. Shedding another skin for us. Flaying us. Our children. And their children after. But never the same again.

Think on it and place it in the proper perspective because it rained the Saturday the show scheduled. And Sunday. Then blue again Monday. No one survived the weekend. We had to start all over again. Lost again. Cudjoe wondering why the weather had been so mean. Whose idea was it to wash away *The Tempest* with a tempest before it ever got started. So one more ring of imaginary, of play around the play because as we consider it further it's only fair to break the news that it never really came off. Cup to lip, but . . .

Begin with a double meaning. If Cudjoe did not live to see his play hatched, he did spin from the endless circles of its possibility that second meaning cached in the drama's tide: time. Borrowed time, bought time, saved time.

So this narrative is a sport of time, what it's about is stopping time, catching time. Watch how the play works like an engine, a heart in the story's chest, churning, pumping, tying something to something else, that sign by which we know time's conspiring, expiring.

What's the point?

Doing it. That's the point. Why not?

Ahmad is quiet but he loves noise. Perfect for the maker of
thunder and lightning. Long sheet of tin to wiggle. A bass
drum to strike. Ahmad's perfect. Swaggers as if one leg's shorter
than the other. Regular little Shango. Tough, cranky, a warrior.
Other kids keep their distance from him. Yet he's a leader in
a way, because they watch him, want to know what he's
thinking, what he's going to do next. Seldom says a word but
when he does, the others sure listen. We'll have him speaking
and leading both. In the thunder's voice. Shake it, Ahmad.
Don't break it. Shake rattle and roll us a storm, son. Tear this
old building down.

Ahmad in the wings. Sound effects. Stage manager.

In the wings? Thought you said you're going to stage it in
the park.

Only way to go. But we'll build a stage. With wings and
tower and a machine for flying Ariel.

Good luck, dude. Better take out lots of insurance on any
them black kids you expecting to fly.

It's going to happen. Needs to happen. Negative shit's bound
to come up. This is the kind of thing scares people. So they'll
be bitching, moaning, and backsliding. But I guarantee you.
It's going to happen.

I think back to the beginning. When the project was just an
idea teasing me. Black kids doing Shakespeare. How impossible
it seemed. Farfetched. Maybe not even a good idea, even if I

could pull it off. Blowing smoke. Talking to anybody who'd listen. Black boys and girls mastering Shakespeare. Bucking myself up by telling everybody how confident I was. Constant PR campaign with me as supersalesperson. At the same time I didn't believe a word I was saying. Underground, in the shadows, sneaking around, inspecting the doubts I wouldn't let my audience see. Trying, like the Chinese person sitting on the fence, to convince myself I could make a dollar out of fifteen cents.

I catch myself staring at one of the kids. At a small perfect skull, still growing, the bone porous so when I trepanned away a side wall my entrance was silent, cunning, a perfect cross section revealed, framed by the curve of the skull's crown, a stage set under a proscenium arch. I sit, unobtrusive as a video camera at a keyhole and observe the goings-on. Melissa is at her kitchen table. She is eleven years old. A tall girl for her age. No one, however, would mistake her for a woman. Even a very young woman. She is defined by long, bony arms and legs. Beyond them, not much to her. If she were standing you might think high-waisted, shoulders thin as clothes hangers, a skinny neck which must be tough and fibrous as a tree trunk to support the weight of the scene we are watching through the peeled-back temple of her skull. One lanky arm flung out flat on the kitchen table. She collapses forward and rests her head on it. Gives in to the sleepiness still abounding in this early-morning quiet kitchen where she sits alone, empty eyes tracking the ceiling then gazing at a cereal box. Though her head is not upright, miraculously the scene inside does not spill and come apart. Some subtle proprioceptive accommodation inside the vestibules of her body—ear canals, sinuses,

tiny reservoirs of fluid strategically spotted here and there—
allows her head to fall, her dream to stand. Her lips move.
She's sounding out words from the box of Cap'n Crunch or
Corn Pops or Sugar Crisp or Frosted Flakes. We cannot read
her lips. The box of breakfast cereal is turned away from us.
They all look alike from the back. From where we have fixed
ourselves for this time being. Her eyes not focused on the box
so perhaps she's not reading. She's mumbling to herself what
she's read a hundred times before. Reciting the box from
memory. Yes. The way one would memorize a part in a play.
So we are encouraged. Continue to spy.

Long as you are able / Keep your elbows off the table. She is
alone but pops up as if at a command. Her own perhaps. Get
it together, girl. Don't be sitting here falling asleep again. Too
much tube last night. Johnny Carson was a doctor and a man
came to him for help and said, Doctor, Doctor. I have a
problem. Sometimes I think I'm a wigwam. Sometimes I think
I'm a tepee. And the doctor he said, Aha. I know just vhat's
vrong vit you. You're too tense. Nobody laughed for a second.
Then everybody start cracking up. And Johnny Carson he
giggling his own self. She didn't get the joke. What was funny
about *too tense*? All she could think of was a frozen river and
snow and tepees neat row after row asleep. Up on a ridge
blue-coated soldiers watch quiet smoke curl from the tent
town. Horses snorting and spurs jingle-jangling the blue men
gallop down a hill, toward the snowy riverbank where Indians
sleeping peacefully cause they don't know what's dropping out
the sky on their heads. Cannon fire. Snow churned blood red.
She thinks of that. The time she'd seen that late movie on TV
and babies running naked in the cold, yelling for their

mommas, their mommas chased by men with swords on horses, hollering, cutting the women down in the snow. One Indian lady naked as the babies, her clothes blowed all off her. Couldn't believe it for a moment. Grown woman hair and titties hanging out on TV like that. She didn't know what was funny but smiled anyway. Smiled because everybody laughing. She didn't want to be dumb. Even though nobody could see her in her own apartment curled on the floor, thumb in her mouth, rubbing her nose with an old end of blanket. Up too late. The house empty because, Mama has got to live too, baby. Going out tonight. Be back before you be home from school tomorrow. You all right here by yourself, ain't you, baby? Mama's big girl. Love you. Don't sit up all night staring at that TV. Don't be late for school.

So she jerks up. No more time for lazy daydreaming with her head on the table like it's a pillow. That's not what a table's for.

Her hair is plaited in cornrows. Took hours and hours. The girls did it for each other when their mamas couldn't. She does her mama's.

Cereal box is her company this morning. She parts the flaps. Digs down and undoes the plastic inner wrapper she'd rolled tight to roach-proof its contents. Whatever the contents are— crunch pops nuggets chex flakes krisps grains pebbles—she sprinkles them in a bowl. Sweet already but that don't count so she sweetens them again, tablespoonful waved, then tapped to spread the sweet dust evenly. Top refitted snugly into the sugar bowl. Only once did she find a big black bug in the sugar. Ate hisself to death or asleep or whatever there he was big and black in the bowl when she lifted the lid. Nasty and black as black could be in the snowy sugar. She screamed when she saw it.

What's wrong with you, girl? You crazy? Nothing but a roach. Close things up tight nothing won't crawl in the food. Now dump that out and eat your breakfast.

Happened only that one time with the sugar but the black hole there every morning after when she opens the lid. She can feel her breath riling up. The scream armed and ready to blast off. Her eyes put the nasty thing in there, then they take it out in less time than she takes to blink, less time than the knot in her stomach takes to unknot, gone before she knows it's there, there even though she knows it's gone.

Her ankles crossed. She's scooted forward so her narrow behind barely grazes the edge of her chair. Hunched forward, weight on her forearms that are parallel, laid on the table like walls of a fort protecting the flanks of her bowl. She nibbles the bowl's chill lip. Rests her chin on the table again. The box upon which she seems to be concentrating is taller than the bumpy silhouette of her gardened head.

How many words does the box hold? How long must she study her part? Is she able to read it or is she saying letters of the alphabet to herself? Is she waiting for the box to speak? Does she unravel the letters on the box each night when others are sleeping and then each morning knit them back together again? Patient. Tireless. Never completing her job because she must hold out till her lover returns. Is it that story or another we get an inkling of, watching her fascination, her rapt attention, the drift of her eyes that signals presences we, with all our privilege, cannot see? She is perhaps enchanted. By her time of life. Neither little girl nor teenager. A few in her class at school have already changed. Sprouted, budded, bled. Some couldn't care less, leap into the arc of the churning rope, the singsong metronome of pipy voices double Dutching like there's no tomorrow. Because there isn't. For some. For this one whose talent we're scouting there is a moment soon when she steps out or is smacked out of the rope's angry wind, the teasing, signifying, tell-your-business rhymes of the other girls, a moment when she's clear, when her turn's over and she knows she's not going back. Maybe once more, maybe ten times. But never going back, not really, not like always before because in that moment clear of the game, the game is miles away behind her back. She can hardly hear it, can't imagine why it's still happening, why anybody'd want to play. Because she knows. It's finished for her. She's done. Sidewalk shudders behind her each time the rope slaps down but it's a sound mize well be on the other side of town. With those screechy voices. None knows her name. Her secrets. None knows the names we know. Penelope. Miranda. The new world she will step into once this long stunned moment between is over. You can't see the cage of rope, but it's there sealed a line at a time. When you're inside you hear it buzzing like a cloud of insects round your face.

Where is she? The furniture, the kitchen walls disappear. Our aperture closes.

I'm asking myself, Who can she play? Or whom? Did she reveal anything in this moment we've stolen from her that encourages me to believe the play can happen?

If I could, I would speak directly to her. Ask her questions. A quiz. What kind of chance do you think we have? Any? But this fakery, viewer and viewed connected temporarily by a hole in a skull, does not allow real questions back and forth. Look, don't talk. Talk is touching, is disturbing the scene. Keep your seats. Don't upset the delicate balance of our fiction within hers within yours within whatever this is twisting and hissing and crackling like a churning rope.

Figure of the rope roped into my design. Playing. Dead serious. Enough to hang me. Us. Together or separately. Let the rope the girls are turning freeze at the height of its cycle. A perfect arch above the pavement. And she too is frozen there, restored, virginal, intact as Coyote one panel after he's been tricked by Roadrunner and smashed to smithereens on the desert floor. Imagine her in sumptuous costume or elflike in next to nothing at all, stepped forward, to the edge of the stage, framed by the keyhole of proscenium arch we've constructed of plywood and cardboard painted and tacked to a temporary platform in the park. We transform this moment of the play to a soliloquy by bringing her stage front, by directing Prospero her father and Caliban her suitor manqué to drift subtly away and back, a fog dissipating as she slides forward, closer to us, nearly in our laps if we are seated in the bright-eyed mob settled on the grass below the stage. The men subside; they are less than they thought, less than we thought, than she thought, less at the center of this speech than some editors have thought who ignored Miranda's claim, attributed the words about to be spoken to her father. As the eyes of the mostly women and children who've settled on the grass in front of rows of benches, sitting on that green margin because they can't get any closer to the stage, as the eager eyes of kids and mothers follow the slow glide of Miranda toward them, Prospero and Caliban should become as insubstantial as possible without actually exiting the platform. If there were lights I'd chance one on her, soft, soft, and a purple-colored gathering of darkness misting the men who should be mere shadows as she speaks:

> *Abhorrèd slave,*
> *Which any print of goodness wilt not take.*
> *Being capable of all ills! I pitied thee,*
> *Took pains to make thee speak, taught thee each hour*
> *One thing or other: when thou didst not, savage,*
> *Know thine own meaning, but would gabble like*
> *A thing most brutish, I endowed thy purposes*
> *With words that made them known. But thy vile race,*
> *Though thou didst learn, had that in't which good natures*
> *Could not abide to be with; therefore wast thou*
> *Deservedly confined into this rock, who hadst*
> *Deserved more than a prison.*

There it is, children. The spurned woman speech. Clearly Miranda, not Prospero talking. This is personal not planned. Testimony to her passion, her suffering to bring forth speech from the beast. Unbeast him. And what did she receive for her trouble, her risk? More trouble. Beastly ingratitude. She offered the word. Caliban desired flesh. She descended upon him like the New England schoolmarms with their McGuffey's Readers, the college kids with books and ballots. Caliban, witches' whelp that he was, had a better idea. Her need, his seed joined. An island full of Calibans. He didn't wish to be run through her copy machine. Her print of goodness stamping out his shape, his gabble translated out of existence. No thanks, ma'am. But I will try some dat poontang. Some that ooh la la, oui, oui goodness next to your pee-pee. Which suggestion she couldn't abide. Could not relexify into respectability. He asked, in short, for everything. She knew she was her father's daughter. A lien on his property. Daddy'd taught her not to give but to negotiate. Calculate and get down on paper all terms of endearment. What's always at stake is the farm. Bargains must be struck carefully. Keep your elbows off the table and your ankles crossed, knees together. Someday, when your prince comes, then you may people this property with property. More. Makes more. In the meantime, go to Vassar. Travel, if you must, during school vacations but not on the Frontier because there are barbarians sleeping at the gate. If we wake them, we must teach them manners. Manners maketh man. Teach them to speak the when spoken to. Are you following me, children? The dangerousness of this speech about speech shoved in a woman's mouth. It's informed by a theme older than Willy or Willy's time. Eternal triangle and wrangle. The Garden where three's a crowd. Monkey in the middle. Who's in, who's out, who says so?

So it's Caliban who gets moved out, exiled, dispossessed, stranger in his own land, who gets named just about every beast in the ark, the bestiary, called out his name so often it's a wonder anybody remembers it and maybe nobody does. But is Caliban the snake on this island paradise or is the serpent wound round old Prospero's wand? Or is it Caliban's magic twanger, his Mr. William Wigglestaff he waggled at Miss Miranda and said: C'mere, fine bitch. Make this talk.

Oh shit. Excuse me. This is not turning out to be a children's story. I could get fired for telling my pupils this one. Expurgate it as you listen. Bowdlerize. Daddy Caliban learned enough to pick out meaty curses. Like starving prisoners in concentration camps straining kernels of corn from do do. It happened. At Andersonville for instance. It happens today, every day, round the world, round the clock, where the wind blows and the cradle rocks, prisoners catching hell, captive populations beaten into submission. Or death. Kid stuff. Elementary. Old as nursery rhymes.

That's why I shove aside both suspected killers, those blue-chinned, hard-knuckled, baldpate cons and con men, expurgate and exile to one side of the stage, or rather each one to a separate side so they won't start a fight to draw attention to themselves while we're trying to achieve, through the guile of dramatic art, our original production in the park, an opportunity for Miranda to talk for once, unencumbered, clear of the shadow of their lusting after the one, the many meanings she suggests with, among other things, what's secreted between her thighs. They will fight over her forever. Not really over her. But she is their excuse. The reason put forward for the storm. The exile. The falling out.

We bring her forward to clear the air, to entertain and instruct the next generation. She's trying her best to be her own person. She wants to share. But she can't. She's a prisoner, too. Hostage of what her father has taught her. A language which Xeroxes image after image of her father, his goodness, his lightness, his deed to the island and the sea-lanes and blue sky and even more than that. The future. Which is also confirmed and claimed in the words he taught her and she taught Caliban, buried of course, unmentionable of course, like her private parts, but nonetheless signified in the small-print forever-after clause of the deed. Her father needs her to

corner the future, her loins the highway, the bridge, sweet
chariot to carry his claim home. Her womb perpetuates his
property. Signs, seals, delivers. Spirit needs flesh. Word needs
deed. And Caliban understands the connections. Wants out.
Wants in. All her civilization whispered in his ear. Her words
on the tip of his tongue.

She whips a message on him. It hurts him. She's also hurt
and mad as a wet hen. Sounds just like her father when she's
angry. Births him live onstage. Turnabout fair play.

Caliban snatches his hand back from her fire. Pain causes
his tongue to thicken and twist. Old injuries cannot be undone.
You hear them every time he opens his mouth.

Yo. Mama. How bout some dat roundeye, sweetcakes? Is it
true your thang runs east to west, stead of north to south? Is
it a fact the hairs grow from outside inside your tickly tunnel
of love? Are you truly Goldilocks below your equator? People
say that when you set your mind on something you subject to
tear up anybody, anything to get what you want. Gingerbread
houses and little minding-their-own-business cottages with
nobody home.

Caliban's blueprint for the future: First, gimme. Then I'll be
much obliged, he says. Flesh today. Word tomorrow is the
proper order of business. Later, afterwards, we'll rap in that
postcoital snuggle and baby-babble each to each, coo-coo like
pigeons, our own aboriginal, lovey-dovey tongue and that talk
elaborated by generations of Calibans will grow up to be a
full-fledged voting member of the United League of languages.
All the talk we'll ever need.

Other way round won't work. I know plenty curses already.
See because while you pouring all that nice poison in my ear,

your daddy shipping my island piece by piece back to where it won't do me a bit of good. You neither, quiet as it's kept. Never met your mama. Nothing against her. For all I know she might be my mama, too. So I ain't playing the dozens but that lying ass wanna be patriarch Prospero who claims to be your daddy and wants to be mine, he's capable of anything. Incest, miscegenation, genocide, infanticide, suicide, all the same to him. To him it's just a matter of staying on top, holding on to what he's got. Power. A power jones eating away the pig knuckle he was dealt for a heart. All his fancy talk don't change a thang. Cut him loose while you still can. C'mon, put away the Magic Slate, my dear, and drop them pantaloons, step out all that funny stuff I see when you wear them dresses the sun comes shining through.

He squints. Like a one-eyed cat peeping in a seafood store. Measures this child, half-asleep at her desk, for a part, a costume. Too much TV. Not enough nourishment. Rickets. Kwashiorkor. Third World diseases in this best of all principalities and powers. West Philadelphia in the year of our dark lord Prospero, 1968. Springtime. The buds bursting. Birds singing. In a language of their own. She doesn't hear that either. Should I awaken her? Is she remediable? Can she play a part?

I'm going to make it happen.

I think it's a great idea. Real guerrilla theater. Better than a bomb. Black kids in the park doing Shakespeare will blow people's minds.

Miranda's age is not given in the play. I think she's probably a little older than you, hon. Two, maybe three years at most. Do you have an older sister? Yes? Couple years older? Yes? Then you know what Miranda's like. Boys on her mind all the time. Thinking about boys even when she's thinking that's not what she's thinking about. You're smiling. You know what I mean, huh?

What's your sister's name . . . that's a pretty name. Do you like the name Miranda? I think her name has something to do with the sea. I'll look it up. Or maybe we'll look it up in the dictionary together. The more you learn about Miranda the better you'll be at playing her. She lived four hundred years ago but try and think of her being somebody you know. Shakespeare's time was different but some things never change. Boys and girls fall in love. Right. Your sister likes boys and Miranda likes boys. Some things will be different, of course. In Shakespeare's day, when he wrote *The Tempest*, girls were married very young. Much younger than is usual today. They started families at an age when we'd still consider them children.

Oh. Your sister does? Twins?

*　　*　　*

Gold smoke twists from the lake this morning. An illusion of fire. The water smolders, reflects the reddish colors of high clouds drifting in from the west. Lower, peach-tinted clouds climb, dissipating in a vault of blue sky. Half a mile away, toward the center of the lake, a bird's flight parallels the horizon, catches light filtering through tattered layers of cloud and flickers on and off, a blazing iridescence, a white chip, a beacon flashing on off, on off as it traverses a cleared space between tranquil blue above, cloud mist and fiery water below.

Through a breach in the low-lying haze a stand of pine trees on the lake's far bank appears snow-laden, a winter postcard in August. A door opening on the wrong season. Frieze of white-draped evergreens asleep on the opposite shore. Ghostly trees, disguised, spray-painted white out of season.

Yeah, but that's another story, another country, it doesn't fit here. You can't rewrite *The Tempest* any damn way you please. Schoolmarms. Freedom riders. All the dead weight of their good intentions. You can't put that on stage. How's Caliban supposed to sass Miss Ann Miranda without him get his woolly behind stung good and proper by that evil little CIA covert operations motherfucker, Ariel? Round-the-clock surveillance, man. Prospero got that island sewed up tight as a turkey's butt on Thanksgiving. Play got to end the way it always does. Prospero still the boss. Master of ceremonies. Spinning the wheel of fortune. Having the last laugh. Standing there thinking he's cute telling everybody what to do next. And people can't wait to clap their hands and say thanks.

Aw, man. That's worse. That's jive. How she gon steal the wand? Even if the bitch did get her hands on it, what she gon do wit it? She ain't nothing but a wimp. Daddy got her so brainwashed first dude from the world she see she think he's god. The girl's ignorant, man. Stone hick. Easy pickins. Kind of chick those big-hat boys in the Port Authority waiting for when she simpers off the bus from Minnesota. What she gon do with a wand? Who's gon believe some trumped-up story like that? You got to do better. Everybody knows *The Tempest* ain't about penis envy. Laugh you out the park, man. Everybody knows can't nobody free Caliban but his own damn self.

Hey. I'm just trying to help, good buddy. I want to see the play happen. But I agree with Timbo. It can't be the girl. Wait. I think I see a way. Prospero. Let me be Prospero. Let him have a change of heart. Prospero realizes he's fucked up and . . .

. . . and what? Gives the nigger forty acres, a jackass and his daughter, too?

No. Listen. I could play Prospero as an outcast, a kind of hippie saint, alienated, hiding out because the world's too ugly. You know. A good guy at heart. Just sick and tired of the bullshit. Weary. Discouraged. So he splits to an island. Sticks his head in the sand. Then one day he wakes up. Something wakes him up.

Caliban's foot in his ass.

No. No. Nothing violent. This shouldn't be a western. See, it's all inside Prospero. The good, the bad, the ugly. He can be anything. A matter of willing it. But he has to work at changing himself. Spiritual discipline. If he turns himself around, he can turn the island around. The play's really about Prospero's guts. Everyman. The inner drama. The war of light and darkness within our souls. The power of the artist to create, transform. Poet as savior.

You're too fat, Charley. Too fat, too white and too old. This is a play featuring skinny black kids. Point of the whole thing is for them to master Shakespeare. To learn from putting on the play. To teach their teachers and families. Maybe teach this whole neanderthal city what kids are capable of. You're something else, Charley. Cudjoe shares his idea with you and what do you do, you try and eat it.

*   *   *

For a long while I didn't believe. Convincing other people I could pull it off was my way of keeping the idea alive. I didn't believe a word I was saying, but if they believed, well I was encouraged to talk more. Bounce the notion off someone else. Easier than trying to convince myself, easier than lying to myself. I can look back now and admit. Yes, I was depending on an illusion. I was strengthening myself by feeding other people a lie. I marginalized myself. If all these other people believe this bullshit, this harebrained project, what's wrong with me, why can't I believe it? Why should I be different? I talked them into talking me into doing it. If that makes any sense. And it probably doesn't. Or if it does, the sense is a scary kind of sense. Something not to be examined too closely. The point is then, at some point I began acting as if the play could be staged. The act became a habit. The habit brought the play closer and closer to life.

Alberto Giacometti revolted from his father Giovanni's aesthetic convention that known reality is identical with perceived reality.

*   *   *

To live on an island. Captive of air and wind and sea. To be
the island. Buffeted by sensuous wind, sound of trees and water,
bird-song, the sun on naked skin, black nights, golden dawns,
sparkle of the sea in late afternoon, a sheet of tin hammered
light and flexible and spread upon the water, so thin the sea
wears it like a second skin and every ripple every breath is
caught and held and silvered, petrified an instant then released
into the vast flat sheen stretching to the horizon.

Ah. Think of it. Your untouched island. Days and days. Ask
nothing of you. Food hangs on trees, grows on bushes, sprouts
from the earth. Best fresh water in the world gushes cool from
an underground cavern. You can't be lonely because you know
nothing but yourself. You are like the island. To prosper you
don't need another island beside you. You are complete. Time
is yesterday never ending, returning again and again. As always.
Your future is each season recycling. What has been, once
more.

You watch the sky crack. You see deep into the night.
Lightning holds for a fraction of a second too long and you
see farther into the darkness than you've ever seen before,
another island, a city of trees and hills, teeming, terraced,
dropping into the sea a thousand miles away, beyond the
horizon line that till this moment has always defined the limit
of your vision. You have seen your face in the water and
understand that trick, understand how the hand reaching up
for you as you reach down for it never cracks the pool's surface.
You must always be the one to go a little farther. Enter its
medium because it will never venture into yours. How all it
takes is the slightest touch, water on your skin, and the other's
gone. You wonder about the island the lightning revealed.

Wonder if it will always remain far away. Would your touch destroy it if some miracle ever brought it closer?

You remember that night, that storm cracking the horizon, that new, pale island hovering an instant before black night slammed shut again, remember it all when one morning you see the wing of a great white bird loom over the edge of the world, falling, falling, but never quite touching the sea as it glides toward you.

One wing of a great white bird, standing tall like a falling tree. Is the other wing buried beneath the sloughing waves? Or is what you see a bird's gleaming breast, puffed, serried with ranks of feathers fluttering, the whole wide shape tilted, staggering back and forth as if the drunken weight of its leaning intends to crash it down into the murmuring water? You have asked yourself a question many, many times before, unable to form it into words but now with this struggling thing whatever it is zigging and zagging toward your island, with it there so unexpectedly, bright, injured, but weaving closer, closer, bearing down on you, you realize that coming *at* you is also perhaps coming *for* you and the nagging question you never quite put into words crystallizes, flashes clear as this slash of whiteness against blue sky. The question says itself, reveals the words always there, familiar as this new thing is familiar now that it finally arrives, finally announces itself: *where did I come from?*

You never knew how to ask the question about your beginning until the end sighted, bearing down on you with studied nonchalance. Then a storm bursts through the needle's eye. A tempest spins round the tall wing, cocooning it. A spitting, kicking raucous web of sound and light and rushing dark cloud. A fist closes upon the intruder and wracks it. Strangely, beyond the fiery ball of tempest and the white bird snarled and tossed in the storm's net, the sea is calm. The elements seem detached, passive spectators of the unnatural squally presence so suddenly whipped up.

As abruptly as it dropped upon its prey, the clutter of storm swirls away. Whirling particles, a million warring pinpricks of light and darkness are sucked into a funnel cloud that instantly narrows to a point, then drains into the sky, leaving no trace of itself, no echo, the harmony of a moment before restored, except on a sandy beach in a broad horseshoe cove two hundred steps from where you stand, becalmed, ancient in your watching as the elements, a crippled something lies mangled. The dark hand that untidied the sky and sea had finished by depositing something there in the cove. And you wait, wondering if the same hand will launch it again, send it scudding over the breakers, back to open water from whence the tempest snared it. You see white. You think of bones. A carcass some beast has partially devoured and caches in the bush until its appetite rises again. You wonder for the first time if your bleached bones will be viewed by another creature. You are chilled in spite of a blazing sun. A draft created by the storm's sudden passing is almost visible, expands in ripples as it reaches you, explores your skin inch by inch, then enters and shuffles through layers, down to the wetness inside the bones and chills that too.

Welcome. Welcome. Are you speaking aloud? Do you know how to talk? Are your words inside or outside? It matters now, for the first time, in a way you never dreamed it could.

*   *   *

You depend on the children's capacity for make-believe. Ahmad will rattle a sheet of tin. Thunder and lightning. A drumroll announcing the play's beginning, the moment when identities slip away. Spirits descend and walk about like ordinary folks. In their mammies' laps, mammies sprawled on the lap of greasy grass bordering the stage, little kids will whoop and holler, shriek with delight. Their enthusiasm will ignite the rest of the audience. We'll all be seized. Players. Play. Audience. Bound together by the screaming children.

Never happened, did it?

No. We were set to go. Then it rained. Two days and two nights.

Too bad.

A lot of hard work went into it. The kids were ready. I know it would have been a smash. They were very good.

Was it ever performed?

Nope. Things happened. Time ran out. I quit the teaching job. Went to grad school. Whole business just petered out. Funny. For a while there in the halls of West Philly, you could hear Elizabethan English. Snatches of Willy's verse in the most unlikely places and times. Scared the shit out of some people. You know. Witchcraft. Possession. Outside agitators fucking with the kids' minds. Wow. You can probably still hear lines from *The Tempest* wherever those kids are, whatever they're doing.

They're not kids anymore.

Guess not. Let me tell you, though. They were good. Iron heads. Never forgot their lines once they memorized them. Good kids.

Too bad. Too sad. It never came off, huh.

Wonder what happened to my beautiful cast.

Wonder if they wonder about you.

I've always felt guilty about deserting them. When I was teaching, every day I'd go home with a sad feeling, a guilty feeling, knowing I should have done so much more. And that's what kept me coming back. It's also what finally drove me away. Running, talking to myself. Tail between my legs.

I understand just what you're saying. Teaching's impossible. Trying to explain what you don't really know yourself. Especially teaching in one of these detention-center concentration-camp rag-ass prisons we call public schools.

They change as soon as they bust out the doors. For a moment anyway, before they remember they don't have any place to go, their faces light up. They're real kids. Children. Free at last. All colors of the rainbow in their faces. All the better things we could be, we could do if we believed what's in their eyes. Then the outside shit starts raining down on their heads and it's as bad as the shit inside the school building. Off they go, half-asleep again. I couldn't keep coming back to that. To failing every day. Little teensy, teensy successes and mountains of failure. Couldn't take it. The play's the best thing we did and the city pisses on us. Rains two days and nights steady.

So you think they're still saying their lines.

I used to believe I'd hear the whole thing, start to finish, the way I rewrote it. That I'd stumble up on it one fine day. The kids still kids, meeting, doing the play in the park. Their secret ceremony. Their way of keeping something special alive. I wonder why I believed that.

I will write you soon again. Can you learn to hope in what seems a hopeless situation? What makes sense? What might help? Where do we go from here. I don't feel I can *tell* you anything. You've been places I've never been, you're facing threats and fears and burdens I can barely imagine. We're different. But not separate. I don't have any choice about that. My connection with you is not something I can think in or out of existence. I'm stuck with you as I'm stuck with myself. If I draw a line around who I am, who I can be, you are inside the circle. I have no choice. Don't want a choice. To be who you are you must draw your own circle. Or rather as you grow, as you become, you'll draw many circles, your sense of who you are, who you must be grows, changes. Right now you must feel trapped. By the terrible consequences of your acts, the frightening portion that seems to be your fate. But if you, if we can preserve your life, conditions, awful as they are, will change. Even if externals might seem to be the same to someone looking at you, the conditions of your life, your feelings about it will change because every day your mind must form a new picture of your circumstances. That picture changes, if only because you've lived through one more day of hell. The next day you'll have a slightly different outlook because you have survived the hell, you are facing what's next, whatever.

I'm not looking to give you consolation. I wish I was able. What I'm trying to do is share my way of thinking about some things that are basically unthinkable. I cannot separate myself from you. Yet I understand we're different. I will try to accept and deal with whatever shape your life takes. I know it's not my life and try as I might I can't ease what's happening to you, can't exchange places or take some of the weight for you. But

I believe you have the power in your hands to do what no one can do for you. Live your life strongly, fully, moment by moment. Make do. Hold on. Each day will be slightly different. Some will surprise you. Pleasantly or unpleasantly. We don't know what the future will bring. We do have a chance to unfold our days one by one and piece together a story that shapes us. It's the only life anyone ever has. Hold on.

PART III

The old town's dying behind J.B.'s back. Rats and fat cats fleeing. City in flames crackling against the horizon. Tuba-doo. You were beautiful when you smiled, child. My baby. My opp-poop-a-doop. A blind man know you're burning now. Don't have to see nothing. Don't have to touch. You smoking, darling. Smoky-doo. Halfway up my goodness nose. Nose wide open. Oo wheee. Shake a hand. Strike a match.

One foot after tother. Shuffle with that store on your back, man. It's your mama told you better be home fore dark, better be here long long before the band starts playing. Dinner be ready bout half past eight you better be on time. Don't be stoppin nowhere for nothing. Ain't slaving in this kitchen for my health. Pots boiling. Greens burping. Set yo foot in the paff. Liff it. Tote it. Motivate it, old man. J.B. remembers her voice, her meaty arms, but there's no home no more. And he stares where the city should be. Hurts like his own eyelash on fire. Blazing away, a roof of tar and feathers crumples, the ridge above his eyepit disintegrates, turns to ash. His name is James. James Brown. They teased him forever when the singer stole his thunder. The jokes got old, but it's still *please, please, please, don't go* his name. Him and no other turning his J.B. back on the famous flaming city and walking away like *shit*, it ain't nothing to me. Petroleum wigged singers, signifying niggers, burning cities, his own scorched, black ass. Don't mean a thing. Don't mean a thing.

At dawn there be another one. Always nother one. Nother city, nother name, nother woman. He misses his Big Mama rising on her elbow a second as she's turning, her bone a cleaver and she's chopping their soft mattress in two. For a second there as she pivots away from him, raised up on one elbow, she looks like she might sink. Her droopy titty. Her sleepy eyes. All her brown weight on the point of her crusty bow turning, pivoting toward him or away from him, God only knows, in the bed. Be another morning tomorrow morning. If he lives that long.

He remembers all the smoke from burning cities he's ever sucked up the four-lane blues highway of his nose. The stink and putrefaction. The flies. He'll miss this city. He always misses them. It hurts to just walk away. Leaving everything behind. Nothing. A vacant lot where he picked a flower for his lady's pompadoured hair.

It's almost finished now. Loud pops of automatic weapons fire scything down naked bodies lined up against walls and fences. Like taking down wash. Only these bodies are dirty and make dirty heaps where they crumple, drawing flies, dogs, crows, stirring in the hot wind of fire storms smashing whole city blocks like bowling balls scoring strikes. The figure wavers. Like a highway in heat. Many, many pekel falling down, falling down. Blown away because they don't suit somebody's purposes, cut down because this is the last morning of the last day and they are victims of terminal boredom, somebody's needing something to do.

This job, like God's, of making a city had wearied J.B. Light every morning to tame. Playing father son and holocaust to the kids running wild in streets and vacant lots.

Who's zooming who? The mayor born in Georgia? The Old South. Red mud country, slow-talking roots. Rumor has it the paddy-boy director of public safety a cracker, too. Imported from Bull Connorsville, given a voice lift, a polyester leisure suit, a slinky, retarded teenage mistress from an Italian slum in South Philly (why can't we write about these things—they're not true, are they?) and carte-blanche, white power to whip whatever heads needed to roll. Carte blanche and the black mayor's dark blessing, chocolate oreo cookie above the director's vanilla brow, so who's gonna get in their way? Zooming whom?

This is an irresponsible way of looking at things. There may be survivors in the bar-b-qued city who require assistance. Better to light one little candle than to sit on one's ass and write clever, irresponsible, fanciful accounts of what never happened, never will. Lend a hand. Set down your bucket. A siren screams. We should stop in our tracks. Walls are tumbling, burning-hot walls on tender babies. And you sit here moaning cause your welfare check's late. Talking about the mailman's a racist, likes to watch you squirm thirtieth of the month. Mama's Day every month, when your body's flayed and you're so broke flies won't even light on you.

What should open now in response to the tragedy of a city burning is the vista of your heart. But you run away every time. You'll turn your back every time. Philadelphia's on fire. You worry about your chest burning. Wonder if smoke's bubbling out your ears. J.B., you've got to get up off your ass. World's out there and it's begging for your attention. What we need is realism, the naturalistic panorama of a cityscape unfolding. Demographics, statistics, objectivity. Perhaps a view of the city from on high, the fish-eye lens catching everything within its distortion, skyscraper heads together, rising like sucked up through a straw. If we could arrange the building blocks, the rivers, boulevards, bridges, harbor, etc. etc. into some semblance of order, of reality, then we could begin disentangling ourselves from this miasma, this fever of shakes and jitters, of self-defeating selfishness called urbanization. In time a separation (spelled in case you ever forgot, with a *rat*) between your own sorry self and the sorrows of the city could be effected. If you loved yourself less, J.B. If you loved your city more. Especially now as it dreams this incinerated, smoking vision of itself. Realism: the stolid arbitrariness of the paltry wares we set out each morning in the market square to make a living.

I love you truly. Truly I do. Like a brother.

J.B. thinks of drops of blood on the pavement. What passes for pavement between these houses owned by pests. He remembers the trading post where you could collect a bounty for rat scalps. Bonus if you brought them in alive. He thinks of young black boys shotgunning other black boys, black girl babies raising black girl babies and the streets thick with love and honor and duty and angry songs running along broken curbs, love and honor and duty and nobody understands because nobody listens, can't hear in the bloody current that courses and slops dark splashes on the cracked cement, how desperate things have become. How straight the choices, noble the deeds.

This is your rap-rap-rap-rapcity rapper on the dial
So just cool out and lissen awhile
Cause if you don't dig what I'm rappin bout
They'll pull your skin off, turn you inside out
They'll pull your skin off, turn you inside out
It's a new trickeration, a hip sensation, divine inspiration
     blowing cross the nation
They peel your skin then you're in like Flynn
Drain your brain so ain't no pain
Makes you feel so real, it's a helluva deal
No money down, easy credit
Skin's gone, you can just forget it.
Dippy-do, dippy-do, rip a dip rip rip
Rippy-dip, rippy-dip do-rip dip
Put their hands in your heart
Rip it all apart
Keep on peeling
For a righteous feeling
You got to die one day
Mize well go this way
You're a separate nation
Under their domination
Takes you for a ride
Peel away your pride
When your skin's gone, children
Are you black inside.

Best to let it burn. All of it burn. Flame at the inmost heart.
The conflagration blooming, expanding outward, like ripples
from a stone to the corners of the universe. One little candle.

The scab above Twanda's eyelid burns and festers and grows concentrically as she picks at it, sworls of white-speckled soreness on her black forehead and it leaps from her brow suddenly as a siren in the middle of the night and we know instantly it's coming for us, we're implicated as its light arcs and flashes in circles, we are infected, finished in the feral swoop of its dirty-fingered stab into the town houses where we are hiding. The gem in her forehead explodes slowly as a rose blooming, dying simultaneously because we neglect to tend it, adore it, praise it as our own.

These ruins. This Black Camelot and its cracked Liberty Bell burn, lit by the same match ignited two blocks of Osage Avenue. Street named for an Indian tribe. Haunted by Indian ghosts— Schuylkill, Manayunk, Wissahickon, Susquehanna, Moyamensing, Wingohocking, Tioga—the rivers bronzed in memory of their copper, flame-colored bodies, the tinsel of their names gilding the ruined city. Oh, it must have been beautiful once. Walking barefoot in green grass, the sky a blue haven, the deep woods full of life. Now the grit of old dogshit ground into the soil lodges in our children's toes when they play in the park. Poison works its way through their veins to their brains. They play cowboys and Indians. Colored and white with real guns. Shots exchanged over Cobbs Creek and one player falls down forever. Real bullets bridging the racial gap, hurtling over the scrufty water and trees that separate two warring villages. The Book of Life exchanges hands. Who will read it next, kill for it next? A red ghost thin as conviction giggles its last laugh. No one rescues the victim. He's shot, drowns, waits for fire. Water turns rusty with old blood. Old, old thirteen-year-old blood, old the instant it begins seeping into another container. Cobbs Creek named for somebody named Cobb who was named Cobb because somebody else was. Named. Cobbs Creek. Where you can always bleed twice in the same place.

Images of years past dog James Brown as he trudges toward the suburbs. He thinks he was at the Salvation Army shelter last New Year's Eve. Like maybe on a folding chair watching with a bunch of other celebrants on folding chairs, what else, TV usher in the new year with lists. Top tens, top one hundreds. Everybody who's able constructs a list. Ten somethings. Lists of ten most popular because that's how many fingers and toes. Little piggies we can wiggle, name. Lists of lists. Lists listing. Lists passing in the night. Lists while I woo thee. J.B. can't recall the items or the lists listing the items. Only flashes of commercials, of blood. News reviews of massacres. A year of terror. Us versus Them. Who's zooming who? Shattered, blood-stained glass strewn in an airport lounge. Mile after square mile of broken glass littering the countryside. Lebanon Soweto West Bank Belfast San Salvador Kabul Kampuchea. Spin the globe and touch it wherever it stops. You'll get blood on your finger. A gigantic jigsaw sheet of glass smashed to smithereens and fragments spattered everywhere nobody can put it back together again. And even if a someone came along with infinite patience and began to gather the grains, the small bits into a heap and chose one speck and began to seek its mate, its match from among miles of wounded glass, if such a patient one and such a rare passion to mend revealed itself, even with the bad luck and patience to live and die a million times moving barefoot through the barbed-wire sea of glass, so what? Don't mean a thing. Even that one couldn't knit it back together.

Smoke gets in your eyes. Smoky-doo. Bye, bye, baby.
Good-bye.

Hey—hey, youall, this rapcity here
Got a tale to tell make you shed a tear
Bout some dreadlocked bloods trying to do their thing
And a evil Empire with a evil King
Not the kind of story I like to tell
Dreads was seeking heaven, all they caught was hell
Didn't eat no meat, let their kids run naked
Got the Emperor uptight, he just couldn't take it
Called his army, his navy, his flying corps
Said: This shit's gone too far, I can't stand it no more
Got to play by my rules if you live in my city
Fuck with the piper, don't expect no pity.
Shame if babies have to burn
But life is hard, they got to learn
Give them primitives five minutes to leave the premises
If they don't comply, come down like Nemesis
When the smoke clears, don't want nary a one
Left standing to tell me how my city should be run
Left standing to tell me how my city should be run
How can I rule with equanimity
When every day them monkeys making a monkey out of
*   me.*
You wouldn't believe the ordinance brought to bear
To drive them Rastas out their lair
Dreads didn't falter, they fought toe to toe
But the odds were too heavy, they had to go
It was like Tyson throwing on a little kid

The kid was doomed whatever he did
Down they went in bullets, water and flame
It was Murder One by another name
Murder One by any name
Uh—uh. Uh—uh, uh—uh, uh—uh
Spleeby—spleeby, spleeby—spleeby, spleeby do duh
I—I—I—I'm the—the—the rapper, the dapper, the last
  backslapper
Wit you on my team we the cream de cream
Don't cry, don't moan, don't pine away
Them Dreadys be back another day
Remember what you heard rapcity say
Them Dreads coming back another day
Hey, hey, hey, hey, hey, hey—hey, hey
Them Dreads coming back, somebody's got to pay
Dreads coming back
Somebody's gotta pay
Gotta pay, gotta pay
Somebody's gotta pay.

When they pee in the weeds sounds like a fire. Weeds knee-high and crackling brown sometimes Alphonso fancied himself trucking through hog hair. Making tracks on a big piggy's bristle back. On another planet, one with hair for grass and seven snout-pussed green moons. A sky with something always in its eye. No fingers to rub shit out. You can shortcut anywhere in the city through these dark empty overgrown lots. Sent by Vator, king of the universe. You go in a phony, stiff-legged, cartoon run like Vator's boys across these raggedy fields and the weeds sound like death brushing your jeans. You are a comb, a pick, a razor styling through this no-man's-land of stinking weeds.

Bunch of us in Old Vats nothing-can-harm-you magic armor. If we bumped into each other be loud as garbage cans falling in the alley. A whole little army of motherfucking bad dudes pissing in the weeds behind the Jew's store. *Whizzing* he heard a white boy call it once in Clark Park. Take me *whiz*, Mommy. Watering the weeds, scalding them and maybe he hears you pissing, maybe it's him, or the ghost of him outside the ghost of his store, old four-eyed Jew above you in the black sky who psyches you into looking up a minute so he can look down on you and say, Shame, shame, on you, boys. His bald helicopter head. Light on steel rims of his specs rotoring, Roto-Rooter round and round the blades of the chopper silently *chuck chuck* spinning, keeping him up there on patrol in the air over top of where his store used to be.

We run him away from the neighborhood. Getting Uzis next week but didn't need guns to stick up ole Markey. Stole the whole cash register when we couldn't make the sucker work right in the store. Snatched it up off the counter and split. Mark the Shark knew exactly who we was. Who else it gon be? No ski masks or stocking caps. What difference that shit make? He knew. The Jew knew. So we bust in broad daylight. Told him, We got to have it, today, old man. Give it up, hymie.

Snatched the motherfucker right off the counter. Broad daylight. All us together. Like we so black and bad nobody could see us less we want them seeing us. No lie. That's the way it went down. Markowitz ain't said a mumbling word. Knows it's his ass if he calls the cops. Like taking lunch money from chumps at school. You got to come back here tomorrow, sucker, so you bet not say shit, you hear. This where you be tomorrow and we be here too. So give it up and keep your mouth shut.

All kinda mess in the weeds. Piece of bicycle, cat bones, cashbox, shoes, a mattress the nastiest thing melting down like a dead body with ugly shit inside when the skin rots. Wonder who been laying up on that thing so many nasty spots look like measles or some spattery diarrhea disease all over it. Jump on it and bounce till one them rusty springs pop through tear up Lester's leg. Gash him from knee to ankle and he howls like a stuck pig. Leave it alone then. Stuffing rot out get wet stink like pus. Be your mama's bed. Be where she sell her pussy. Roaches and water bugs and spiders be crawling in there too. One them slimy black bugs be your daddy. See, you ain't cool you cut your whole damn leg off running through here be glass and shit and a stove, a Cadillac fender, a kitchen sink. Dog dukie, junkie puke, soft banana kinda mess you slip in and fall. Wasn't there five minutes ago. These warriors pissing a river. Nuff pee pee drown you you come running through here when we finish. Wasn't nothing a minute ago then you come flying cross the lot be knee-deep in piss, you be drowned before you know it.

Pee creeping like fire through a jungle. Every animal scared, hollering its holler. Haul-assing out the way. Big ones stepping on little ones. Little ones mashing their babies trying to get out the way.

Like fire. Or rain when it drops all the sudden big as eggs. Drops hurt you if they hit you. Bombs. That big, brother. I ain't lying. So big sound like bricks hitting the cement.

Tomorrow night we taking over downtown again. Wait till the movies let out. Charge them chumps while they still half blind. Cop a feel. Run your hand up the bitches' clothes. Anywhere you can grab a handful. Grab ass. Grab pussy. Squeeze some tit. Off the dudes' money. Be on they ass so fast ain't time to holler. We gone before they catch their breath. Long gone. Biff. Bam. Thank you, ma'am. Cop and blow.

Wish them people was a wall. So you could spray them with your mark. Those paddy-girls girls' thighs. Those screams. The tough guy you punch in the face just cause he ain't acting scared enough. Cause he's calling you nigger before you rob him or touch his ole lady. Be nice to leave your mark so you could go back next day and see it still there, show the fellas you ain't lying.

You swoop down. You the blade, they the grass. Got your hands all in they clothes, under they clothes. No secrets. You take what you want, got it and gone before they know it's took. You hear them squealing behind you. Your legs never get tired cause you're one of Vator's boys. Trick's over that quick. Be nice if you could rewind it. Study it up close. Your mark big as life right where you left it, right where it ain't spozed to be. Girls wearing nothing under them see-through, peek-a-boo tops. A handful of that, sure enough. A stinky finger you steal away and write her name in the air with it all the way home. Be nice to go back and play it over and over. That was you and me, babe. Remember? Member what we did? Member all the fun we had?

My army stuffs them chumps. Right up the gut. Down to the bone. Jam city. They squeal and scatter like they the rack, we the cue. Bomb them motherfuckers. Set a fire under they asses. We the fist. Rammed up their giggies. The hard black fist. Hit them hard, real hard. Knock some on the ground. Take everything they got. Wave your piece in the faces of the ones left standing. Back. Get the fuck back, while you strip the ones on the ground. Stand shoulder to shoulder. Hard black brothers. Swoop in like Apaches, like Vietcong, hit for the middle. Grab a few. Knock a few down. You know how to pick the good ones. You know the chubby wallets, chubby bums and titties. They on the ground cause ain't nowhere else to go. Got em trapped and we on they asses tight as white on rice. My army swoop down like thunder. Like a storm and nowhere to go but down on that hard cement. Then we on top, taking what we want, what we came for, what we find. They belong to us the minute we close down. Give it up. Give it up. Nothing you got is yours anyway. You know you stole it. Know you ain't spozed to have it. You lied and cheat and steal to get it. Mine now. My fingers in her silky hair and silky panties. My hand in your money box, Mr. Markowitz, hymie motherfucker. Oh yeah. I be here. Where I always be. Today. Tomorrow. Wind in the weeds. Fire. In your pocket. In your ass.

Talk to me. Lion.

> *In the park called Clark we rule the dark*
> *Live like Noah in his ark*
> *They tried to shoot us, bomb us*
> *Drown us burn us*
> *They brought us here, but they can't return us.*
> *We the youth, the truth*
> *You better learn us*

You know we're right, don't start no fight
Any chump can tell we was born in hell
Cooked lean and mean in the fiery furnace
Lean and mean in the fiery furnace

Don't boss us, cross, throw us no bone
Git the fuck out the way, leave us the fuck alone
We own the night, gonna rule the day
You brought us here and we're here to stay

                                        here to stay
                                        here to stay

A kite flutters blocks away over the low compacted roofs of my suburb. A jack-in-the-box, free at last, free at last, the kite jiggles and shimmers like a neon message. From this distance it's one thing, then just as quickly another and the first thing again as I watch it cavort. I test my memory of its history, the bodies it cycles, swaps, retrieves, recycles, forgets. Yes. Just seconds ago it was a watermelon-headed, octopus-armed minstrel man, his torso a snake, his giant hands, white-gloved like Mickey Mouse's, flapping and waving, a three-headed dragon, a fish, a beanstalk bearing three seed-pods swaying in the air to sweet melodies only it hears. The long tail shakes, rattles, roils. There must be a string anchoring the beast because it sails horizontally without rising, reversing itself, whipping back and forth along the same path like a typewriter carriage. Farther east, beyond the last housetops, below the chimerical kite, there are hills deeply greened by trees. I think, when I need to think, of the peace those low hills might contain, if this world were other than it is, if it

were a pet you could tame and diminish, if you could teach
it your name and its name and teach it to come when you
called with your slippers in its mouth to your easy chair
beside the picture window where you're sipping your three
fingers of Cutty Sark after work.

I am alone in the house. Nothing new. The usual in fact.
Mine eyes have seen nothing more exciting lately than the
coming of the kite. Wavering, flickering, silly, ominous, blowing
in the wind.

Invisible, three or four stories below the kite, there must be
a hand holding the kite's string. Whose hand, I wonder. Whose
toy? Whose game? A child perhaps. An adult entertaining,
instructing children. No matter. The hand, whosever, moves
back and forth, back and forth, short, jerky tugs that translate
into the kite's broad rippling sallies, writing the lines of its life
then erasing them as it tacks in the opposite direction. Wiping
the slate clean. A slate it dirties with each line of fiction. Then
removes. I can almost hear the old-fashioned banging chime
as it shifts. The story appears, letter by letter, then's gone.
No-fault divorce. A film run backward to its conclusion, which
is its beginning now and perfect end.

Here is the story it writes: I am an informer. I tell tales on
my friends. Who become my enemies. Because I am a snitch.
I squealed on my former soul mates, my comrades huddled
in the arms of the Tree of Life. Squealed to the pigs. Revealed
all our good hiding places, secret springs of potable water, the
edible roots and berries. Translated our secrets, stored in the
sacred Book of Life, into the grunting, rooting, snarly pig
tongue. Stood by aiding, abetting as Porky Pig snouts bulldozed
and leveled and angry pointy Porky Pig hooves stomped.

I betrayed our good mother Earth. Betrayed her anointed, dreadlocked King. Switched allegiance, planted incriminating evidence, stranded my good brown brothers out on a limb, high and dry.

I feel terrible. Together, black and white and yellow and red and brown together, all the rainbow children of Life, all born to Life's bounty, Life's sacred trusts and duties, together we learned the message of the Book. To read it and pass on the teachings and keep the Tree alive. So when I turned, when I shifted loyalties, the most hurtful twist was the knife in my own guts, the disemboweling hari-kari wrench of my own self exposed inside out and stinking to high heaven.

Forgive me, brothers. I didn't know what I was doing. Still don't. Never will. Forgive me.

When the fires blaze highest at noon, smoke rolls in from the west, till it's dammed by that upthrust of green hills. Smoke thickens to a wall, then slowly disintegrates during these long summer afternoons. A dusky kingdom suddenly risen then gone to rags and tatters which night swallows. I watch it intently. Read the smoke again and again for what it says about me, my fate. The only truly interesting, engaging story anyone can tell me, after all. My fate.

My friend the mayor is expected for cocktails. Somewhere. Perhaps here. Perhaps we will watch the smoke dying together. At this window, drinks in hand, the perfect couple.

If I see him again, it won't be in his inner city after dark. Not for all the snow in Chinatown. My last trip into the nighttime city was definitely my last. I didn't believe anyone remained who'd recognize me. After that trial, life sentences, the fire. So in I went for drinks, dinner, a movie. Cynthia accompanied me. We saw *Hud*. I fell in love again. With Newman not Cynthia. Mind love. Perfect because unrequited, impossible. The idea of him ravished me, though of course I preferred nights with Cynthia. It's just that one needs a friend these days. Gender bonding. A gang. And Newman would make an irresistible kingpin. Other studs would be attracted. Enough for a softball team and beers afterward in our favorite hangout and once, after we capture second place in the park league slow-pitch tourney, an evening of stag videos. Donkeys and dogs and Rhine maidens all in a row. I know he's that kind of class guy and I miss him so much, even as Cynthia's hand rubs mine in the box of popcorn we're sharing in the theater. She reaches farther down into the pit between us and strokes my leg. My trousers are fawn colored, pressed and clean as driven snow. I hope there's no butter on her fingers. But I like it. I like it, her fingers kneading my fleshy thigh, and the evening of love I anticipate begins to play across the private screen of my mind, her big, teddy-bear body naked as a pea as we romp to exhaustion; her hot sweet hungry mouth closing on my pecker, my first four fingers up to their ears in her sopping wet twat. She lets me know she's ready too in that millisecond concupiscent caress of our fingers in the burbly box of hot buttered popcorn. She's a good girl. In the dark she'll lick her fingers clean before squeezing my thigh. The smell of popcorn is the smell of semen, don't you think, after you've been at it awhile and the first juicy waves have dried on the sheets, starting that palimpsest you build layer by layer and you hate to shower hate to wash your linens because it smells good to the last popcorny stale drop, your smell you suddenly recall and connect as you reach in the box and pop a handful of popped kernels in the dark.

Image a city called the City of Brotherly Love. Consider the pretension of that greeky compound, tinker with the sound till it becomes brothel-ly, City of Brothelly Love. Imagine old tumbleweed, tumbledown James Brown, J.B., living there. What was the name of the first city? At this very moment someone at the University is achieving academic prominence puzzling out the answer to that question. Was it Jericho? Our professor gathers shards of pottery. His computer swallows every bit of evidence—telexed phoned mailed modemed cabled punched faxed—from across the globe, evidence it will digest and excrete in graphs, plots, statistical tables, colored projections, Mercator maps, holograms, laser-printed bulletins, updates, summaries, reports, inching forward the known in a shorthand that is tolerated as an acceptable translation of the unknown, because nothing ever stops happening, pieces of information, sources of information proliferate, crossbreed, cyberneticize, competing claims from every corner of the earth, track the birth of the first city, keep the blessed event happening, Mama's baby, Daddy's maybe. The first citizen passes out cigars on the first street corner in the first city anyone ever dreamed. Jericho lives, but its crackling imminence, its buzzing persistence in the birth canal of computer tapes, relays and flashing lights has little to do with J.B. today because now his town is definitely Philadelphia, last time he looked anyway, and it's neither first nor last but it's all he's got, and he must feed body and soul so he's on his way to work but there is no work so he stops in the middle of Market Street, three blocks from City Hall, and decides since the mayor's black, blacker by far than dreadlocked coffee-colored J.B., he, Mr. J.B., ought not to be out on the street, desperate as he is, nowhere to turn, on a flimsy day like today and people passing him like there's no mayor in an office in City Hall blacker than J.B. Like white people still think they own everything they see and still don't give a fuck about none of it. Least of all J.B.

For the record, J.B. wears army fatigues, camouflage issue, big thigh pockets, pocketed also in the rear, buttons, snaps, elastic waistband, funky, filthy from six months in the field. His sweat, piss, shit, the miscellaneous stains earned from encounters with the ubiquitous sludge of the city blend into brown green black tan swirls designed to render him invisible to his enemies. On land. Who cruise the air. A T-shirt which may have been olive drab but now the colorless color of an oil slick complements his baggy trousers. He searches for a job that will pay his bills, feed his wife and kiddies, even though for years now he's ceased believing his kidnapped family could be alive. Inside bamboo compounds guarded by brothers in creased khaki, pitiful hordes of women and children are spoiling like raw meat left out in the sun. Guards plug their ears and noses and wear thick black shades. What you don't know, don't hurt you. Death rules on the other side of the electrified, poison-staked stockade where J.B.'s people are detained. Enlisted men wear tiny transistor radios stuffed in their ears. A dance boogie shuffle, a distant attentiveness separates them from officers who stand rigidly surveying the compound, thinking whatever they think about behind their gold-rimmed ever-lasting dark glasses.

Nothing much to do. The men, whose women and children are captives, refuse to return from the jungle and work the rubber plantations. That means their families remain as hostages behind the bamboo walls. Rules say guards must not feed or water the hostages unless their men surrender and milk the rubber trees. So it makes for long days. Women and children dying of thirst and starvation inside the compound, you dying of boredom out here in the stubbled clearing. Except once a week it's your duty to retrieve and bury the dead, and once every two weeks you must cut back the encroaching bush. Hours in the sun swinging machetes. Nigger work in the fields again. No one feels like singing. Stripped to the waist, fighting back the jungle that never sleeps, that circles the compound where you've been exiled to preside over the slow death of babies and their mamas and old folks not worth saving to cultivate the rubber trees.

Always a threat their men may return to rescue the hostages. Rumors of camps overrun, guards impaled on bamboo stakes and roasted alive. They bullshit you with such tall tales to keep you alert. The missing men, the ones who claim they want freedom, who dress like bush natives, who call themselves rebels, are, as they've always been, cowards and fools. Enemies of your tribe a thousand years. Tall tales about all that too. Stories of better times when your enemies were worthy enemies and you met them in pitched battles, thousands of warriors a side, to gain honor and captives. Long ago when the land belonged to gods and the gods loved those who were fearless and steadfast and right living. A time when our clan spoke with one voice and followed the ancient ways. When drumbeat and the ululations of our women filled our hearts with the Lion's blood, when our flesh was a fit vessel for the ancestral spirits, when the invisible ones rode us and we leaped over rivers, galloped across plains, stepped over valleys, when our splendid headdresses scraped the clouds. Old sad stories because now we are fallen, laid low. Not as lazy and worthless and low as the missing men of our captives. Not offal, not flies who circle the death stink of this camp, moaning and buzzing and pleading when darkness shrouds the forest. Not slugs who hide under rocks in daylight, pretending their women and children are not baking in the pitiless heat, no shelter, no water, their tender, naked bodies raked by the sun's claws.

No, we are not fallen as low as our enemies, but this guard duty drives you down. The stars grow more distant each night. It hurts to crank up my neck to view them. Muscles whine all day, supporting the weight of East German helmets, Israeli arms, British uniforms. Not much, you say, but all day every day, the weight accumulates, a certain weighty bitterness tangible in the slightest exercise of our duties. You may say the heat is getting to my brain but I swear, pulling this uniform off and on is like undressing a fresh wound. I lose skin and scabs, my blood runs every time. I would sleep in my uniform if regulations did not require crispness, creases each morning at parade. Perhaps it is truly as they preach to us: spit and polish, the crispness of our shorts and tunics, our weapons polished and oiled are all that separate us from our degraded enemies, all that protect our dear, distant women and children from the fate of those we guard.

1ST MAYOR (WHITE): How many dissidents fit on the end of a pin?

2ND MAYOR (BLACK): Depends on the size of the pinhead.

1ST MAYOR: You twist everything into a racial issue.

2ND MAYOR: No, you do.

1ST MAYOR: The color of dissidents don't faze me. Dissidents is dissidents. They all gotta go.

2ND MAYOR (who's disguised himself as 1st Mayor): Then it's the size of the pin.

1ST MAYOR: It's the man behind the pin.

2ND MAYOR: There you go playing racial politics again.

1ST MAYOR: And there you go playing me.

2ND MAYOR: Let's put the past behind us. It's a new day. We must ask new questions. How many dissidents fit on the end of a match?

They say Jericho's mighty walls brought down by trumpets. They say this Republic's built to last, blood of twenty million slaves mixed into the cement of its foundations, make it strong, brother, plenty, plenty strong. They say there are veterans' benefits available. J.B.'s not a vet, his name not scratched on some goddamn cold-ass black-marble slab in DC, but half his crew who went to war killed over there in the jungle and half the survivors came home juiced, junkied, armless, legless, crazy as bedbugs. Fucked over good in Asian jungles whiles this Philly jungle fucking over J.B. and the brothers left here to run it. Casualties just as heavy here in the streets as cross the pond in Nam. So J.B. figures. Shit, he's entitled to something.

He totters toward the first official he sees, a white man, late thirties, business suit, striped silk tie, Clark Kent glasses, just in off the Chestnut Hill local for a day at the office. J.B. doesn't know this man's name is Richard Corey today, that the pitiful sonbitch intends a swan dive at noon from the nineteenth floor of the spanking new Penn Mutual Savings and Loan Building that's taller than Billy Penn's hat. So at this juncture of his last morning, what Mr. John Doe, A.K.A. Corey, sees is not bright cityscape exfoliating around him as he rises from the dark subway cavern. He is silently weeping and hot tears have fogged his specs. He is regretting a movie, a wall of smoke, a mugging. As J.B.'s scruffy, African-American mug looms closer, unseen but felt, like all the pedestrian traffic rushing this way and that around Mr. Corey, as J.B.'s shadow detaches itself from the crowd and J.B. thrusts his meal ticket—*I am a vet. Lost voice in war. Please help.*—into the low-riding clump of somber fog enclosing Richard Corey, Corey's lank fingers grip his briefcase tighter. He considers the pistol inside. A Walther automatic, chosen because some hero or another, he can't remember the movie, they all look alike, carried this particular weapon to shoot discouraging holes in teenage subway predators. A caution after the horror of the movie-queue mugging. His wallet ripped away. Cynthia's unladylike panty show as she squirmed on the sidewalk. Could a woman be raped in ten seconds? Why was she bawling? Why didn't she bounce up and cover herself after her assailants fled? Boo hoo, boo-hooing, her skirt hiked up, her orange frilly underwear showing as the crowd of curious citizens gathered around her where she lay. C'mon, honey. Are you OK? Did they hurt you? Here, let me help you up. But she just lay where they pushed her down, pinned in the yellow spotlight of the marquee, crying her eyes out like a big boo-hoo baby, like she didn't understand a word he was saying or see his helping hand, like she didn't mind showing her orange bloomers to anyone who cared to look.

The Walther if he needed it nestled in his lamb-leather briefcase. He sometimes wished he hadn't indulged in lamb. Attractive appearance but didn't wear well. Every scuff showed. Impossible to clean. Next time a pebbled black finish. Impervious to hard usage. So what if it made him look like FBI or CIA.

Next time?

He'd promised himself he'd never use the pistol on a human being. He purchased it as a deterrent. To halt the growing spiral of violence. In dire straits he'd draw it to scare off a thief shoo away one of his old comrades who held a grudge. Never any intention to harm a soul. And absolutely no way, even though the gun is conveniently close and efficient, he'd blow his own brains out with the Walther. He tightens his grip on the smooth handle of his lambskin briefcase, blinks the black face and black-printed white card into focus. Reads this street person's tale of woe.

I am a vet. Lost voice in war. Please help.

Corey contemplates stopping here and now, reciting his own gory story. Would the black derelict listen? Would he laugh? Take pity? Be outraged and angry? Would he understand one word? Maybe they could start all over again. Both of them with time to spare. He had no pressing engagements before noon. And this floater dunning him the very image of idleness. Corey could tell the long version of his tragic history. How he'd been born blind, under a cruel star. Then learned to see. Then taught others to see what he'd seen. Second sight. The beautiful Tree of Life. Lions and lambs lying down together under the rainbow arc of its branches. Then struck blind again. Everything grainy and jerky as a silent movie when his vision was restored. Oh shit. Oh shit. I'm so sorry. He spilled his guts to the cops because they were the only ones with power to kill the terrible seeds he'd sown. Weeds bred from the seeds were choking the city. Columns of greedy black insects, fattened on the weeds, were marching through his veins. Gnawing at the gates of the temple of reason. The Life Tree is wizened, gaunt, crooked, dying at the top, dripping sickness in dead leaves that are drowning the city. I was born under an unlucky star, doomed to a terrible fate. Wicked little hoodlums, kids who should have been home in bed at that hour, stomped me. Treated me like dirt under their unlaced sneakers. My name and Cynthia's name winked from the marquee, our faces in lurid color leering from all the coming attractions. I watched her grovel and snivel on the pavement then forget to cover her shame. I was embarrassed. Bikini panties. Orange, frilly etched. Snatched down on one hip so they slant across her tummy. You couldn't see all that by the time the crowd gathered. Her naked belly with its fleshy folds already. They's why he'd never marry her. Only twenty-five and you could pinch an inch. She'd rolled over to her side and a triangle of orange underwear showing but thank god not the tubby belly.

Was there time to narrate the long version of his life? Maybe over coffee in the White Castle. A place where this fellow traveler would feel comfortable.

You see. my friend, when you think about it, when you go beneath the skin, beyond appearances, we're very much alike. Brothers of sorts. Don't you agree? We're victims, aren't we, both of us? Stuck playing roles we have been programmed to play. You never had a chance; neither did I. We've turned out the way we were supposed to. And soon we'll both be dead meat and the same wagon will scrape us both off the street and the same high-stepping, high-heeled shoes will trot over the stains we've left. Brothers after all in this City of Brotherly Love. But let me begin back at the beginning. Then you'll understand what I mean. Two coffees, please. And a couple of those delectable double-Dutch chocolate-fudge goo-goo doughnuts for my amigo here. What did you say your name is?

J.B. does not say. J.B. plays deaf and dumb. Thrusts his calling card in the dude's face. But this cat's far out. A goddamned stingy Republican like most of these three-piece private-enterprise trickle-down pee-pee commuters. J.B. wants to scream at the owlish incomprehension. Can't you read, motherfucker? Goggle-eyed white boy's on another planet. Don't see card, don't see J.B., don't see shit he don't wanna see. Peckerwood like some groundhog pop up here blinded in the light. J.B. would curse the sombitch out but then somebody else might hear him and call a cop when J.B. lays his handicap card on them. So he shakes his head and moves on, a wave of pedestrians parting before him like he's brandishing Moses's rod.

A few blocks farther on, in the alley behind the golden arches, sits the best Dumpster for half a mile in any direction. Full of boxes and packets that seal flavor in. Almost like buying your own meal. Surprise. Surprise. You open a discarded orange-and-yellow-striped box and anything could be inside. Hunks of snow-white bun, lettuce, pickles, cheese, tomato, special sauce in finger-licking good puddles. Plastic envelopes with seals unbroken. You bite into them and smear the virgin goodness over your lips. Ketchup. Mayonnaise. B-B-Q. Sweet and sour. Mustard. French fries you've come to prefer cold, the way you find them mashed and broken in the boxes, salty grease stiff as icing you save under your fingernails and suck later. You're grateful for boxes which keep the treats safe inside the Dumpster's rotten maul. You feel blessed because someone packages each morsel, each ingredient in its own individual container. Grateful for paper and plastic that protects each meal, that preserves and delivers leftovers a second time around. If worse came to worst, you could probably live on boxes, napkins, bags, packets and sheaths. Enough food smeared, soaked, micro waved, wiped, slopped on them you could survive just chewing the wrappings.

J.B. is about to turn a corner into the Dumpster's alley when he hears a siren. Very near. Is it a squad car dispatched to prevent the late-morning garbage raid? He thinks not. Cops must have better things to do: collect payoffs from the dealers and numbers runners, hit the whores up for booty, chase black kids out department stores. But also thinks it's only a matter of time—one bright morning they'll decide to come for him. If not today, tomorrow, soon. His life no use to anyone and just by breathing and taking up space he's breaking every law on the books, according to some important folks. Just a matter of time. J.B. and his tribe of gypsies shuffling like zombies through the streets to cop a meal. Boom. Pow. One big net snares them all. Police wait till they settle down with their little piles of boxes, the whole scummy swarm back in the alley getting down to business, peeking into their bags and boxes, chitchatting, catching up on who's in, who's out, who's gone to glory overnight. A big net sails over them, captures them unawares, this one chewing, that one running a finger round a cardboard rim, Phoebe mining grains of gritty meat from a napkin crumpled elaborately as a conch shell. Caesar smiling and stuffing a transparent bubble of honey in his pea-coat pocket. Kwame bemused by the timpani of his guts. J.B. recording everybody's business, in no hurry to explore his share of the loot, saving what he'll find in his nearly intact box, daydreaming its contents. Maybe he's hit the trash-can lottery. A five-course meal, shrimp cocktail, T-bone steak, soup, salad, fries, baked Alaska and somebody's Cartier watch, credit cards and keys to a new BMW.

Gotcha. The noose slips silently over their unwashed, uncircumcised necks. They cry like babies. Cops herd them with cattle prods into the holds of unmarked vans. Black Marias with fake shower heads in their airtight rear compartments, a secret button under the dash. Zyklon B drifts down quietly, casually as the net. Don't know what hit you till you're coughing and gagging and puking and everybody in a funky black stew rolling round on the floor. J.B. dies frustrated, wondering how his life would have been different if he'd availed himself of the opportunity to open that last box.

Two kinds of people in the world. The ones who eat the part of the meal they like best first and the ones who save the best for last. Gobblers or savers. Humankind divided into those two species. Observe a person and it won't take long to figure out whether they are gobbler or saver. J.B. the King of Savers. If all the fine women pouring out those office buildings and stores on Chestnut Street at the end of the day begged J.B. to fuck them, he'd line them up naked and the one looked best to him, he'd save for last. Working his way through the others, he'd be anticipating what was still to come, knowing there was more and better ahead while he's humping the one whose turn it is. Savers enjoy the best lots of times before they get to it. Licking their lips. Saving the best for last.

Siren's overheated now. Must be stalled in traffic. Bleating, squealing, the red knot on its forehead pulsing, ready to burst. Other cars don't know whether to stay still or move out the way. Siren screaming at drivers, drivers screaming at each other, pedestrians jammed up at intersections, afraid to step into the tangle of vehicles.

The snarled cop car jolts forward, skitters sideways, jumps a curb, bears down on some poor fool in the wrong place at the wrong time. Cop car spurts through two lanes of traffic where there didn't seem to be spurting-through room. Gone again, the yo-yo wailing of its siren crashes against brick and stone, shatters them, brings down the walls.

As plate glass explodes around him and clouds of black dust boil higher and higher, J.B. sings the blues: *Poor boy long way from home. Poor boy long way from home.*

Picture the man of steel in a cartoon. He shoots from the pavement, a blue cannonball into the Gotham sky, one knee flexed, one arm ramrod straight, aiming for the stars. Pow, a crimson jet stream hisses from his toes in their streamlined red booties. Now reverse the film, slam the superhero into the cement as fast as he rose from it. Watch him plummet backward, watch the stream sucked back into his feet. Watch him explode on impact. A fountain of blood whacked from his wrecked insides. Bright tub of blood big enough to swim in. As we look down on what's left of him our vantage point is nineteen stories above the city streets, a window in the Penn Mutual Savings and Loan Building, same window our hero, Corey, exited after enjoying one last extended view of the dying, ungrateful metropolis he had attempted to save from itself.

Poor boy long way from home. Poor boy long way from home. J.B. knows what goes round comes round and what goes up must come down. And what comes down comes down sometimes a whole lot faster than it goes up. And when you least expect it. Unless you could fly like a man of steel, getting to the nineteenth floor CEO suites takes as long as it takes, but coming down, shit, any fool can step out in the thin air. Zoom. Express don't stop till the bottom. And don't really stop there. There's down under down down under there.

Because he skulked at the rear of the crowd, as close as he cared to be, as close as the crowd wanted him to approach, J.B. saw what they missed, a mutilated lamb briefcase under the fender of a Buick Regal where it had bounced and skittered and ended up throat slashed, scalped, but cradling its load still, a gunmetal blue gun, the Book of Life.

Two hours later even the most desperately curious have departed the death scene. The fans who had attended live and in person, while the body still as warm as theirs, were long gone about their affairs, retailing the tale to whomever will listen, embellishing it, exaggerating their role in the urban drama, growing increasingly confused as the event subsides, the body cools, about what they'd actually witnessed on the corner of Sixth and Market and what they wished they'd seen. Early shift replaced by fresh faces as news spread. Each wave of spectators moves on quicker and quicker as the props of the scene disappear. No body, no cops, no emergency vehicles, fire engines. The crowd thins, the story flutters like a last gasp-candle in fourth- and fifth-hand recitals. Finally, only a vague hesitation, an undefinable uneasiness, then rapid strides away from the scene of the crime, as passersby sense something's wrong here, but don't really remember what.

Thank god the Buick hasn't moved.

J.B. retrieves the souvenir no one else noticed, stuffs the briefcase under his T-shirt, into the elastic band of his camou-flage pants. In spite of the heat he wishes for the anonymity of his suit of many coats, multiple pants, many layers, folds, pockets, tunnels, habitats for livestock, warrens, hives, caves, the labyrinth of his winter gear that could swallow the briefcase without a burp. No telltale bulge to betray him to his enemies. Looked like a pregnant kangaroo now. Good news was nobody left milling around to pay him any mind. No ambulances, cops, meat wagon, no TV camera crews, sirens, stretchers. They'd immediately draped a rubber sheet over the corpse, so only a lucky few observed firsthand what a wreck the jumper had made of himself. One young woman couldn't stop crying. Weeping and wailing and people trying to prop her up, sit her down. She drew her own miniaudience, stares and whispers and good samaritans because she was large busted, trim legged, attractive, doubled over by grief or fear or sick at the stomach, her long hair distraught. She's not dressed for hysterics in the street, she's one of those women you know you couldn't touch with a ten-foot pole when they click past you downtown. But suddenly she's somebody else. She's vulnerable after all, and the crowd loves it.

No one notices a funky derelict emerging from an almost invisible wedge between two buildings, an alleyway J.B. had chosen as his vantage point to outlast crowd and cops. No cop with nothing better to do than hassle a bum is around now to spot a suspicious-looking figure lurking in a shadowy recess. Hey you. Stop right there. What you got under your shirt? Up against the wall, scum. Spread em.

If you stink bad, the cops don't like to touch you. Won't frisk you. Except with their nightsticks and boots. Less personal. Hurts but you like it better than the pawing, slapping, shoving, their fingers punching through your skin.

You would have thought it was the birth of Christ the way people fought for a view of the dead man. Crowds smell blood. Like sharks. Like mosquitoes. Everybody craves a piece of the action. Like it makes people feel better to see one of their own kind mangled or dead. Another one gone and thank goodness it's not me. No. Blood and guts everywhere, but not mine. Yes sirree it's dangerous and mean in this city of brotherly love, but I'm still here. People dropping like flies. But not me. I'm holding on.

Tape measurements and photographs. A figure chalked in the street, where the suicide made his clean landing. With cars parked both sides the street and high-noon traffic and pedestrians, how'd he miss hitting something, somebody on the way down? Didn't get runned over, either. No second or third superfluous death. Roasted in a torched car. Drowned by a berserk hydrant. No extra work for the meat-wagon crew. Smooth sailing through the needle's eye. Happy landing right on target. J.B. was proud of the jumper. Whatever else the guy'd fucked up, he'd done this right. A slick, professional job. Bet the dude's wearing clean underwear.

Only one consequence of his own inevitable wipeout in the city streets bothered J.B. The goddamned morgue people thinking they're superior to him just because his underwear's not clean. If he had one thing to say about the fatal accident with his name on it, he'd ask to be wearing clean white underwear the day it comes down. Dishrags, newspapers, rummage sale, Salvation Army castoffs, feathers, fur, didn't give a fuck about what covered the rest of him, but please, Lord, when they peel down to the skin, when they laid him on the cooling board where they hose you down before cutting and sawing and pulling out your guts and setting them on the scale, he'd love to shock the sonbitches, remind them they ain't so smart, ain't no better than other folks. Clean underwear. Where'd this one find clean underwear? Who is this masked man?

Shake em up a little bit. One flunky with big scissors and a clothespin clamping his nose holes shut, snip-snipping away, and, look out, up pops the devil. Clean white drawers. Oh shit. This other shit must be disguise. They stop in the middle of what they're doing. Wonder for once who they're doing it to. J.B.'s revenge.

Honk, hoot, and ohhh, ahhhh. Ooop-poop-a-doop. The jumper sure gave them something to talk about. Bet he makes the six o'clock news. White, well dressed, a gentleman caller dropping in unexpectedly. The whole world in his hands, what's he got to go do something like this for? In the middle of the city so we have to step around him, over him. So we have to gawk and squawk and tie up traffic for blocks. Commuters home two minutes later than usual. You can calculate the cumulative effect of accidents like this one, the ripple outward that stymies the flow of cars emptying the city at rush hour. Disturbances, chaos like this don't just quietly disappear. They shake up the whole shebang. Put all our plans at risk. Disrupt the schedules of trains, buses, planes, spacecraft. A wild hair. A willful, selfish plunge upsets countless applecarts. Good citizens should pass the corpse stony eyed. Refuse to be discombobulated. Resent the intrusion. Don't give him the satisfaction. Who does he think he is, anyway?

J.B. can relate to being despised and ignored. Commiserates with all those lonesome corpses, uncovered, unattended except by flies, buzzards, creepy-crawlies. Were you sporting clean skivvies under your nice suit, my friend? J.B. envies him if he is. Of course they wouldn't produce the same effect as clean white shorts on J.B.'s crusty behind. On a gentleman like the dead man immaculate undergarments taken for granted.

J.B. stares at the drawing of the jumper, the crude chalk outline barely visible now, larger than life, in the center of Eighteenth Street, the door the dead man slammed open in his hurry to get through to the other side. Whatever other side there is, lurking under the asphalt. The drawing's not very accurate or flattering. All square corners, straight lines. Nothing round and squashable. The officer executing the drawing didn't have to bend. His chalk marker was attached to the end of a long stick. He paced around the body, outlining it with his magic wand. Sketched something that resembled a kite, a mummy case. A hopscotch shaped vaguely like a man. Man shaped obscurely like a hopscotch.

Paramedics had rescued the hysterical pretty lady. Smelling

salts. A squeeze, a hug, pats on her pretty back, comforting words to restore her as she tottered like an invalid in the blond arms of one of the men in green singlets with a name stenciled across the chest. They all looked like patients to J.B. Love at first sight. Love among the ruins. Paramedic and pretty lady would name their first-born after the dead guy. What was his name anyway? Was his identity embossed in the asphalt? A death mask Xeroxed there? Person or pizza under his blue hair? Would J.B. have recognized him if he'd landed face up? A fellow graduate of the University who like J.B. had picked a rather unconventional channel for employing the wisdom imbibed in those ivied halls? Who would believe that under that lumpy black rubber sheet slept a man capable of reciting French poetry and successfully calculating differential equations? To graduate the University during J.B.'s time the jumper would have also been required to pass his seven-lap swim test and a fine arts elective. Maybe he'd taken art history with J.B. J.B. had loved the darkened lecture hall, slide projector's hum. When the lights went out the silver screen was a train window and the midnight express glided faster than thought past cities, villages, cathedrals, countryside, castles, mountains, oceans, intimate interiors with all the inhabitants frozen stiff as dolls, clouds of angels, daisy chains of fire-breathing demons. People and places J.B'd never dreamed of seeing, his Europe, his Greece and Rome and British Isles, rearranged every minute through the window as J.B. lay back in his retractable armchair, invisible, practicing the art of letting the wide world pass him by.

Perhaps the dead man sat next to him in Art History 105. In the dark all students the same. Devoured by transparencies flashing on the screen. Easy to tune out the instructor's droning voice-over. Who the fuck cares what he named the picture? Pictures belonged to nobody. The paintings were just there, floating on beams of colored light. Nobody's property. J.B. could make what he wished of them. He took some home. Pieced them together even now on this street corner, squeezed a scene into focus, fine-tuning his slide projector till an image freezes bright and precise on this screen. In the dead man's fluids blotted on the asphalt were all the chemicals needed to paint *Déjeuner sur L'Herbe,* Venus on the Half Shell, vultures pecking the liver of Prometheus, Balthazar in his splendiferous robes, always the sharpest Wise Man. *Colors of my mind.* Whose song was that? Maybe J.B. sat behind the suicide when the dude's blue hair hung down in a ponytail. Men were starting to wear shit like that in those days. Lots of far-out costumes and weirdo hairdos. Art history drew the oddballs, the counterculture. Colors of whose mind? Humpty-Dumpty's shattered shell littering the mayor's nice street. All the mayor's horses and all his men can't paste poor Humpty together again.

The clumsy chalk sketch could be anybody. Reusable, recyclable. It would do for J.B. when his time came. More or less. If a shoe's not perfect, J.B.'d learned to wear it anyway. Shoes tougher to come by than feet. If the shoe don't fit, it will soon enough.

The crowd had dispersed. J.B. doesn't disperse anymore. He is always everywhere at once. Never a rush, a reason to leave here and go there. He inhabits many places, no place. Not really a difficult trick. No trick at all. The end of tricks and trickery because he is no one, no where. An accident had occurred and he hadn't survived. Everyone agreed that's what had happened. Unanswered questions about the tragedy remain, but nobody's on the case.

Lost soul. If found, return to sender.

Too bad J.B. wasn't first on the scene. Before anyone disturbed the dead man he would have pinned one of his hand-printed cards to the suicide's back. Pinned it if he'd owned a pin.

I am a vet. Lost voice in war. Please help.

Shit like that not really funny. J.B. knows better. He'd been educated. Brought up right. Bad luck to laugh at another's misfortune. What goes round comes round. But you had to laugh sometimes, didn't you? I mean, doesn't hurt the dead man, does it? Dead man pretty far past hearing anything. Or being insulted by it. Besides, the crowd had dispersed. J.B. the last hanger-on. Who'd care if J.B. laughed? Who'd notice? Nobody else giving a good goddamn now. Just faithful J.B. Even the bitch shedding goo-gobs of crocodile tears, where was she now? Probably popping little greenies or reds or yellows with her savior, whooping and bouncing while he cries giddyup, giddyup, slapping her trim thigh as he prongs her in the ass. Only J.B. mourns the shadow drawn by a man with a big stick.

Grim reapers and lady weepers. Mr. Peepers and high-wire leapers and on and on and on J.B. raps to himself. Make everything rhyme if you got the time, the time to rhyme, rhyme the time, time rhyme, rhyme time.

Meanwhile, much later, J.B., after a day of foraging, napping, marching, slouching, observing the city clean up after one of its suddenly dead, a day he's spent delaying a full inspection of the briefcase and its contents, saving it for later, for that ugly time when nothing's shaking, when he's the only person left alive and must explain, account for the next breath he bites off, the space he occupies on the planet, even though no one's listening, no one remains to care, J.B. heads towards Independence Square.

Savers save for rainy days. Saved because you could pretend there'll be goodness in the last drop, even if every swallow so far had been bitter, bitter going down. In the courtyard of City Hall, near the door to the Mayor's Office, where he'd parked himself a few fine minutes in the afternoon sunshine before a cop chased him away, J.B. had been tempted to peep inside the case. Just a little tease there in that toasty sunlight, a nip of what he was saving for later. In the courtyard people were puffed up like penguins with their own importance. They bustled and hustled because they wanted their fellow citizens to see them on their busy way somewhere. J.B. chose a spot where he could ignore them conspicuously, self-important as any of these chumps, absorbed by his business, part of which was paying them no mind. Let the chumps wonder. Let them dig. More to life than slaving in some office. More to life than dressing up pretty for the people. J.B. sneaked a peek inside the case but resisted temptation. Saved it for later.

Much later as things worked out. Saved it for that betwixt and between hour when J.B.'s habit is to sit in Independence Square, at Sixth and Market, contemplating his sins. Too late to be sorry enough for all he's done and undone in a lifetime. Fuck it. Two words he usually settles for as he tries to reason why. Or why not. At least once a day he's bullied into this familiar dialogue, forced to admit he has no life worth thinking about and forced to admit he'll continue saying yes to it. On

with it. Another breath, another step, not because a gun's held
to his head but because he can't think of anything that's better.
No one to blame but himself. He's the stubborn one who
chooses to hang on to his collection of nasty habits. The worst
habit hanging on when no reason to hang on. Except he'd
managed to hang on yesterday. So here he is today. Hand full
of gimme. Mouth full of much obliged. Swallowed one breath
of air. Got to have more. Wakes up screaming because he
dreams he's a baby and a big white cat's in his cradle, sitting
on his face, sucking the breath out his body. Fur in his mouth
and he's hollering like he got something to lose.

Shit, grit, motherwit. Was he the baddest of the bad, freest
of the free? Lone Ranger roaming the high plains where nobody
else dared. Or was he scared? Chickenshit. Chickenheart.
Tossing everything worth anything away so he'd have nothing
to lose. No strings. No fear. Not quite. He was still a saver.

Saved the briefcase. Saved it till it's quiet in the square.
Everybody in Philadelphia asleep or dead and that unforgiving,
god-awful voice starts to nag him and J.B. says, G'wan away
from here. No time for you, motherfucker. Can't you see I'm
busy? Got this book I've been saving to read.

Looked like Frankenstein's monster shuffling around with
the briefcase stuffed under his clothes. Felt good to sit down
and pull it out. Good to have company in the empty square.

The gun had worried him. Scared it would blow off his balls.
The thing loaded no doubt. Big vicious bullets fat as thumbs.
A murder weapon. If the cops find it on him he's in a world
of trouble. They'd third-degree his ass till he admitted shooting
a dozen people. Hit man for the black mafia.

He extracts the book gingerly, inch by inch so's not to disturb the blue volcano of gun slumbering in the depths of the bag. Fifty times today he'd heard the weapon explode, the red rip as a bullet unzippered his scrotum. Like walking on eggs. How do you walk when a pistol's pointed at your prick? Gently. Gently, Boss. One teensy, soft step at a time. Dynamite in his guts. Nitro. Stay away from crowds that jostle. Keep out of traffic that might force you to run to save your life. The brief-case had chafed his thighs, scratched his navel. Time to see if the damn thing worth the trouble.

He inches out the book. Sets it across his knees. Tries to remember the last book he's read. Run. Spot, run. Look at Spot run. The case with the gun inside leans against his ankle. If it discharges now all he'll lose is a toe, a foot. Ocular proof of disability. More pity, more profit when he flashes his card at strangers.

I am a vet. Lost voice and toe in war. Please help.

The book's a kind of journal or diary. Handwriting squinchy small. J.B. holds it close, then at arm's length, then pulls it toward him till it wavers into focus. Like art slides materializing from a dusty beam of light. Quiet in this quiet place. Night's falling. He can't tell if the city's still out there, surrounding the empty square. Wind reams the narrow spaces between build-ings. Fluorescent tubing crackles. J.B. maneuvers the book into the yellowish light.

The Tree of Life will nourish you. You need only learn how to serve its will. Its will is your best self speaking the truth to you. The seed of truth is planted in all of us. You only need to listen. Let it grow . . .

J.B. started reading somewhere in the middle. A few lines at the top of a page. A block of black writing cramped into a space not much larger than a postage stamp. Rest of the page untouched. Waste of paper, J.B. thinks.

He tries again. Lets the pages flutter. His finger leads him to this.

It's time, my friends, to reap what's been sown. The Children's Hour now. The Kiddy Korner. What have they been up to all this time we've left them alone? Over in the shadows with Buffalo Bob. Mister Rogers. The Shadow knows. But do we? Are we ready to hear the children speak? Ready or not we shall be caught. We are pithed. Feel nothing. Children have learned to hate us as much as we hate them. I saw four boys yesterday steal an old man's cane and beat him with it. He was a child, lying in his blood on the sidewalk. They were old, old men tottering away.

The handwriting's too tiny. Light's too poor. It's been a long day and two or three attempts to decipher the manuscript are enough for J.B. He shuts the book. Shuts his mind. Nods off. Doesn't awaken till he's swimming in pee.

He smells something burning. Old rags. A shitty, oily stink singeing his nose, his lips. He gags, needs to throw up instantly. Then he hears the pitter patter ha ha ha ha of little ha-ha feet. A hot fist snatches his whole body. Icy cold talons dig in. He knows he's on fire then, burning from his tennies to the nappy crown of his skull.

He is burning alive and he rolls over and over on the hard ground. Jerks to his feet and scoots as fast as he can fanning the flames as he goes helter-skelter arms flapping, legs kicking, a jiggedy-jig beeline toward the fountain at the center of the square, even though he knows as he pumps his legs and pumps his heart and pumps his scorched lungs and clutches with his fingers for white flutes of spray, by this time of night the water's been turned off for hours.

When he's exhausted and his strength returns, he washes his bloody hands and listens to the cool waterfall behind him. He's seen it all before, or read about it or dreamed it or maybe he saw the movie in one of the all-nighters on Market, maybe it was somebody else's dream in a book, maybe a book he, J.B., was writing. All were possibilities, possible worlds he was sure he was remembering, one or the other because here he was ha ha ha the pitter patter of little sneakers laughing, little white boys drenching him in kerosene and throwing a match ha ha ha laughing, running away pitta patta and he's shaking his fist but they have the Book, the briefcase, running away, disappearing, are not there, never were there and then he's thinking movie or TV show or in a book, this shit is funny but this ain't one bit humorous ha ha ha my ass. Remembering the book that promised things would get better. Remembering kids scooting down green sheets of water. Squealing. Screaming. Remembers sun hot as fire under the asphalt cooking his bare toes. Lawd. Lawd. He jumps like the spirit got holt to him. Hopping on one leg. Then the other. Hippy-hop down the bunny trail. And then there is a commercial break. And then a tape of his own screaming he lip-syncs. The tape stops and it's live broadcast time. He surveys the multitude. Begins to preach.

This is my story. This is my song.

The book he's singing from snaps shut. Is smoke in his hands. Ashes. He beats down flames on the crackling pages.

When he reaches the fountain he trips over its raised lip, plunges, flailing into its dry center, a belly flop all the wind goes out of him when he hits he gushes like a man slammed across the stomach with a two-by-four, he's prostrate, flat out, clenching his fists, kicking his toes raw against the cobbled bed of the fountain as wave after wave breaks over him and he riffles like a deck of cards being mixed, like a field of amber grain undulant in the breeze, a snake swallowing a frog, a flag rampant planted in the territory of somebody's chest.

First they ordered the bad guys out of town, then they buried them in dungeons. Next they were transported in sailing ships to the other end of the known world. Convict societies clinging like lichen to barren rocks in a land upsidedownunder. The last act space travel launch motherfuckers Roman candle style to the stars, deep space warp drive ain't never coming back never coming back shiny bullet-nosed buckets of blood and the bad guys inside baaa baaaing like black sheep crossing from Asia Minor to Greece just in time for Easter dinner. Goody-bye. Goody-bye. And if nothing else works, if evil's still inside, not *out there*, not *them*, if stocks and blocks and locks and pox and rocks and flocks and docks don't work, you can always light a match.

*   *   *

Less than an hour before the memorial service for the dead of Osage Avenue and Cudjoe is surprised to see the square's nearly empty. For a second he populates it with ghosts. All of Philadelphia crammed into Independence Square. It's 1805, a Fourth of July rally. In their customary place at the rear of the crowd, dressed in their Sunday best, toting picnic baskets and jugs for this annual day of feasting, speeches, fireworks and merrymaking, black Philadelphians, descendants of the 150 slaves who arrived in 1684, emigrants and migrants who'd been drawn by the Quaker promise of tolerance, are out in force to celebrate the nation's liberation from British tyranny. It's 1805 and before the party begins that year, blacks are hooted, shooed and beaten from the square. Cudjoe sees them haul-assing in their old-fashioned clothes, brass-buckled shoes, hoopskirts, bustles, aprons, bonnets, cutaway coats, tricornered hats, wigs, stockings, tripping over crackling good pieces of chicken they'd fried, straw-covered bottles of wine, panicked, fleeing, clutching the hands of their children who are dressed just like the adults. Mad rush and scramble out of the square into narrow cobblestone streets and twisting, dead-end alleys, pursued by their howling fellow countrymen, the thunder of thousands of feet, sticks and stones and curses like hail pelting their heads, like a storm spoiling their holiday outing. Yes. God speaking. Chasing them home. Where they'd better stay, if they know what's good for them, behind locked doors till he speaks again. The square's cleared, the platform festooned with bunting, banners, mikes, wires is empty. A few stragglers here and there whose presence is a sign of greater absence, the square more abandoned, more desolate because they wander purposelessly, as if lost, as if something must be wrong with them that keeps them in the deserted square when everybody else is someplace else.

The emptiness of the square means something has already happened that Cudjoe should know about, but doesn't. So here he is expecting lots of people to be gathered and instead of a crowd greeting him, hiding him, confirming his reason for arriving, here he is out in the open with a couple other fools. Something he doesn't know about must have happened and it's a big something cause everybody with good sense knows it happened and didn't show up here. He doesn't like being exposed, out of place, out of sync, like the few chumps milling around in the square. The Fourth of July mob had turned on its shadow. Swept it away. Sun-baked stones of the square had been purified. The owners will be back any second to claim them. Cudjoe slinks down into himself, his brown skin retracts under his clothes, his bare face, bare arms and hands that would betray him, disguise themselves as wood, as stone. Ghosts in funny outfits rush pell-mell past him as he freezes, wonders what the hell's going on, retreats from the entrance to the square.

On Market Street he pulls the rolled program from his hip pocket and checks to make sure he's got the right day, right time and place. *Through observance, atonement, education, and cultural expression we aim to confront and move beyond the horrors of that terrible day, to contribute to healing the wounds of our city and its inhabitants, and to aid in the development of humane and peaceful methods of resolving our community's problems.* The flyer confirms everything he was already sure of. Yes, there's a party. Problem is, looks like Philadelphia ain't coming.

To kill time he strolls up Market toward City Hall. All-night movie houses are gone, replaced by new glass storefronts with no stores inside the glass. The all-night movies always smelled sickly sweet like those pastel cakes of deodorizing soap hanging in wire halters in urinals. Continuous shows, twenty-four hours. Did they ever air those joints? Uniformed ushers herd derelicts, pimply-faced kids, stray husbands, perverts, college lads, transients, runaways, whoever else is huddled down in the rows of soggy seats, out on Market once a year. High noon and the exiled patrons mill around nervously ill at ease in the sunlight, blinking, heads bowed, hands deep in pockets, necks scrunched into collars, pavement like hot coals under their feet while fumigators spray the corners and crevices of the Palace. A disgruntled bunch sure enough, yanked from sleep, from love bouts with the twenty-foot-tall ladies on the screen. Crusty immigrants disgorged from steerage, gawking and grumbling, light of day like some social worker's merciless interrogation. The area below City Hall had grown seedier and seedier once the movies switched exclusively to X-rated flicks. No raunchy porn houses and peep shows on Market anymore but nothing much else here either. Another party and nobody showing up. Thick plate-glass windows cloudy, greenish, like the walls of abandoned aquariums. Sawhorses, lengths of plywood and Sheetrock in some of the interiors. Others totally blank. An entire block boarded up. Scaffolding, temporary sidewalks. Hundreds of homeless people could bunk in these storefronts. Did businesses occupy the upper floors. Time of day office workers should be streaming out of buildings. Secretaries in miniskirts and high heels. Cudjoe used to trolley downtown to catch the show. Women in this city knew how to dress. To carry themselves. Philly folks were sharp. Thousands of young ladies looking good, piling out of gray buildings

between 4:00 and 5:00. Bottled up all day then free to strut
their stuff. A special time. Like the moment the 2:30 bell
released Cudjoe's students from school. Cudjoe loved the
women's touches of style, a rainbow silk scarf, a leather strap
spiraling around an ankle, coils of necklace draped where you
wouldn't expect necklace to be, a purple suede purse slung or
dangling or clutched. Outrageous hats. Heels elevating them
so they clattered by proud as a duchess on horseback. Mize
well have been mounted on horseback when they trotted past
you on those spindly spike heels. If you pinned a bushy tail
on their high, tight behinds it would have sashayed back and
forth, working hard as a windshield wiper in a storm.

More ghosts. No whip-tailed Philly fillies on the street in
skimpy sixties costumes. Too late for rush hour. Gaggles of
footsore, see-through tourists giving up for the day. Street
people. Drinking people. Little knots of men hanging at the
entrances of bars. Not night yet. Not day. The city catching its
breath between shifts. Cudjoe out of phase again. Maybe he
could recruit a crowd for the memorial service. Pied Piper
returning with a mob of misfits to fill Independence Square.
Hey fellas. It's about youall. Listen, brothers. If they offed them
people on Osage yesterday just might be you today. Or
tomorrow. Look at yourselves. If you'd appeared in the vicinity
of 6221 Osage that day the bullets and bombs were flying, if
you'd sauntered or hip-hopped or swooped down on the neighborhood with your dreadlocks and bare chests hanging out
your silk tank tops and baggies and Egyptian sandals and PLO
headbands and Indian belts and African jewelry and hair
shaved and sculpted or high and wild as Don King or Fred
Douglass, youall wouldn't be congregating here on this corner,

grinning at the white gals, smiling at black gals, scaring the piss out of everybody else, surly as you want to be, your fingers round their throats, their wallets, up their asses. No, brethren, you'd be burnt and boiled and blowed up like the rest, if you showed your bearded faces, your narrow behinds on Osage Avenue because that day in May the Man wasn't playing. Huh uh. Taking no names. No prisoners. A hot day like this, my soul brothers. And here you are again making no connections, taking out no insurance. C'mon. Follow me. Before they decide to sweep your corner clean.

Cudjoe nods. Nobody pays any attention. He isn't buying or selling. What the fuck you want, man? Why you looking at me, lame ass? Doo-wop rags circle their foreheads. Could be the old times again. Hair marcelled. Shiny and ripply as Karo syrup drooling on a stack of pancakes.

He doesn't speak. They don't answer. Music trails him. Raps at the boys gathered in the doorway. Music tars and feathers his unguarded back. He can't help feeling naked. Known. The burden of returning is remembering he has no secrets. No answers. Boys on the corner speak to him as plainly as he speaks to them. Exchanging nary a word. A mumble.

Hey bro.

Hey homey.

He leads no parade back to the square. This is the ho-hum hour the city empties itself. Regular as a tide. Everybody who has a home splits for home. Goody-bye. Goody-bye. Why should they stop today. For a microphone, some black crepe paper, a semicircle of chairs on a platform.

More people in the square now than when he left. A TV news van. Two girls in T-shirts, jeans, black Adidas high tops unrolling a spool of cable. More mikes. Undercover (ha ha) cops in suits and ties with cameras round their necks.

News teams, mobile cameras, pretty boy and girl reporters with clipboards and remote microphones. Activity onstage. Respectable citizens have taken charge. Cudjoe watches the event stagger into place; he's a spy, a noncombatant. An insta-cam helicopter buzzes over once, high above the action. If a chopper had hovered over the rally in 1805 the view of the throng transmitted by its video camera would have been like the cross section of a fancy piece of chocolate candy, gooey white inside a dark rim. Then like a balloon bursting, the neat figure flies apart. The center melts, spreads. Dark envelope novas into scattered fragments. Red ants and black ants scurry through a maze of streets along the waterfront. Blacks outnumbered twenty to one never had a chance. Some lie stiff where they've fallen. Others crawl off, disappear into underground bunkers. The victors repossess the square. Continue their celebration.

Cudjoe leans against the edge of a fountain. Not quite part of the meager gathering in front of the temporary stage, not exactly part of the busy indifference of the city behind him. Sunshine. Blue sky. It's not weather keeping folks away.

The fountain, a huge dish with an abstract steel sculpture in its center, is dry. Traffic is moving but few pedestrians on the streets. Maybe it's just the wrong time of day. Someone should have hired jugglers, majorettes, a brass band to grab people's attention when they got off work.

A microphone is tapped. A quavering, tentative voice amplified across the stones. *I guess it's working. Ha ha.* Cudjoe's offered a candle by a pasty-faced woman. She's walked a good ways to reach him, around the fountain to the periphery of the small crowd where he's stationed himself. She is his mother's age. She's overdressed for the heat. Cudjoe doesn't want to feel sorry for her. A faint mustache he tries to ignore above her determined lip. Her thin mouth curls into a smile. He picks a candle from the box she extends. Each pale candle wears a pale paper cup impaled on its shaft. Cudjoe grasps his so its collar rests on his fist. He wonders if the lady purchased the candles. Someone's job would have been estimating attendance at the rally and ordering an appropriate number of candles. That number, a hope, a wish, that number minus the few candles Cudjoe saw people holding today would leave stacks of boxes unopened, surplus candles, cups, matches. Simple arithmetic that could break somebody's heart. The lady in the dark dress, dark turban wound round her hair had passed on, circulating through the forty or fifty Philadelphians who had stopped to see what was going on in the square. Why wasn't the entire city mourning? Where was the mayor and his official delegation from City Hall? The governor? The president? A dog hit by a bus would draw a bigger crowd.

People file onstage, occupy the semicircle of chairs. Each one supports a large, hand-lettered poster with the name of a victim against his or her knees. A brace of light-blue helium-filled balloons tethered to the back of an empty chair bump their heads together, dancing sprightly in a late-afternoon, early-evening breeze.

A gritty swirl of scrap paper and trash blows across the square. People shut their eyes. For a moment it seems everyone stops and listens to the scraping, the aimless flutter. Like the ceremony's over before it begins, Cudjoe thinks, and this silence is coming after, a benediction when the square's deserted again and the litter left behind by the mourners plays itself to sleep. Night when the balloons will return, shrunken to black specks in the black sky, each speck heavy as a galaxy.

Wind can't lift the heat but it teases and strokes, a promise of fall coolness dashed across Cudjoe's sweaty face. Long shadows from buildings to the north have dropped over one edge of the square. In forty minutes the witching hour. The exact moment when the bomb exploded atop the row house on Osage Avenue.

Two black men, chests bare, dreadlocks to their shoulders, drum their way into the ceremony. They sit facing each other, above and behind the stage, on the steps of one of the monumental buildings that enclose the square. A slow, easy rhythm rises from African drums clasped between their knees. Cudjoe's program doesn't mention them. Invited or not, they become as necessary, as natural as a heartbeat to the event.

The first speaker, a tall, fiftyish, elegantly brown man in a gray suit, glances over his shoulder at the drummers. Is he considering asking them to stop? If so, he thinks better of it and turns, speaking about those who are absent, explaining to those in attendance why the whole city should be gathered here.

Cudjoe sees people lighting candles. Clever, clever. The cups push up to shield the flame. He edges around the fountain's rim, closer to others in the audience so his candle can be touched.

Share your light, brother. He hears someone say that. A fingernail of flame gutters in the cup a man holds up for Cudjoe and two others. Another man gets a hit from Cudjoe. His face is close to Cudjoe's, close enough to bump heads as they peer down into their cups, verify shivery points of fire.

The younger man speaking now into the microphone clearly belongs to the tribe of the drummers. Natty dreads. Naked above the waist except for a crocheted tricolor vest—green, black, red—draping mahogany shoulders. He chants and the drums respond, punctuating his phrases. He echoes them, pounding a fist into his palm. Fire. Fire. Fire. A hymn to death and rebirth by fire. Fire the word each time his fist smashes into his hand. Fire the chorus prodding the drums louder, faster. Fire Fire Fire. As you live. So you shall die. By fire fire fire. And those who kill by fire shall die by fire fire fire. And then there are no more words, only the power of the pounding drums, pounding heart, the fist pounding the anvil where fire burns and is transformed from word to force by this man's chant and curse and prophecy.

Two black women read short poems. White college kids riff and scat an elegy for four voices. Then the dreadlocked priest up again, demanding the release of eleven of his brothers and sisters locked in the devil's prison for the murder of a cop they didn't commit. Then he intones a dirge for the ones gone who must not be forgotten whose names face us today crying for vengeance, justice, for vindication and peace. Drums rumble behind him again till he looks at his watch and raises his arm for silence and begins the countdown.

Chopper's over the house now . . . cop in a flak vest riding shotgun with a Uzi in his lap is the bombardier . . . checks the satchel of death . . . guides the pilot down closer, closer . . . rotors chuck chuck . . . he sees gasoline cans on the roof . . .

closer closer . . . inside the house they hear it chuck chuck . . . just seconds now 10 . . . 9 . . . 8 pig grins and says this is gonna be something . . . 3 . . . 2 . . . 1 . . . Hit it! Fist . . . slams into his palm. No word. No drumbeat. His head is bowed. People rise from the arc of chairs, lift their placards. Wear names like giant masks. Shins and shoes all you can see of them. The first speaker releases the balloons. They soar upward. Divide into two groups. The larger bunch explodes, rising, scattering in every direction. A smaller group of three seems to be traveling together. Their ascent is more gradual, stately, after they separate from the others. Cudjoe had not understood the fall sky's blueness, its depth, how it arches like a floating vault over the city, the numbing distance of it, till these three sacks of air paused as if caught on the rim of something, hesitating, gathering courage to launch themselves, to plunge into the limitless reaches stretching blue above them.

The three balloons have formed a kind of family, hovering above the stage, resting, trapped. Afraid to let go. To be gone. For a few moments it seems they'll never leave. Stuck under some invisible ledge. Bound by a string that loops them and connects them to the earth. They bob, spin, their tails dangle. Then a breeze catches them. They bounce once and shoot off. Soap bubbles. Air bubbles. Climbing to find the others that are mere dots already, miles above the highest thing in the city.

The invisible string mooring them had unraveled from Cudjoe's chest. As the balloons raced away they emptied him. His lungs. His heart. He knew the precise moment when the string snapped. A kind of twang, pop. He has no more to give. The string's played out. He lowers his eyes. Can't stare after the balloons any longer. They can't carry him on their flight. He can't anchor them to the square.

From the platform the victims' names are being recited. As each name is called Cudjoe wonders why words are so heavy. Why didn't words rise and fly like balloons? Words are shell, husk, earth-bound. He heard the names fall. Watched the mourners drop one by one back onto their chairs as the man at the mike reads the names on their posters.

A hush again after the last name. Then the drums commence a meditative rifling. Faster. Slower. Faster. Slower. Smack and thump and shuffle of skin on skin. People onstage and in the audience sense there's nothing more to say, to do, the program's over, it's time to go.

Cudjoe wants to run. He doesn't know what to do with the candle in his fist. Will the candles be collected and saved for another day, to commemorate another massacre? Will they be recycled next year, same time, same station.

He checks the sky. It remains serene and seamless. No sign the lost souls have been welcomed or refused. What had those balloons been to him? Why had he been tied to them, drawn after them, emptied, when they swept away? Eleven had died May 13, 1985. He couldn't say their names now. The heavy names. He'd stared at the posters, trying to memorize the victims' names. No time to learn them before they became something else, whisked away, elsewhere, where they would always be, waiting, gone.

Fire . . . Water. Earth. Air. Names bound those elements, twisted around them, held them close, breathed life into their combinations. Binding. Pulling.

The man in the suit said pray for them. The dreadlocked

man promised more fire next time. Drums bound them, braided them, infused them with the possibility of moving, breathing, being heard.

Cudjoe hears footsteps behind him. A mob howling his name. Screaming for blood. Words come to him, cool him, stop him in his tracks. He'd known them all his life. *Never again. Never again.* He turns to face whatever it is rumbling over the stones of Independence Square.